Praise for *In the Han*

"The book is a page-turner from the
larly gifted at writing about the natu
rural Alberta."—*Globe and Mail*

"Characters are compelling, realistically drawn, and three-dimensional. Vibrant."—*Quill & Quire*

"Compelling."—*Alberta Views*

"A lovely and loving exploration of hope and human connection."—*Times Colonist*

"Eriksson weaves her story with a natural simplicity. *In the Hands of Anubis* is touching and poignant."—*St. Albert Gazette*

"An engaging novel about love and loss."—*National Post*

"A lovely little book. It seems at times to touch on all the humor, the sadness, the joy of the human spirit."—*January Magazine*

Praise for *Decomposing Maggie*

"A luxuriously visual rendering . . . Eriksson's writing grows rich as the story develops. Gorgeous and powerful depiction."
—*Canadian Literature*

"Ann Eriksson shows an assurance beyond what might be expected from a first-time novelist."—*Vancouver Sun*

"Grief is as individual as a fingerprint. Unblinking and original. Maggie's mourning is absolutely her own—and every reader will identify with it."—Katherine Ashenburg, author of *The Mourner's Dance*

"Ann Eriksson's first novel is as heart-wrenching as it is life-affirming."—*Herizons Magazine*

falling from grace

ann eriksson

Library and Archives Canada Cataloguing in Publication
Eriksson, Ann, 1956–
Falling from grace / Ann Eriksson.

ISBN 978-1-897142-46-2

I. Title.

PS8559.R553F36 2010 C813'.6 C2009-906896-6

Editor: Kathy Page
Cover image: © Fotosearch
Proofreader: Heather Sangster, Strong Finish
Author photo: Gary Geddes

Brindle & Glass is pleased to acknowledge the financial support for its publishing program from the Government of Canada through the Canada Book Fund, Canada Council for the Arts, and the Province of British Columbia through the British Columbia Arts Council and the Book Publishing Tax Credit.

The interior pages of this book have been printed on 100% post-consumer recycled paper, processed chlorine free, and printed with vegetable-based inks.

Brindle & Glass Publishing
www.brindleandglass.com

1 2 3 4 5 14 13 12 11 10

PRINTED AND BOUND IN CANADA

For Gary

A lifetime can be spent in a Magellanic voyage around the trunk of a single tree.
—E.O. Wilson, naturalist, 1994

Grace: The attractiveness of charm belonging to an elegance of proportions
—Oxford English Dictionary

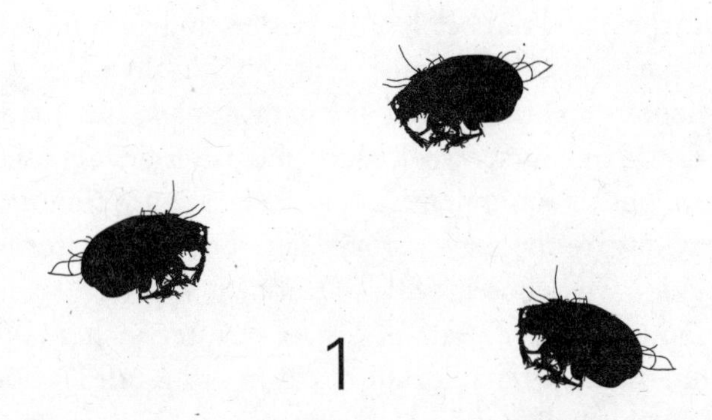

1

I climb trees for a living. My mother, Grace, a woman of great compassion and little tact, claims I climb trees to make myself taller. She likes to relate to anyone who will listen how as a child I climbed anything, my stubby arms and legs wedged crablike between door frames, scuttling up the lattice to the garden, the china cabinet, the drainpipe to the roof. She is mistaken, my intent not to be taller. When my feet leave the ground, I rejoice in the release from gravity. If I could fly, I might, like the marbled murrelet, never touch the earth, setting my feet only on the highest branches of the tallest trees. What I seek most is solitude in the company of trees. Connection with another being.

My trees are not garden varieties or boulevard specimens. The trees I climb are wild and old and tall. Trees of the ancient rainforest: western hemlock, Sitka spruce, Douglas-fir, western redcedar. *Tsuga heterophylla*, *Picea sitchensis*, *Pseudotsuga menziesii*, *Thuja plicata*. I take comfort in the naming, in knowledge itself. When I stand surrounded by these massive conifers, I understand how Tolkien conjured the Ents, the tree beings, who unearthed their limblike roots and thundered across the landscape to fight the armies of Saruman. Their centuries-old trunks are my avenue to the forest canopy, where few venture and much remains a mystery. My job, my life's passion, is to explore this uncharted territory, bring a small part of it to earth, and attempt, in my own limited way, to understand it. My subjects are the inhabitants of this arboreal world, the mites and beetles, the spiders and ants, that dwell in the suspended soils and moss mats high in the oldest of trees. The hunters and the hunted, the parasites and the scavengers.

I don't, of course, work alone. Logistics dictate otherwise. The weight of equipment. Safety. I choose my climbing partners with care the way a storyteller chooses her stories. And this story was chosen with the utmost of care. This tale is not about me, Faye Pearson—three feet, ten inches tall—little person, dwarf, woman of short stature. This tale is about subjects much smaller and much bigger than I.

I met Paul at the end of a long fruitless day of interviews. When he walked through the door into my office, I could have sworn I smelled cedar boughs, as if he trailed the forest into the room after him. I found myself reluctant to let go of his calloused fingers, which reminded me of the texture of bark. The way he folded his tall, lanky body into the chair gave me the distinct impression he didn't belong indoors. His first words: "I'm thrilled to meet you, Dr. Pearson."

"Thrilled?"

"You have a great reputation." His eyes were the same dusty shade of green as the lichen *Lobaria*.

"I work in a great field," I answered, painfully aware of my reputation. The previous applicant had left no illusions, a farm boy from the Fraser Valley, his interview promising, until he asked if he would have to do all the climbing because of "your arms, you know." "No, I don't know," I shot back. "What's wrong with my arms?" I regretted the flush of embarrassment on his face. The irony of a person like me studying microscopic bugs at the top of massive trees does not escape me. I could imagine his skepticism. After all, I stood no higher than his navel, my feet propped on a stool under my desk. But I was tired of explaining myself, educating the ignorant.

And I expected civility. He tripped over his own feet as he left the office. I scrawled a giant red NO! across the farm boy's application form and filed it in the trash. I wished I were up a tree hunting for bugs. A task much less taxing than finding a suitable assistant.

"You've done a remarkable amount of research." I flipped through Paul's resumé, impressed by his credentials. "Arborist by training?"

"That's right."

"Tell me about your last position."

"I climbed for Nadkarni on her cloud forest project in Costa Rica," he answered. "We studied epiphytes."

Plants that grow on plants. "Nalini's a close friend of mine." I smiled, my train of thought sidetracked when he smiled back. I forced myself again to the sheets of paper on the desk in front of me. "Eucalyptus forest in Tasmania, marbled murrelet nest sites in Oregon and Washington, arboreal lichens in Alaska," I read with approval. "Contracts in Chile, Argentina, Ecuador. Impressive."

"Climbing, yes." He shifted in his chair. "But I'm no scientist. I have no degrees. You're the pioneer."

"Yes, well, no more than my colleagues elsewhere." I fiddled around with the pen in my hand, flustered by the unexpected praise, and closed the folder. "I need a skilled technical climber. You're more than qualified." I took a breath and asked him the one question I really cared about. "How do you feel about working with me?"

He blinked, wrinkled his forehead, stroked a wispy, fledgling beard, and considered my question for a moment. "Not a problem." He leaned forward. Flecks of gold in his irises caught the light. "I'm surprised you asked. It would be an honour to work with you."

I excused myself and put a note on the door. Research Assistant Position Filled.

If I had known what would happen, I never would have hired him.

2

A black bear burst from the trees and barrelled down the slope and across the road. I slammed on the brakes and the car skidded to a stop in a rain of gravel and dust, the startled white of the animal's eye visible, sun glinting off its spring coat, rump muscles working under the loose skin as it disappeared into the brush on the other side of the road.

"Close call," Paul said. "Great driving."

"Call me Lyn St. James." I shifted the car into first gear.

"Who?"

"A nickname from my brothers," I said. "They taught me how to drive." I related to him how Patrick and Steve had shown up on my nineteenth birthday at my university dorm room and presented me with keys to a dented four-door sedan, powder blue, with new sidewall tires, a purple bow taped to the door handle. "You're crazy," I had objected, kicking one stubby leg into the air. "I can't drive." Steve had handed me a package and I tore open the wrapping to reveal three shiny metal brackets. "Pedal extenders," he announced. "They're adjustable." Caught between tears and an urge to cartwheel a circle, I blubbered onto their sleeves. Never in my wildest dreams had I imagined driving a car. "You'll be like damn Lyn St. James," Patrick had drawled. "Best female race driver in the world."

"You're lucky to have family," Paul said. I didn't tell him my brothers had also rolled me drunk as a lord into my bed after midnight. I woke up in the morning with my first hangover to find a note on my desk. *Sorry about the botany exam, Lyn. If you fail, you can always join the race car circuit.*

I pulled over again to allow a hulking truck loaded with logs to pass, the fourth that morning. The dust from the eighteen-wheelers lingered in the air. Paul closed his window and I inched the car along until the view ahead cleared, the road bone dry from a week without rain.

Paul pointed out a distant ridge where a single tree stood sentinel like a missed hair on a shaved head. "Why the hell would they leave only one?"

"Must have an eagle's nest." I shook my head. "No doubt it'll fall this winter in a storm."

He scrutinized the map. "Here's our turn."

We had tried four sites in the past two weeks; two inadequate for our study needs, the others threatened by logging. Otter Valley was our fifth prospect, promising because of the provincial park that protected an extensive stand of old-growth forest along the creek.

We entered a narrow track through the trees, cringing at the squeal of overhanging branches along the side panels of the car. Twice we stopped to move fallen saplings that barred our passage. At the river, the wooden planks on the one-lane bridge rumbled and banged under the car, the white swirl of water visible through the cracks. A clearing at the side of the road provided parking. We stepped out into fresh, moist air; the rush and tumble of the current. An impenetrable green wall of old-growth forest bordered the road. A wooden sign announced the boundary of Otter Creek Wilderness Park. No facilities.

I opened the back hatch to unload the gear. When I turned around Paul had disappeared. "Paul?"

"In here."

I followed the sound of his voice through an overgrown gap between two trees to find him perched high on a fallen hemlock, the girth spread wider than he stood tall. "Big trees in here." He whooped and jumped to the forest floor with a muffled thud. "Let's go."

We shouldered our loaded packs, a pile of climbing and camping equipment left for a second trip. I led the way up the path, a rudimentary map to big trees—sketched on the back of a bar coaster by a colleague—tucked in my pocket. The trail along the river was wide and well worn, the ground cleared and flattened here and there for campsites. Shafts of light filtered through the branches. The blue ribbon of Otter Creek sparkled on the other side of a wall of falsebox and salmonberry. We passed giant conifers, head-high sword ferns. Our spirits rose with the possibility we'd found a secure study site where logging was forbidden.

We scrambled across a dry creekbed on to a narrow trail overgrown with underbrush, then pushed through a patch of willow to find our way obstructed by swiftly flowing water. Above us to the left, a waterfall cascaded in a turbulent froth into a deep pool, to our right the main stem of the river and before us a boulder-strewn rapid.

I checked the map. "We have to cross the river," I yelled over the din of the waterfall.

"Through the rapids?" Paul's eyebrows lifted.

"Your initiation," I joked.

He dropped his pack in the sand at the water's edge and undid his belt. "If I had known I'd be fording wild rivers, I'd have worn my best gonchies."

I studied the bubbling froth ahead, the water deep and fast. "I'm sending you over with a rope."

He saluted me playfully, then stripped to his underwear. He tied one end of the rope to a sturdy sapling, slung the remaining coil over his shoulder, and waded into the current, paying out the line. "It's ice," he hooted. The water rose to his knees, then to the middle of his thighs. He picked his way over and around rocks slippery with algae to the opposite bank and scrambled out, hairy legs pink with cold. He hobbled barefoot up the slope, wet body glistening, and wound the end of the rope around the trunk of a young Douglas-fir. He gave me the thumbs-up and flashed a smile, then waded back into the current, pulling himself along the taut line. I couldn't help but notice his muscular shoulders and the trim of his waist, the dark hair plastered to his chest by the river water, the V disappearing into the waistband of his shorts. I realized I was staring and looked up, but he was concentrating on his footing. I let out a mischievous wolf whistle—another skill learned from my brothers.

"Sexual harassment," he protested with a grin.

"You should have seen what I did to my last assistant." I laughed, glad of his sense of humour.

Paul stepped out and shouldered a pack. I waded cautiously into the river, my grip tight on the suspended rope. The frigid water soon rose above my waist and I gasped at the cold, the current stronger than I had anticipated, the rocks underfoot treacherous. I tightened my grasp and fought my way to the far bank, thankful for the security of the rope; I lost my hat to the current in the process. Paul ferried the gear across and made another trip back to the car. I set up camp and changed into dry clothes. An hour later tea water boiled on the camp stove, tents up, wet clothes drying in the sun.

"Great spot," Paul commented, filling my mug with steaming dark liquid.

"I imagine you've seen lots of great spots," I said. "The amount of travelling and wilderness work you've done."

"Sure, but not many as hard to get to as this place," he replied. "We hiked three days into a site in Borneo."

After lunch we bushwhacked our way from river to ridge. Giant ancient trees appeared one by one: Sitka spruce in the sediments of the flood plain, trunks dripping with lichen and moss; thick-barked Douglas-fir rooted into the well-drained slope, and on the ridge a dozen western redcedar reached skyward, as big around as cars. Hemlock everywhere. Paul and I paced opposite directions around the perimeter of a mammoth cedar. We met halfway and beamed at each other. We had found our study site.

We assembled our equipment at the base of a massive hemlock. I threaded fishing line through the end of a rubber-tipped bolt and notched it into a custom-made high-powered crossbow mounted with a casting reel. I took aim from a patch of sword fern where I had a clear view of a large limb a third of the way up the tree. I braced myself against the recoil and squeezed the trigger. The bolt hissed through the air; the fishing line snaked behind, the reel singing as it spun.

The arrow cleared the limb and dropped down the far side. "Yes!" I raised my fist in triumph. I slung the crossbow over my shoulder and ran across the rough ground to the base of the tree where I searched the lower foliage for the dangling bolt.

Paul jumped from a fallen log and waded through a patch of salal. "First shot. You're a pro. I don't know what you need me for?"

"My safety net," I said.

"Here it is." He pointed out the bolt hanging a metre above his head. I paid out the line from the crossbow reel and the bolt descended to the ground. Paul retrieved it from the grasp of a devil's club and untied the fishing line.

I watched him knot the line to a coil of light parachute cord, pleased with his apparent skill and comfort with the equipment. He pulled the parachute cord over the branch and repeated the procedure with a climbing rope strong enough to lift a Volkswagen Beetle. I secured one end around the base of a nearby fir while Paul geared up to begin the tedious process of rigging a tree. Ascend to the limb, shoot another line higher up, climb, shoot, until he reached the top where he'd install a permanent pulley and anchor webbing to support the rope.

It took three hours to rig the hemlock. Our lives depended on the care with which we placed the rope higher and higher in the tree.

When done, Paul rappelled to the ground and we took a break against an arm-thick root that emerged from the trunk above us, looped over our heads, and wormed under a mass of moss, shoulder-high salal, and Alaskan blueberry.

We reviewed our safety procedures over a bag lunch of sandwiches and fruit.

"Have you ever had problems?" I flicked a carabiner clip closed with a click to test its spring.

"No," he said. "I don't take chances. But I've scraped a couple canopy cowboys off the ground. I watched one guy crater. Half equipment failure, half brain failure." He glanced up from the nylon webbing he was knotting into a loop. "I think he clipped his descender onto the wrong side of his rope."

"Did he live?"

"Yes, but it wasn't pretty. How about you? Any problems?"

"Not yet," I said. "Knock on wood." I tapped the gnarl of root behind me. A few months previous a reporter had interviewed me for a story about canopy research. The woman had crossed her legs and scrutinized me in silence, hesitant, I knew, to ask the burning questions. *How do you climb giant trees with your stunted limbs? How do you wipe your bum?* "Let's say I manage," I would have assured her. *How do you lecture a class, carry a pack, drive a car, tie your shoes? Make love?*

The tape recorder hummed on the table between us. She finally spoke. "Tell me, Dr. Pearson. How many canopy scientists are injured or killed every year while climbing trees?" I wanted to scream at her, at the stereotype, at her fixation on the sensational.

"It's the falling, not the climbing that gets 'em," I had answered wickedly in my most professional voice. The reporter's face turned blank in confusion. "With proper training and equipment, tree climbing is safer than driving your car to work. And we never climb alone. Would you like to see my climbing gear? In fact, why don't we gear you up?"

We never got around to talking about bugs, the reporter and I. Few people understood my passion for segmented bodies and multiple appendages, armourlike exoskeletons so unlike the soft fleshy exterior of the *Homo sapien*, the ability to moult.

Paul loved to talk about bugs. He seemed to know an enormous amount about them. He had informed me that morning on the drive into the site that a flea can jump one hundred and thirty times its own height. That a house fly hums in the key of F and mosquitoes are attracted to carbon dioxide. That one species of moth exists entirely on cow tears.

I tried my damnedest to steer him away from the trivia toward my own passion. Arthropods.

"What do you think we'll find up there today?" he asked, double-checking my equipment.

"Mites." I snapped the chin strap on my helmet closed. "Lots of mites."

In climbing gear, I resembled one of my specimens blown up to gargantuan proportions, a creature from space. Helmet, safety glasses, hiking boots. A harness heavy with carabiners that dangled with ascending equipment called Jumars, foot straps, and a descender. I stuffed the pockets of one side of my dork vest with a soil corer, plastic sample bags, field notebook, and a pencil; the other side with a compass, handheld tape recorder, walkie-talkie, digital camera, knife, and a bag of chocolate chips and soy nuts. I took a pee behind a snag before I headed up; I expected to work in the canopy for several hours.

Paul and I bounced from the end of the rope like toddlers in a Jolly Jumper, to test the ability of the rigging to hold the weight of two people.

"All set." Paul knelt and held the bottom of the rope taut to give me purchase. I clipped my Jumars onto the rope and climbed: slide the top ascender as high as I can reach, sit in the harness, lift the bottom ascender along with my feet, stand in the foot loops. Top ascender again. Repeat. Hump, stretch, hump, stretch, I jugged up the rope the way a worm inches along a tendril of honeysuckle vine. Early on in my career, tree climbing presented a challenge for me. My elbows did not straighten, each stride up the rope with my short arms and legs inadequate. An entire tall tree exhausted me. I worked out, swam to increase my endurance, practised yoga asanas to loosen my shoulder joints and hips and watched my weight. It wasn't until I understood climbing was more technique than strength that I was able to swarm up most trees in ten or fifteen minutes. Paul nicknamed me *the human arachnid*, although he beat me hands down, one-legged, a single stride to four of mine, up a tree in sixty seconds flat.

The going today was easy; the tree devoid of lower branches, the redundant appendages shed over time, no longer useful, the bottom third of the trunk straight and uninterrupted. I followed my progress against the red-brown scales of the bark a half metre away. I stopped, hung in my harness, and ran my hand across the rough surface, my fingers coming away sticky with clear, amber-tinged resin, the scent a mixture of herbal tea and paint thinner. I recalled the reporter's view of canopy work as sexy and chuckled to myself. Sap stained my clothes from years of mounting trees, my arms and legs bruised, hair decorated with plant life shed from branches. I laid back and looked up. The rope wound from the ground, between my thighs and through the ascenders, to disappear into the lacy foliage of the canopy high overhead.

I resumed my ascent and entered a maze of plant life. The light brightened and filled with birdsong: the *suweet* of a towhee, the spiralling whistle of a thrush, a raven's *kraah*, and the soprano *tsee* of a creeper. Each limb wore a cloak of vegetation as varied in colour and texture as a weaving. Forty metres up and out of sight, in the sunlight above the dense canopy, I knew the top of the tree drooped like all hemlocks, the way the tallest person in the room hangs his head in a vain attempt to appear shorter.

My radio crackled and Paul's voice floated out, frightening all the birds into silence.

"How's it going, boss?"

"Great," I replied. "Why don't you rig the cedar while you wait? And don't hit me with a wild shot, eh?"

"I'll do my best."

I continued up, stopping at five-metre intervals to take core samples. My perceptions were sharpened, the sounds louder, the smells more intense, the bark under my fingers an extension of my skin. I lost myself on a climb. Lost my limitations. Lost my name, my past. I opened up to the world in a way I never did on the ground. It was as if I became part of the tree. I twisted the corer, a section of open-ended pipe, into the thick mats of moss and soil, growing more and more excited at the prospect of what I would find once back in the lab with my microscope. New unnamed species of arthropods? Unique to the canopy? To this tree? Little was known about the high dwellers of the temperate rainforest.

It wasn't until I reached the pulley and tied myself in that I noticed the world beyond the intimate space of my hemlock. I radioed to Paul with one hand and fished the bag of nuts from my pocket with the other. "I'm at the top. I'll take a snack break before I head down."

"What's it like up there?"

"Spectacular." Through the crown branches, a sea of green stretched out to the horizon. "Trees as far as the eye can see." I swivelled my head around to the east. "Shit." My voice dropped an octave at what I saw.

"What's wrong?"

"Bloody goddam clear-cut." From my vantage point I could see the destruction across the river, the ridge at the top of the slope bare of trees, and if I concentrated I could hear the distant roar of chainsaws and yarders.

After dinner, we stood on the pancake boulders in the wide, lazy mainstem of the river near our campsite, the current sluicing around us.

"How far away is the logging?" Paul said. His eyes followed the trajectory of a bat feeding on mosquitoes high above our heads.

"Can't be more than a kilometre." I flipped a pebble into the water. "Thank God for the park." I sat cross-legged on the rock, its surface like human skin, warm and smooth against my hands. I took in the beauty of the valley, the hushed light of day's end on the water, the cool green of the forest. A

Garden of Eden. Every surface, every nook and cranny, above and below ground, brimmed with life. Last winter on a whim, while writing a talk on canopy research for an outdoor group at a church, I downloaded the King James Version of the Old Testament from a website and searched for references to trees. *SEARCH*, the striking of a single button on a keyboard. The computer counted three hundred and twenty-eight. I found and read them all. *FIND*. The process took me a week, the initial reference—the prime reference—was to the *Tree of the Knowledge of Good and Evil*.

Was it old? Did its limbs drip with lichen and moss? Did spiders spin their webs between its branches; did mites go about their business of decomposing organic matter in the accumulated soils, the tiny chelicerae hard at work? Did beetles wriggle under the bark and armies of ants build galleries in between its roots? Did Adam and Eve climb into its canopy when they ate the fateful fruit?

Did it live in a rainforest?

"What species of bat do you think it is?" Paul shaded his face from the glare of the setting sun.

"Hard to tell from here." I lifted my binoculars and watched the animal fly figure-eights through the air. "A long-eared?"

"You have a boyfriend?" he asked without warning as he crushed a mosquito against his cheek, a smear of blood left behind when he lifted his hand away.

"Me?" I lowered the binoculars, surprised by the question. "No. Too busy. You? A girlfriend . . . or boyfriend?"

He laughed. "I'm a ladies' man," he said. "A lonely one. I travel too much." He paused. "Know any nice women?"

I studied his profile, more comfortable than handsome. His attention was on the bat. All I knew about him were small details from his resumé and the fragments of his personal life I'd gleaned on our long drives together. His older sister married and moved to the States when he was a kid. His parents both dead, a fact he shared while deciphering another sketchy map to another study site drawn on the front of an envelope.

"I'm sorry." I regretted the foolish personal question.

"No worries," he'd answered. "I think we turn here."

I could slip what I knew about him in one pocket of my jeans. "Personal policy. I never make matches for my employees," I quipped. *Or date them.*

I'd heard sex described as the bite in the forbidden fruit responsible for the expulsion of humans from paradise. Before sex, each living thing was a clone, its genes identical to its parent.

Without sex, there'd be no dwarfs.

I changed the subject. "Tell me about the amulet around your neck."

He fingered the object at the hollow of his throat. "This? It's an orangutan tooth from Borneo."

"Good luck charm?"

He untied the leather thong and handed me the tooth. "They spend almost all their time in trees. Orangutan means 'person of the forest.'"

"I suppose you know they're endangered." I examined the yellowed piece of bone, the grinding surface worn flat, then handed it back.

"Yeah, going the way of the Dodo." He retied the amulet around his neck and zipped up his jacket. "What do people say when you tell them you climb trees for a living?"

"Leaves most of them speechless." I laughed. "My mother thinks I climb trees to make myself taller."

"And is she right?"

I admired his candour. "No. I just love trees. The search for knowledge. Defying gravity."

"For me it's the adventure, the body rush." He cocked his head to one side and listened. "Murrelets," he whispered.

A pair of small mottled birds the size of robins appeared over the tops of the trees to the west. The birds shot over our heads, the whirr of wings audible, calling a high-pitched *keer, keer*, and disappeared into the canopy on the other side of the river.

"Amazing they fly this far to feed their chicks." I searched the visible branches with the binoculars to see if I could detect the nest, the secretive seabirds choosing mossy limbs high up in old-growth trees, commuting at dawn and dusk with food for their babies. "We must be twelve, fifteen kilometres from the coast."

"In Oregon we found marbled murrelet nests seventy-five kilometres from the sea," he said. "No wonder it took decades to find out where they nest."

Within an hour we detected more than thirty murrelets flying upriver.

"I bet hundreds nest in this forest," Paul said, jumping from rock to rock to reach shore. I followed him, the sky growing too dark to see bats or birds.

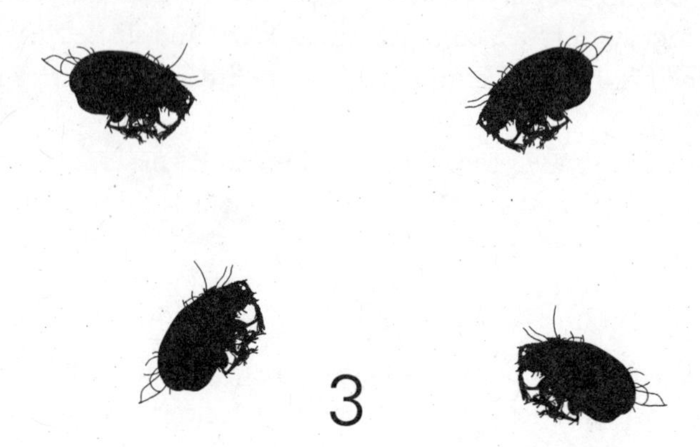

3

I knocked the last tent peg into the root-riddled ground, the nylon shelters wedged between huckleberry bushes laden with flowers. I stood and breathed in air pungent and fresh with spring growth. It was early June, the start of our third field season in Otter Valley. We had given up fording the river long ago in favour of a natural log bridge upstream of the waterfall and moved our base camp to the clearing near the road for ease of access. Three large hemlocks guarded the camp. An enormous fallen spruce thick with moss and bristling with seedlings provided protection for our make-shift kitchen—a portable propane stove balanced on a plank supported by two stumps—where Paul was fixing dinner. Muted evening light angled through the canopy, the air cool. Steps away the river current sang its journey west to the ocean, the stream bank thick with red columbine and false bugbane in bloom, the delicate white and yellow flowers of the bugbane showy against the dark green fans of leaves that left painful red blisters on the skin. Few people came to the valley, the odd hiker or bevy of teenagers out for a drinking spree. Paul and I considered Otter Creek our own.

We were tired. We'd left town at six AM to ensure we'd reach the site by nine, then spent the day in our trees, setting aerial traps, collecting moss samples. Otter Creek had fulfilled its promise. We had negotiated a buffer zone outside the park boundary and adjacent to our study site with the company that held the timber rights. Pacific Coast Forestry had agreed to forgo logging there for the years it would take us to complete our work. A significant tract of undisturbed true, old growth forest was essential to our research, and we had it, a biological paradise where diverse tree species grew together, upstart saplings and hoary veterans centuries old supporting lichens and mosses in the high canopy, shrubs and herbs flourishing at ground level, the forest floor a nursery of decaying logs and debris. A complex and multilayered collaboration between the living and the dead. An ideal wilderness laboratory.

We planned to stay two weeks.

I settled on a log with my laptop to enter the afternoon's data. As the machine chugged through its startup, I watched a common merganser fly downstream above the large flat rocks at the river's edge, wingtips skimming the water's surface. Intent on its passage, I was unprepared for the female voice behind me. "Hello?" I turned. A woman materialized like a sylph from between the trees at dusk. She reminded me of a waif out of *Les Misérables*, her face frightened, dark eyes huge and innocent, dreadlocked hair as wispy and wild as the arboreal lichen, Methuselah's beard, that hung from the branches above her head. I would have taken her for a child but for the baby in her arms—cheeks stained with tears, hair white and loopy with curls—and the girl at her side, about six or seven, who clung to the woman's long worn skirt. The girl wore pants under an ankle-length skirt of her own, an old Cowichan sweater two sizes too big, and mud-caked boots. Her straight dark hair stuck out in impulsive tufts from under a pilled handmade toque.

"We've come to save the trees," the mother said.

Paul and I exchanged glances. Save the trees? Paul stood from his crouching position beside the camp stove, a ladle in his hand. "What do you mean?"

"They told me if we came here we could help." She gazed at her feet and then behind her as if she'd be grateful to fade back down the trail to the road.

"They?"

"The people in Victoria. From the coalition."

"Coalition?"

"I'm in the wrong place." She blushed. "I saw your car and the trail . . ." Her voice faded to nothing.

"How did you get here?" Paul asked. We heard all the infrequent traffic on the road—forest company trucks, the odd hiker's four-by-four. "We didn't hear your car."

The woman's face flamed crimson. Her daughter glared at us, hands on her narrow hips, and said, "We walked."

Walked? Eleven kilometres of logging road from the closest secondary highway? Forty more kilometres from the closest town? Three hours drive from Victoria?

"You're kidding," I stammered.

"We hitchhiked to the lake," the woman blurted out. "Then we walked." She shifted the baby on her hip. "You're not the protest camp, are you? It must be farther. We should go." She took her daughter's hand and backed up a step.

I hesitated, but Paul spoke up. "No, wait. Don't go."

He walked over and sat on his heels in front of me. I could see the beginnings of wrinkles at the sun-weathered corners of his mouth, the new growth of moustache on his upper lip. "We can't let them leave, Faye. It's dark in an hour."

"Not our problem." The thought of playing hostess to a trio of children made me weary.

"Where will they go?"

I scanned the three huddled together on the trail, their ragged clothes, the inadequate bag the woman carried over her shoulder. I couldn't ask them to bed down with the bears and cougars. "Just tonight." I didn't bother to hide my annoyance.

Paul jumped up. "I'll cook more rice."

He urged the three into the clearing, moved a jumble of gear off a log, and gestured for them to sit. The woman smiled shyly and her weary face transformed with a fragile beauty. She stuck out her hand. "I'm Mary."

"Paul." He grasped her fingers. "And Faye." He tilted his head in my direction, and then squatted in the duff in front of the little girl. "And you, madam?"

"My name's Rainbow." She inspected his face with her chocolate eyes as if to judge his merit. "Because one was over our house the day I was born. I was born at home, you know, in the bathtub."

"I didn't know," he answered, unfazed by the information. "Sounds like fun. Pleased to meet you, Rainbow. And what's your sister's name?"

"Brother," she growled. "He doesn't have a name yet. We're waiting. Until he can tell us." She paused. "We call him Cedar."

"Was there one in the yard the day he was born?"

She pushed out her lower lip and wrinkled her brow. "Hmmph."

Cedar, whose blond hair curled below his chin, hid his face in his mother's neck when Paul held out his finger and said, "You're in fine company. Lots of big cedars around here." The baby, about a year old and beautiful as a Raphaelite cherub, pawed at his mother's shirt. She eased off her pack and settled onto the log, then lifted and peeled back layers of clothing to expose a bare breast. The baby grasped the white flesh with chubby fingers and latched on to the swollen pink nipple. "Thanks for letting us stay," Mary said.

"No problem," Paul answered. "We'll figure it out in the morning. I'll help you put up your tent after we eat."

Mary bit her lip. "We don't have one."

"No tent!" I blurted out. We were on the wild west coast of Vancouver Island.

"I'm sorry." Her lower lip trembled. "They said they'd have lots of room for us." She pointed at her pack. "I have sleeping bags."

"It's okay," Paul said quickly. "We'll manage."

I raised my eyebrows and cleared my throat. Paul ignored me.

"How?" I demanded. Paul and I slept in two lightweight backpacking tents. "If you think I'm shar—"

"We'll figure it out," he interrupted.

"Did you bring food?" I shifted my laptop to a stump and stepped out from behind the log to face them. Rainbow's eyes widened, her mouth opened in a perfect O, and she gawked at me until her mother noticed and tugged on her sweater.

Mary shook her head, cheeks growing redder with each question. "They . . ."

". . . said they'd provide food too?" I finished her sentence. "They told you lots of things. What did they tell you about this protest?"

Mary smoothed the baby's fine hair with the tip of a finger. I strained to hear the woman's soft voice. "A man handed us a leaflet outside the library. It said the logging company is cutting the last big trees." She turned to Rainbow. "Do you still have it, honey? This was Rainbow's idea. To come and help."

The child reached into the pocket of her jacket, pulled out a crumpled pamphlet, and held it out to Paul with a grubby hand. The photograph on the front page of the cheap photocopied brochure showed the massive trunk of a Douglas-fir encircled by a ring of people. The caption read: "Save Big Mama and the Ancient Giants." The inside text described the imminent clear-cutting of the upper valley, a surprise move by the forest company, licensed by the government without public notice. The group called itself the Ancient Forest Coalition.

Paul and I exchanged a troubled look.

"You must be mistaken"—I pushed away a mounting uncertainty—"We haven't seen any group."

Paul handed the pamphlet back to the little girl. "We'll help you find them tomorrow."

Dinner with Mary and her children tried my patience. When Paul handed Rainbow her bowl of canned tuna, rice, and cheese, she crossed her arms, pointed her nose in the air, and announced, "We don't eat other animals. We're vegetarian." Paul cooked a new pot of our precious rice and served it with cheese and rehydrated vegetables. My shoulders ached with irritation, our meals planned down to the number of slices of cheese allowed per person per meal. The leftover tuna casserole would moulder in a garbage bag suspended in a tree or in the back of the car away from prowling animals until we managed to drive to town for supplies. I needn't have worried though, Paul wolfed it down, apologizing to Mary and Rainbow for his barbarous ways as he licked the last of the sticky tuna off the spoon.

We finished dinner in the dark. I lit the kerosene lantern and heated water for dishes on the camp stove. The orange glow of Paul's headlamp shone through the translucent wall of his tent, where he played peek-a-boo in a sleeping bag with a delighted Cedar. Their silhouettes danced like puppets on the pale green nylon, Paul's gear scattered on the ground outside the tent. I sloshed the bowls and cutlery around in a pot of water and biodegradable soap and slapped them on a log to dry. I didn't dare to ask him where he planned to sleep. The car? A head too short for his six-foot frame. His bivy sack? The air smelled of rain.

A shadow fell across my arm and I jumped. Rainbow, her finger in her mouth, stared at me out of dark pupils colourless in the glow of the lamp.

"Don't ever sneak up on me again," I growled. "You scared the shit out of me."

Rainbow removed her finger and twirled a lock of hair around it. "You sweared."

"If you don't go away, I'll swear again," I said. She didn't budge. In contrast to her brother, I found her plain, with a nose too tiny and lips too narrow for her square face. Her brown hair appeared without substance, drab and flyaway, but her eyes, large and intense, burned with intelligence. I turned back to the dishes.

"Mary says you're not one of them."

I plunged my hand into the grey and greasy dishwater and hunted around for the last few pieces of cutlery. "One of whom?" I pulled out a cheese-caked spoon.

"Snow White's dwarfs."

I groaned. I worked in the wilderness to avoid conversations like this.

"Mary says you're a regular person, but small like me."

"And what do you think?" I glared at the child's upturned face.

"Do you want to play dolls?" Rainbow pulled two naked plastic dolls—one white, one black, each the size of a thumb—out of her pocket.

"No, I don't want to play dolls," I snapped. I attacked the spoon with a wire pot scrubber.

"Then you're not like me." Without another word Rainbow skipped off toward Paul's tent, leaving me holding the spoon and the scrubber in the air, soapy water dripping onto my foot.

I stared after her. Paul nudged my shoulder as he walked by with a second pot of water. "You've got soap on your boot," he teased, setting the pot on the stove.

I threw the spoon onto a plate, carried the dishwater a dozen steps away, and dumped it out in the middle of a sword fern. "I hope you're making tea."

"Nope." He grinned. "Diaper water."

Mary travelled light. Besides the lack of tent and food, she carried only two cotton diapers for Cedar. "One to wear and one to dry," she explained. The woman failed to understand she had walked her children into a rainforest, a place where dry is a relative term. A place where three or four metres of rain falls each year. Where trees grow continuously in the mild temperatures, where it's never too hot or too cold, where it's too wet for forest fires. *You're a fool*, I wanted to scream at her, *can't you see*? Every surface dripped with life, green in a million shades, ankle thick moss, slime moulds, curled sheets of lichen, head high prehistoric ferns, cream and gold mushrooms at the base of every tree, bracket fungi clinging to mouldy trunks—dripping, creeping, clinging, crawling, sprouting, peeling, rotting.

It turns out Mary had neglected to bring another item for her children. Rain gear.

4

I woke in the middle of the night to the plop of tentative raindrops on the tent fly. Within five minutes, the rain had accelerated to a deluge. I unzipped the door halfway and shone a flashlight beam around the clearing. Through the curtain of water I could make out the blue polyethylene tarp protecting the kitchen and climbing gear, and the second tent where Mary and her children slept. The afternoon I'd spent in my back yard in Victoria sealing the seams of the two tents meant we would stay dry. But Paul, curled up like a fetus on the gravel bank in his bivy sac—a cocoon of waterproof nylon—was exposed to the elements. He'd chosen the spot with his usual care, away from the trees that dripped water long after a storm passed, and well up from the winter flood level.

"Why don't you sleep under the kitchen tarp?" I had suggested when he spread his bedding out on the ground, flipping stones away with his foot.

"You know I'm wild about stars. Besides, it's only one night," he answered.

Thick, heavy cloud now hid the constellations. I aimed the flashlight at the orange bulge of nylon. In reaction, it folded in half like a caterpillar and Paul squinted against the glare from the draw-stringed opening, beard glinting with droplets of water.

"Sorry." I redirected the beam. "Are you okay?"

He yawned. Water streamed from the slope of his hood and dripped off the end of his nose.

I unzipped the door of my tent wider and held the flap open. "Get in here," I ordered. "I'll make room."

He disappeared back into the bivy sac, the cocoon writhing about on the ground like a giant worm. Could he breathe? "What are you doing?" I couldn't make out the muffled answer. He stood—a shiny teetering phallus in a sheath of nylon—hopped across the clearing and wriggled out of the bag into my tent, naked but for a pair of briefs, bare skin luminous in the diffuse light. He drew his sleeping bag out of the sac like a rabbit out of a hat and spread it, still dry, in the space I had arranged between my bedding and my gear.

"What took you so long?" I zipped up the tent door, shutting out the weather.

He chuckled, his long body sliding back into his sleeping bag. "Are you sure you want to know?"

"Yes."

"I had to find my underwear."

"What do you think about this protest?" he asked once settled.

"I don't know," I answered, acutely aware of his body next to mine. "It's possible. Environmentalists have been fighting clear-cutting on the island for decades. Remember the blockade at Clayoquot ten years ago?"

"I was in Australia. Big news down under," he said. "Lots of arrests."

"I'll ask Roger about the pamphlet," I said. Roger Payne, the PCF forester, had helped me select our sites in the buffer zone. "He'll know. But I bet it's nothing."

Paul drifted into sleep. I lay awake on my side, facing him, aware of his breath, the gentle hiss in and out of his nostrils, the smell of rain on his skin. As my eyes adjusted to the dark, I could make out the contours of his face, the high, smooth forehead, his odd nose with its narrow ski jump bridge. I knew the acne scar on his right cheek, the way the trough of his upper lip vanished into moustache, the colour of his beard, a riot of red, blond, and brown shifting from long to short depending on his mood. After two years of working together in the canopy, Paul and I had formed a close friendship; I trusted him with my life. I worked hard to keep myself from wanting more from him. Not only was I his boss, but Paul collected women. A continuous string of smart, gorgeous women—tall women—who never lasted, their demise a faint hope for me at best. After long stretches of time together in the field, I had become his confidante.

"I don't know what I did wrong," he'd moan over the latest loss.

We'd mull over the possibilities, the insecurities of the woman in question, the nature of his work. Or the one I never brought up: his lack of resistance to a shiny new treasure passing by.

"Some women don't appreciate nice guys," I would assure him, unable—or unwilling—to complete the logical progression of my statement. *The right woman will come along one day.*

"The right guy will come along for you, Faye," he would say in response to my few unsatisfying stories about men. Les, my date for high school grad, an IQ of one sixty and an inability to maintain a conversation for longer than thirty seconds. A desperate and mismatched couple for one brief night. Bob, the brother of my one university friend Laura, who disappeared overseas to do aid work. Laura passed on the Dear Faye letter, a short hand-scrawled note I interpreted as, "I needed to go halfway around the world to avoid you." Will, who asked me to dress up in child's clothing the third and last time we slept together. All average-height men. I'd never met another dwarf in spite of the urgings of my mother. "There are organizations," Grace had insisted. I hadn't dated anyone since graduating with my bachelor degree. A master's. PHD. Post-grad work and a tenure-track professorship. Ten years since I'd last felt a warm body next to mine.

I longed to slide a finger through the brown mop of hair Paul seldom combed, but I didn't dare, his behaviour toward me invited nothing more than friendship. Last fall, he invited a new girlfriend, Tessa, along on one of our research trips. A perfect match for him, up for anything, amiable, polite. She loved to climb. Tessa didn't bat an eye when she met me. I couldn't stand her. The nights were torture. Paul moved their tent a discrete distance away, but not far enough. When I couldn't stand the grunts and moans, the sighs and murmurs any longer, I sat by the creek where the sound of flowing water drowned out their lovemaking. Paul always apologized in the morning. "Did we make too much noise, Faye?" he'd ask with all sincerity. I finally admitted to hearing them. On our next trip into the field, Paul strung two climber's hammocks close together high up in the trees on the edge of the camp. He and Tessa ascended at dusk and didn't descend until well after sunrise the next day. It was quiet, but I spent a sleepless night imagining what it must be like to make love in the canopy. I caved to Grace's pressure and signed up for an internet dating service for persons of short stature. In a week I had my first email from Bryan, a geologist from Saskatchewan. His most recent message had gone on far too long about his dog. Not promising. I rolled onto my back, burrowed into my sleeping bag, and listened to the rain on the fly until the sound lulled me to sleep.

The rain continued through the morning. No climbing possible. Paul delivered oatmeal, powdered milk, and tea to Mary in the tent about nine. Rainbow, dressed in a green garbage bag with holes torn out for her head and arms, and a wide-brimmed rain hat of Paul's, crouched by the edge of the stream and searched the pools for water walkers and frogs. After a frustrating hour spent adjusting the ropes supporting the kitchen shelter, I drove twenty minutes along the road to a spot where I had discovered I could get half-decent cell phone reception. The one tolerable use for a clear-cut. I organized my portable office—laptop wired to the cell phone—and turned on the system. It was a decent day for reception. A decent day meant rain. I sent a pointed message to Roger. *Are you cutting in the upper valley?* My inbox held three new messages: one from the biology department with a list of questions about my fall courses, one from Grace reminding me to send Patrick a birthday card, and one from Bryan with a lengthy description of an extremely rare rock he'd discovered. *I'm thinking of coming out that way and was hoping we could meet.* I resisted telling him the possibility was rarer than his rock; instead I thanked him for the photos of his dog, Mercy, attached to a previous email. At least Mercy was a living, breathing being. *I'm not much of a one for dogs myself.* I wrote. *They can't climb trees, although our neurotic border collie of my childhood used to run up the trunk of the apple tree in the yard and hang by its jaw from the lowest limb.* I went on to say that we were discovering rare things too, dozens, possibly hundreds of new species unique to the canopy. *We used to think temperate rainforests contained less biodiversity than tropical rainforest. No longer true. Bugs rule!*

I signed the email F.P., then paused, deleted the impersonal initials, and typed simply, Faye.

The rain quit on my way back to camp where I found lunch ready, Paul eager to get to work, the sun filtering through the ragged fingers of mist rising off the soggy earth. We ate lunch in the sunshine, and Mary hung Cedar's clean diaper on a tarp line to dry along with Rainbow's wet socks. We cleaned up, organized our climbing gear and some snacks, and strung our food bags from a limb too high for bears. Rainbow hovered nearby while Paul and I checked and packed our gear.

"Can I come?" Rainbow said. Paul and the girl both turned to me.

"No," I said. 'We've got lots of work to do."

"Please," the girl whined.

"Mary could come," Paul broke in and I swung around in surprise at the suggestion. He pointed hastily at the child. "For her . . . to watch Rainbow."

"Doesn't Mary want to find her protesters?"

"She'll want to watch too. I know it," Rainbow said. "And I'll help carry," she offered, a rising hope in her voice.

"She has a point," Paul said. A static rope long enough to rig a single tree weighed twelve kilos and filled a large hiking pack, not to mention the rest of the climbing and collecting equipment. A doctor once cautioned me against carrying a pack for fear of spinal compression of the neck. I chose to ignore the advice. But how much could a child carry?

"Please, please, please," Rainbow begged, palms pressed together, eyes pleading.

What a drama queen. "Help?" I begged Paul. A jubilant smile spread across his face and I threw up my hands. "Okay, but I take no responsibility."

"No problem," Paul said. "I got her." Rainbow squealed and hugged his leg.

"No asking a million questions," I ordered.

She waggled her head back and forth.

"And no wandering off. Bears and cougars live here."

Her expression widened. "I promise."

"Your mother has to watch you." I handed her a daypack full of carabiners and harnesses. "Paul and I have work to do. If you're any trouble, I'll send you back to camp."

She beamed, slipped her skinny arms through the pack straps, and scampered off, the pack banging low on her hips, equipment jangling inside. She returned minutes later with Mary, Cedar tucked into a sling wrapped around his mother's torso. Paul handed Mary two water bottles. He himself wore a large pack weighing close to thirty kilos, the crossbow strapped to his back.

Rainbow examined the bow. "Are you one of Robin Hood's men?"

"My old job," Paul joked.

"He was nice to poor people," she answered brightly. She laced her fingers around her pack straps. "I'm ready."

Paul led the group into the upper valley on the park trail, then turned northwest to cross the creek to the far bank, where the trail to our site was marked by a limp strip of orange flagging tape tied to a branch. Single file, we started up the steep slope where the trail quickly deteriorated. Paul helped Mary and the baby up the incline, but Rainbow refused any assistance, soldiering along behind me until we reached gentler ground. We stopped to catch our breath. The forest floor ahead was a labyrinth of felled limbs, debris, and downed trees. Paul and I had not yet had time to clear the route of winter fall. Guided by occasional strips of flagging, we made our way over, around, and under logs, our boots caked with mud from slogging through pockets of bog filled with yellow-leaved skunk cabbage.

An uprooted fir blocked our passage ahead. Paul climbed across with ease, then turned around to receive my gear. I heaved my pack across the thick-barked crevasse between us. The orangutan amulet dangled at the open neck of his muddy brown T-shirt. He'd shaved off his beard a few days earlier and appeared far younger than his thirty-two years, his newly exposed skin untanned and smooth, the line of his jaw more pronounced. His pupils were always a deeper shade of green in the forest. A wave of longing washed over me.

"Well?" Paul said, mouth upturned in an amused smile. "Are you coming or are you going to climb that sapling over there instead?"

"Sorry, daydreaming." I ignored the offer of a hand and slithered across on my belly, thankful I didn't have to suffer the indignity of crawling beneath the log on my butt. Paul held out his hand to Rainbow.

"I don't need help," Rainbow crowed, scrambling across on all fours like a bear cub. "I can do it like Faye."

"Dr. Faye to you." I readjusted the pack, already feeling the weight in the small of my back after a winter away from hiking.

"Wow," Rainbow exclaimed and pointed ahead where an enormous trunk shot up out of the undergrowth, towering above us like a skyscraper. We stopped, sweaty and panting beside the colossal specimen. A second mammoth loomed out of a tangle of salal. Beyond it a third. Our study trees. We had twenty-two trees from the flood plain to ridge top marked on our site map, each tree numbered on a grid for easy reference.

"Which one?" Paul tilted his head back and peered into the canopy.

"SS-1-3," I said. "I want to check the aerial traps."

We continued on until we reached a Sitka spruce we had measured at sixty-seven metres in height. Paul estimated it to be five hundred years old or more, older than the printing press, older than the Renaissance, a seedling when Christopher Columbus made his voyage to the New World. The tree was already rigged and we hunted around in the undergrowth for the parachute cord.

"What's that?" Rainbow asked.

"Didn't I say no questions?" At her wounded expression I explained. "It's cord for pulling up our ropes. We never leave our expensive climbing ropes in the trees."

"Would the squirrels eat them?"

I shushed her and sent her over to her mother, who had settled onto a log where she was already nursing Cedar, white breast showing at a gap at the edge of her sweater.

"Listen." Rainbow jumped up and down, pack thwacking on her back.

"I don't hear anything but you, Peanut," Mary answered dreamily.

"Why is the ground bouncy?" The girl sank to her knees and dug her fingers into the spongy layer of moss.

Paul scanned the path of the cord up into the canopy. "Because"—he tugged on the lightweight black line—"this forest is thousands of years old and under us are layers of rotted dead trees, roots, and needles grown over with moss and lichens and ferns and other plants and baby trees and nosy children." He gave a sharp yank and the cord ran free.

"Centuries?" Rainbow sat back on her heels. "Older than my grandpa? What's a lichen? What's that thing?" She pointed at a marker embedded in the base of the tree.

"SS-1-3." Paul opened the top of the pack and pulled out the end of the climbing rope. "It's the name of this tree. Sitka spruce, Site 1, Tree 3. See . . . markers all the way up."

"SS-1-3?" She craned her head back to view the row of aluminum discs the size of dollar coins nailed into the thick bark at regular intervals up the trunk. "What a funny name. I like Bruce the Spruce better."

"No talking," I scolded. "Hand me that pack and sit." To my surprise, Rainbow sat, laced her hands over the folds of her skirt, and watched Paul knot the ends of the parachute cord and the climbing rope together with a half-dozen clove hitches. Together Paul and I hauled the rope up through the pulley at the top of the tree and down the other side; the rope coiled out of the top of the pack like a charmed snake. While Paul anchored the leading end of the rope around another tree with a bowline, I donned my climbing gear.

"Ready." I clipped the ascender to the rope. "Stay back from the bottom of the tree," I warned Rainbow and Mary. "Watch for falling branches."

"If you hear us yell 'headache,'" Paul added. "Dive for the bushes."

He double-checked my harness and I started up. Paul continued along the trail to the next rigged tree, the goal for the afternoon to check a dozen suspended Malaise traps for captured arthropods I would identify in the lab back at the university during the winter.

I climbed steadily, pausing once to catch my breath. I reached branches at twenty-five metres and hooked my leg over a limb. Below, Mary and Rainbow, faces upturned, appeared as diminutive as Rainbow's two dolls. From the top of the tree they'd shrink to specks of colour through the foliage below, if visible at all. Rainbow stood and waved.

I reeled in the aerial flight-interception trap suspended on a pulley midway between two trees. The fine gossamer net—designed to intercept flying beetles and ants—was empty. The second trap five metres higher the same. The third trap yielded a handful of rove beetles and three types of spiders; one I suspected was a new species of dwarf weaver, awash and dead in the pool of alcohol. I was surprised to find a live green darner dragonfly clinging to the mesh high up in the trap. "What are you doing here?" I said. "You belong below near water." I reached in and pressed its silvery iridescent wings together with care, struck by the solid texture of the lacy fabric, and drew it out of the trap. Its emerald green thorax shimmered in the sunlight and I turned it over to examine the garnet stripe running along the turquoise abdomen. I wondered how I appeared to the darner through its bulbous compound eyes. A grainy pattern of light and dark dots? As fascinating to the darner as the darner to me? A giant? I should have collected it, returned it to the lab, and mounted it on a board with a pin for future reference. I didn't have the heart. I opened my fingers and the darner zipped out of my hand and headed off, darting back and forth, in the erratic way dragonflies do. I fished my field journal out of my pocket and made an entry. *Unusual occurrence of* Anax junius *at thirty-five metres, Site 1, Tree 3, Malaise trap #3. Specimen released.*

My radio crackled and Paul's voice cut in and out.

I stopped climbing, retrieved the hand-held from my pocket, and depressed the transmitter button. "What?"

"I think you better come down."

"I've hardly started."

"Come down," he answered and the radio cut out.

I looped a bite of rope through my descending equipment—a loop of metal called a whale's tail—tested my weight on the line, then unclipped the ascenders so I hung freely from the descender. The procedure took concentration and care, the transfer from ascenders to descender a vulnerable time for a climber, the danger of tying in to the wrong side of the rope an easy but potentially fatal mistake. I let the rope run slowly through my gloved fingers and the whale's tail, and dropped from my perch, the sensation the closest to what I imagined flying might be like, except I was on my way down to earth rather than up to sky. I had the ability to stop myself at will with a simple twist of the rope against the descender, but I loved the freedom of the long, smooth glide and rappelled to the base of the tree in one continuous slide. Mary and Cedar were asleep on Mary's sweater. Rainbow stood next to Paul, our spare climbing harness dangling from her slender hips.

"Can I try?" she asked the moment my feet touched the ground.

"No way." I unbuckled my own harness. "Too dangerous. And you should have a helmet on."

"I like climbing trees. Kids like climbing trees. You do."

"This is not the same. This is work, not playing, and it's climbing a rope. Not for kids."

"But you're a—"

"No, I'm not." I unclipped from the rope and shrugged my gear off in a heap. "What's up?" I said to Paul, who was watching me with an expression I couldn't read, hands slack at his sides as if he didn't know what to do with them. "Paul?"

He tilted his head in the direction of the trail and said, "Rainbow, stay with your mom."

I followed behind, alarmed at his uncharacteristic gravity. A dead body? One of our trees fallen in a storm? He led me upslope past four of our study trees and stopped at the base of Tree 7, our oldest, a redcedar, five metres in diameter, the crown split into three leaders that reached for the sky like a candelabra.

I sucked in my breath. "What the hell," I said, astonished to see a violent blue cross of spray paint marking the trunk. A blue timber tag on a tree meant cut me down . . . and soon. "We're still within park boundaries, aren't we?"

Paul spread his hand over the centre of the mark; the tails of the X extended beyond his fingers like arrows of blue light. "Yes. And besides, there's the buffer. They shouldn't be logging anywhere near here."

I sat on a nearby log. I couldn't tear my eyes away from Paul's hand and the threatening slash of paint beneath.

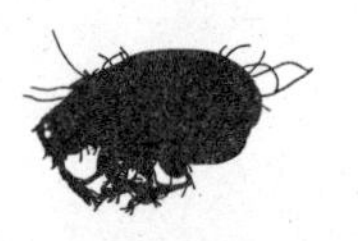

5

I steered my car along the rough gravel road in a light drizzle, avoiding potholes and on the watch for deer. On either side of the road, tall trees towered overhead.

A loaded logging truck careened out of a side road and I slammed on the brakes. The truck roared on ahead, mud and rock chips from the sodden roadbed spitting up behind its wheels onto the windshield, adding another pockmark to my already pitted view of the world. My anxiety rose again at the size of the giants piled on the truck bed—three enormous logs filled the truck to capacity—as they hurtled down the road from the upper valley, an area not slated for logging for years, an area planned for possible expansion of the park. An area where the sound of chain saws should be as rare as a marbled murrelet on the ground.

The car left old forest and entered clear-cut. I winced at the flat glare of light under overcast skies and the kilometres of stumps and splintered wood, streambeds clogged with debris, the ground ripped and heaved from the weight and churn of heavy machinery and the impact of hundred-tonne giants crashing to the ground. They couldn't do this to Otter Creek. Parks were sacrosanct. Moonscape, bomb site, ground zero, every cliché of devastation travelled through my mind. I understood the need for logging on the island; after all, as an academic I used more than my share of paper. I knew the industry supplied jobs for small rural communities. I accepted the concept of sharing the forest land among loggers, scientists, and hikers. But leave the big trees alone. Especially my big trees.

Ironically, PCF's regional field office had been built in the heart of a mature forest. The yard, an expanse of cracked pavement, was empty, loggers no longer housed in the drab green and white trailers that lined the edge of the clearing, but driven into the cut blocks each day from town in a company crummy. A pick-up sat outside the management office.

"Faye." Roger Payne rattled down the wooden steps, a wide smile on his boyish ruddy face, hand extended. "Chasing bugs again?" Roger, a transplanted New Zealander, lived in Duncan, the closest town, his wife pregnant, their third baby due in November. The day we met, he, like most people, appeared embarrassed and uncomfortable beneath a polite veneer, but over the time spent mapping out our buffer site together we'd become friendly. "What brings you all the way out here?"

"Did you get my email?"

"Haven't checked yet today."

"We found timber marks on one of our study trees inside the park boundary. Any idea why?"

"In the park?" His surprise seemed genuine.

"Yes. Our oldest tree. A seventy-metre cedar."

He took off his cap and scratched the top of his head.

"There's a woman at our camp who says she's here for a protest." I watched him for a failure to meet my eyes, the clearing of his throat. "And one of your trucks just about ran me off the road on my way out here, loaded, coming out of the upper valley. You weren't going to log in there until the park issue was resolved."

"Oh that." He laughed and I heard it—the catch—the microscopic hesitation in his response. He folded his cap in half and flapped it in and out of his palm. "We're taking a few loads out above the canyon. Keeping the guys working. We have a permit. Nothing to worry about."

"I respect your right to log, but my study relies on intact stands of old-growth at least five hundred metres from disturbance. We agreed on my long-term plots and the buffer. I can't lose those trees. Will you find out about the tag and let me know what's going on?"

"You bet." He shoved the offending hat into the back pocket of his jeans.

"I'd appreciate that," I answered, but his words didn't ease the knot that had formed in my stomach at the sight of the timber marking. "Soon."

"Sure, but don't worry your head over it. I'm sure it's nothing."

I wanted to believe him, he'd always been one of the nice guys in the company. I turned to go, then caught myself. I'd forgotten my manners. "How's your family?"

"You should see Pam," he said with a broad grin. "She's a house. I think it must be triplets."

On my way back to camp and halfway through the clear-cut, I pulled over to allow another oncoming logging truck loaded with old-growth cedar logs to pass. I brooded over Roger's twitchy reaction to my questions. *A few loads?* Were they taking them all out in a day? High grading the best and the biggest trees? I stepped on the gas and steered the car through a puddle. Mud and water sprayed up from the wheels onto the rear window, obscuring the view of the clear-cut behind.

Over dinner—chicken and vegetable stew minus the chicken—we learned a few facts about Mary. She was on her own, for one.

"No, I don't have a husband. Or a boyfriend," she explained with temerity and no apparent discomfort about the lack of a father for her children. "A woman has all a child needs."

"What do you do for money?" I asked, skeptical about her sincerity.

"I don't believe in money," she said, polishing off a second plate of our stew. "We go to the food bank and live in a room in a group house for a work trade. Rainbow and I clean the house once a week and keep the veggie garden, don't we, honey?"

"I'm home-schooled," Rainbow crowed, hopping on one foot on a stump. "Want to hear me count to a hundred? One two skip a few ninety-nine a hundred," she chanted in time with each hop.

Mary's idealism reminded me of my mother, forever a cause on the go. Grace had dragged my brothers and me around from protest to protest for most of my childhood: the annual peace march, the anti-nukes campaign—save the seals, save the oceans, save everything. When Grace campaigned to send money for starving children in Africa, we had eaten porridge three meals a day for a week. "It's more than they have, and without a nice home. No complaining." She'd cajole me and my brothers into donating our allowance to charity: Vietnamese boat people, rebels in Guatemala, flood victims in Bangladesh, and when word of an impending energy crisis reached her ears, she turned off the heat and, while we sat around the living room in our winter coats, explained how contributing to the oil-hungry western war machine was a sin. My father, Mel, disappeared during these times, taking refuge in his office at the community college where he taught math, working late in warm comfort with the cafeteria down the hall and a coffee machine outside his office door. I don't recall Mel ever standing up to my mother. I don't recall him ever standing up to or for anything. Including his daughter. When I would run home in tears from school, distraught at the teasing, he'd turn away, his reaction hidden behind thick glasses, and I would dry my face and pat him on the knee. "Don't worry, Dad, I'll figure it out."

Paul disappeared to the dug latrine behind an upturned root wad. Mary floated off to bed with Cedar asleep in her arms and Rainbow slid across the log to sit beside me. I nursed a cup of tea and tried to ignore her.

"Would you fix Tracey?" she asked, her dirt-smudged face tilted up with anticipation.

"Who's Tracey?"

"She." Rainbow held up the black plastic doll.

"What's wrong with her?"

"A bear bit her on the foot."

I took the tiny figure in my hand. "Why do you think I can fix her?"

"You're a doctor."

"Not a medical doctor."

She took the doll back. "What kind of doctor?"

"Doctor of philosophy in forest ecology. I went to school for a long time."

"Are you a tree doctor? Can you fix trees?"

"No, I don't fix trees, I study them."

"You are like me."

"I'm not a kid," I replied.

"I know." She slid her hand onto my knee. "But we both love trees."

The next day Paul found two more timber markings on trees in our buffer zone. After eight hours in the canopy, we returned to camp, dirty and tired.

"Roger insisted it was a mistake?" Paul stacked samples into a waterproof bin.

"That's what he said." I pulled off my muddy boot and moaned with pleasure at the release.

"He's a company man." Paul snorted. "A peon."

"I'll have to drive over to talk to him again." I sighed, another morning of sampling lost.

Paul put a pot of water on the stove for pasta. I set up my laptop—the battery freshly charged on the drive to the PCF camp—to transcribe entries from my field notebook into a database, our study too far along to risk losing data. Why would the company go after our study trees? It couldn't be a mistake. They had maps. I stopped typing and pondered the growth rings on the stump. The buffer kept our study site pure, dark and quiet, light subdued, the earth muffled in deep layers of litter and decomposed organic matter. Let in more light and species would be displaced by others that preferred sunnier, drier conditions. I watched the passage of a spider across its web strung between a branch of salal and the bark of one of the large hemlocks next to me. The delicate strands shone silver-gold, illuminated by a shaft of evening sun. Would the spider survive a disruption to its simple existence, at risk from a few extra rays of sun each day, a few millimetres less rain in a year? I turned my attention back to the computer screen and typed a quote from a colleague in Washington State. *Unlike people, trees give back so much and require little in return.*

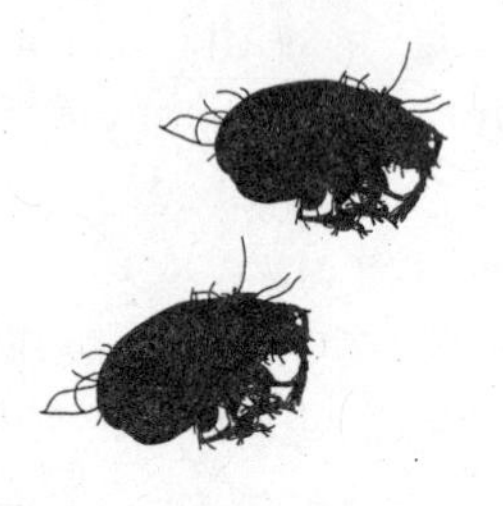

6

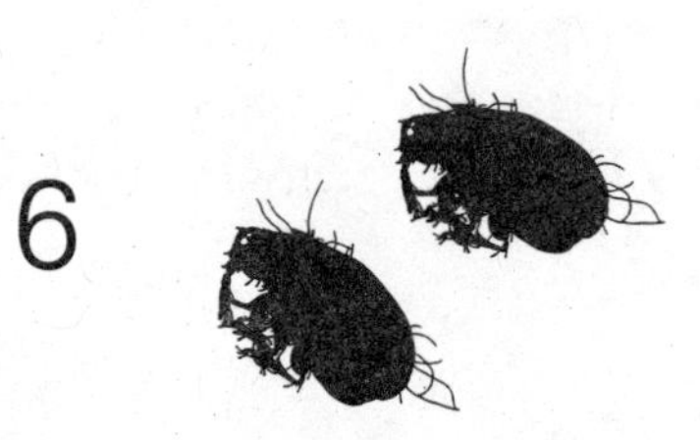

A second trip to PCF's yard the next morning proved futile, the trailer empty, Roger's pick-up nowhere in sight, a hand-scrawled note taped to the door. *Baby on the way. Back in a few days.* Rain pelted onto the windshield on the return drive to camp. The wipers slapped back and forth on high speed, the defroster on full to keep the window clear. I stopped in clear-cuts along the way three times to try calling the company regional office on my cell phone but couldn't get a decent signal.

The rain had lifted by the time I reached the bridge. Five mud-spattered vehicles were parked at the trailhead and I squeezed my car into a narrow spot ahead of them. The number of vehicles surprised me and I hoped they belonged to hikers travelling through, the idea of more strangers depressing. I walked the trail to the edge of camp and stopped in mid-step, stunned by the transformation. Eight tents, two tarps, and a second outdoor kitchen had sprouted up in my absence, the ground littered with stacks of boxes and equipment, people everywhere.

Rainbow tripped over a log in her hurry to reach me. She scrambled to her feet, cheeks flushed, hair in her eyes. "Dr. Faye. They came, the tree-saver people came."

I went in search of Paul. Rainbow straggled behind,

chattering non-stop. We found him with Mary and Cedar, staking down the fly on a large purple and white tent.

"Paul, what the hell's going on?" I demanded.

A fleeting cloud of guilt crossed his face before he offered his most disarming smile. "They showed up an hour ago."

"And you said they could set up here?"

"I didn't have much choice," he argued. "It's a public park."

"Dr. Pearson?" A head appeared in the door of the tent and a young man, dressed in a fleece vest, long-sleeved shirt, and cargo pants laden with multiple pockets crawled out. "You're Dr. Pearson?" he stammered.

"I'm her." I groaned inside at the all-too-familiar reaction. "Is there a problem?"

"No, I wasn't aware . . ." His voice trailed off and he struggled to his feet.

"That I was a dwarf?"

"Yes . . . I mean no. I didn't expect . . ." His clean-shaven face flushed scarlet under his tan.

"And you are?"

"Terry. Sorry." The man wiped his palms on the seat of his pants, crouched until eye level, and focused on the middle of my forehead. "Terry Seybold from AFC." He held out his hand. "My apology for the intrusion. We weren't aware you were here. Paul said you wouldn't mind . . . considering the cause," he added.

I ignored his extended hand and glared at Paul, who grinned sheepishly and lifted Cedar from Mary's arms.

"I'm not sure why you're here. I talked to Pacific Coast a few days ago and they assured me we have nothing to worry about."

"We understand the company plans to cut the upper valley this summer and fall," Terry said. "All of it."

"They can't," I insisted. "He explained they were only taking out a few truckloads."

"Can't they?" He riffled around in a box on the ground and pulled out a photocopied sheet of paper. "Here's a copy of their licence to cut, issued last week."

I took the paper from him and tried to focus on the text, distracted by the thought of blue slashes of paint on my trees, my life coming apart like the interwoven strands of a severed climbing rope. One by one.

Paul spent a third night in my tent. He claimed he couldn't find anyone else willing to accommodate Mary and her children.

"Oh?" I zipped my bag to my chin. The splat of raindrops on the tent fly promised another cold, wet night. "I'll need to drive to Duncan tomorrow to call the PCF office. I'll take them to the bus tomorrow. I can't imagine she'll want to stay under these conditions with those kids."

"I think she's here for the duration." Paul hesitated. "You don't mind if I share your tent for a bit longer, do you?"

"No." The blood rushed to my face and I was glad for the cover of darkness. "I don't mind." *Stay as long as you want.*

"It's getting pretty exciting out here," Paul said, cramming his jacket into a stuff sack to create a makeshift pillow.

"Exciting?" I snapped. "Aren't you worried about our trees?"

"Of course"—he wriggled into his bag—"but it's fun to have more company."

"You think it's fun to get arrested?" I argued. "There are better solutions."

"Like trying to get PCF's attention?"

"I thought you were on my side."

He was quiet for a moment. "I am," he answered, then paused. "The protesters are too."

"We rely on co-operation with the company."

"A deal with the devil?"

I rolled away from him. "I'm a scientist, Paul," I said. "I can't get political. Good night."

Paul was right, Mary wouldn't leave. I managed to get an email out to PCF from the clear-cut early in the morning. We spent the day in the canopy, returning late, hungry and tired after hours of climbing, to discover another twenty protesters and a dozen more tents crowding both sides of the stream. A line of cardboard signs propped against a log bore slogans painted in a rainbow of colours. *Trees Not Pulp. Stop the Greed, Save the Ancient Giants. A Tree Farm Is Not a Forest. Big Trees Not Big Stumps.* The group was gathered in a circle under the kitchen tarp, Terry pacing, talking into an expensive-looking radiophone. We stopped and stood at the back of the crowd, unable to reach our food or cooking supplies on the other side of the gathering.

Terry slipped the phone into his backpack and surveyed the waiting group. "I got the word," he announced. "We're to have the blockade up by dawn tomorrow. They're sending in a half-dozen loggers, a couple of yarders and of course the trucks later in the day."

"Will we get arrested?" a red-haired woman dressed all in lime green Gore-Tex asked.

"Not yet," Terry answered. "The company needs a court injunction against us. Our lawyers in Victoria will deal with that. Our goal is to stop the trees coming down, one day at a time."

Paul nudged me and whispered, "See, they have lawyers."

"How about tree spiking?" a young man in dreadlocks, standing not far from us, addressed the crowd. A piercing glinted in his eyebrow. "How about monkey wrenching? It's all they'll listen to." A current of discord surged over the crowd and a few people yelled out their agreement. I didn't like the way this meeting was going.

A huge man rose to his feet, big shouldered and well over six feet. "No. No tree spiking. No harming people or property," he said in a booming Québécois accent. 'I'm here for peaceful protest, eh. I am against logging, not loggers."

"Marcel's right," Terry said. "No reason to think the blockade won't work. It has in the past. Remember Clayoquot."

Several people nodded. One woman yelled out, "I was there!" Excited chatter broke out.

Terry raised his hand for silence. "Remember, our group advocates non-violent civil disobedience. Violence of any kind will not be tolerated"—he addressed the speaker with the head of dreadlocks—"Cougar, if you feel you can't abide by the rules, I will have to ask you to leave."

Cougar scowled and crossed his arms. I could see his right hand tucked in his armpit, middle finger extended. An involuntary shiver ran down my spine.

"And"—Terry turned to the group—"in case you didn't read our conduct policy before you left Victoria, no alcohol and no illicit drugs. Tread with respect on this park. Be a credit to us, not a liability. Okay." He raised his voice and his arm in the air. "Are you ready for tomorrow?"

"Yes," they cheered in response. The whistles and clapping that followed reminded me of a pep rally at a high school football game.

Terry called for silence. "Unless you have questions, get a sound sleep and see you at five AM. We have trees to save."

After dinner I carried a cup of hot chocolate to the edge of the clearing and settled on a log. Paul was off with Mary and the children to find space, I hoped, in one of the new tents. The camp bustled with activity like a nest of ants. People scurried around with armloads of equipment, talking and yelling to one another. A trio of young adults kicked around a multi-coloured crocheted Hackey Sack on the gravel bank. I longed for peace and quiet, Paul and I alone with our routines. The tall Frenchman, Marcel, spotted me and waved, then wove his way between the sea of tents, stepping across lines and tent pegs, leaping over logs, more nimble than I would have guessed for his size.

"I'm Marcel," he said and offered his hand, as large as four of my own, the palm yellow and calloused. "The little girl she say to call you Dr. Faye."

"Faye's fine."

"Faye it is," he said and sat beside me. Up close, I could see a stubble of coarse black hair on his chin, his teeth stained with nicotine. He offered me a chocolate chip cookie. "I'm addicted." He pulled his pocket open to reveal a half dozen more. "Better than smoking."

"Trying to quit?"

He nodded. "I smoke my first cigarette when I was nine. Ma mère she tell me the smoking would stunt my growth, eh." The log shifted beneath us with the force of his laugh and I steadied my mug to avoid a spill.

"How tall are you?" The top of my head reached no higher than his belt.

"Six foot five," he said. "Ma mère, she is four foot ten."

Technically a dwarf.

"Seven kids, three of us over six feet. Can you believe I was preemie?"

"No, I can't." I bit into the cookie. Crumbs dry as dust cascaded down the front of my jacket.

"You and me. We're the ones responsible for average."

"What do you mean?" I brushed the crumbs onto the ground for the night cleaning crew of deer mice.

"Human statistics. Without tall ones like me, the average for people would measure the height of ma mère. And without small ones like you, average would be six foot or more. I tell people who give me a hard time about my height, without me, the human race would be nothing." He roared with laughter again. "Seriously"—he hung his arms in mock despair between his legs—"you don't know how hard it is to get a girl when you are big as me."

"They don't know what they're missing," I teased.

He held out his hands, one large enough to span my entire back, fingers like sausages. "I give excellent massage."

"Where are you from?"

"Quebec. A village in the Gaspé. I live in Montreal for years while I take a master's degree in philosophy at Université de Montréal. For the last fifteen year, I live in Newfoundland."

"Teaching philosophy?"

"No, I study the philosophy of resource extraction. I worked fishing."

"Fine use of a degree," I said.

"Shameful, oui." He stretched, arms extended like maple limbs. "No more. The fish, they are all gone. The cod, the halibut, the shad," he said. "A tragedy."

"What are you doing here?"

"I try to prevent the same thing from happening to these magnificent trees." He gestured around the grove. "They speak to me, these trees. For once I feel small. I was too late for the fish. I must help these trees."

"I guess you'll get your chance tomorrow."

He slapped his knee. "Oui. And that means Marcel must sleep." He heaved himself off the log, towering above me. Without warning he bent, lifted me off the ground, and squeezed me to his chest.

"Marcel, put me down," I sputtered, nose full of beard. "Don't," I ordered once my feet touched solid ground, "ever pick me up again." I felt like I was chastising the Friendly Giant.

"Okay,' he said. "Je m'excuse, eh? You remind me of ma mère. Your blue eyes, they are like hers."

I walked to the riverbank in search of solitude. The rains had swelled the river, the current swift and strong, and the shoreline had retreated up the bank. My favourite rock was almost submerged, so I settled on a sandy spot at the edge of the trees. Dusk was falling, the perfect time for wildlife viewing, but I wasn't hopeful with the amount of noise coming from the camp. I wondered what my father, Mel the mathematician, would think of Marcel's analysis of average. Scientists discarded outlier data—measurements falling outside the normal range of variation—as suspect and unreliable. I expected Marcel already knew the scientific term for average was *mean*.

I jumped when Paul plopped down beside me. "I've been looking all over for you," he said. "Would you take Rainbow?"

"Where?" I answered.

"In your tent."

"What?" I stammered, unsure I'd heard him right. "What for? She's happy enough with her mom. That tent's too small for three of—"

"Two."

"What do you mean? Two. Where are you going?" His eyes

slid from mine and I realized what he wanted. "But . . . what about . . ."—I groped for a name—"What about Tessa?"

He shrugged. "Will you?"

I didn't answer. He didn't know what he was asking.

"Please," he pleaded, touching my shoulder. "I'll owe you. Big time."

A few minutes after he left, Rainbow stomped, crying, into the tent and threw her sleeping bag onto the spot vacated by Paul. Eyes red-rimmed and swollen, her words caught in her throat as she ranted.

"I h . . . hate him," she declared. "I'm n . . . not inviting him to my b . . . birthday. And if he ever gets m . . . m . . . married . . . . . . I'm not c . . . c . . . coming to his wedding and my . . . my mom stays . . . r . . . right here with me." She stabbed the floor of the tent three times with her index finger.

I helped arrange her bedding, not bothering to assure her Paul would move on soon enough. "I need to sleep, no talking." I felt oddly motherly as I tucked the edge of the bag around Rainbow's chin. My lecture about peace and quiet was unnecessary; she rolled away, chest still heaving with her anguish. I hesitated, then patted her thin back, struck by the feel of the sharp edges of bone under the shabby cotton T-shirt she wore for pyjamas.

The protesters rose before dawn and I listened from the tent while they fixed breakfast and headed out for the road, Rainbow a motionless lump beside me. Her bare feet stuck out from the top of her bag and, worried she would suffocate, I zipped the bag open. I dressed, crawled outside, and made myself a cup of tea. Paul and Mary were still asleep, their shoes tucked under the tent fly. *So much for her convictions about trees.* Before making the long drive to Duncan to talk to the company, I decided to try an area upriver where I'd had intermittent success receiving a cell phone signal in the past. I was in luck, the signal weak but adequate, I punched in the number for the PCF office and listened to it ring. When the receptionist answered, I explained my situation.

"If you leave your phone number, someone will call," she assured me.

"I can't be reached by phone. Can't I talk to anyone in charge?" I said.

"No one's in."

"Can I make an appointment?" I said, irritated at the run-around.

"I'll have someone call you," she repeated.

"You can't call me," I yelled into the phone before hanging up. "I'm in the middle of freaking nowhere."

Furious, I hooked up my laptop and pounded out an email to the company CEO, another to Roger, but it seemed futile, my last few pleas to them had gone unanswered. An email from Bryan appeared in my Inbox. I opened it to find another picture of him and his dog, Mercy. I rolled my eyes; I'd have to compete with a dog if I got involved with this man. He wore boots, khakis, and a hard hat, a rock hammer in one hand. *Dear Faye: I'm in the Badlands in southern Alberta hunting for fossils for an archaeological outfit. How's the research coming? I'd like to hear more about your high-flying career. In person?* I groaned. I should tell him to give up. I hit Delete, shut off the laptop, and headed for home.

I calmed down on the walk back to camp, only to find Rainbow outside the tent, crying and lacing up her boots.

"They left me behind," she sniffed and wiped her nose on her sleeve, leaving a smear of snot on the cuff. "I want to save the trees too."

The camp was deserted; Paul's tent empty, the camp quiet for the first time in days. The stream bubbled along, the breeze rustled through high branches. A winter wren chirped from a huckleberry. *Chit chit.*

"A wren." I pointed at the bird, hoping to distract her, but she was already marching down the path to the road. "Whoa, where are you going?"

"I have to save the trees." She didn't stop.

I ran up and caught her by the arm. "I can't let you tromp around out there alone."

"They left me."

I regarded her pinched face, flushed from crying, jaw set like the Rock of Gibraltar, fists clenched by her sides.

"Do you know the way?"

She stretched out her arm and pointed her finger up the trail.

"And then where?"

Her shoulders slumped and a pitiful sob shook her body. My heart dropped and I sighed, mourning the lost hours of solitude. "Come on," I said, nodding back toward camp. "Let's have breakfast and I'll take you to your mother."

The parking area was empty when we reached the trailhead. My car was nowhere to be seen. "Looks like Paul took my car," I said, annoyed. I glared up the road, then back at the trail. Above, the sky was clear and blue through the breaks in the canopy, the sun warm. "Want to walk?" I asked.

Rainbow's face brightened.

I walked, Rainbow did anything but. She skipped, ran, twirled, hopped, and sashayed. She squatted to examine a banana slug crossing the road, poking her finger in the thick gluey trail of slime. She picked a fireweed from the ditch and smelled it. Every dozen steps or so, for no apparent reason, she would jump straight up in the air and waggle her feet back and forth. Her constant motion made me dizzy. And she talked.

"What's this?" She pointed to a pile of dried dung at the side of the road.

"Bear scat," I answered.

"What's scat?"

"Shit."

She poked at it with a stick, flipped it over, and peered into the woods.

"It's old," I explained.

She threw the stick into the ditch and skipped on. "Do you have a dad?"

I considered saying no. Other than the biological imperative of most male mammals to sire and nourish offspring, Mel hardly qualified. On my thirteenth birthday—a Pearson right of passage, the magic doorway to the mysteries of adolescence—

Mel took me out for lunch. He didn't want to go, a fact I gleaned from an eavesdropped argument between Mel and Grace in the living room the night before my birthday while I did homework in the kitchen.

"It's not the same," Mel said.

"Of course, it's the same," Grace countered. "She's your child too. No different than the boys."

"Come on, Grace. She's not like the boys. What am I supposed to say to her," he said. "I have no idea what she'll go through as a teenager."

"Tell her . . . tell her you love her." I could hear the exasperation in Grace's tone. "She's waited for this day since you took Patrick to lunch six years ago. We've always talked about the birthday lunch with Dad. Don't disappoint her."

The next day at noon we walked to Sally's Diner. Mel lurched along on his spider legs, shoulders hunched like a vulture, bracing against an imaginary wind, his hands in his jacket pockets, head topped by the Tilley hat he wore whenever he went out in "the weather," as he called it. By the time he reached the diner in a parking lot at the edge of the beach, I trailed half a block behind. He waited at a picnic table for me to catch up before we went inside.

Contrary to what my mother thought, I had dreaded this lunch with Mel since Patrick and Steve related their experience to me one night in the back yard. Their main advice, "Take a book." But in the back of my mind, I maintained a faint hope my father might one day meet my eyes and ask, "Tell me one important thing about your life."

We ordered fish and chips and ate in silence. Mel gazed out the window at the ocean, at his food, around the room. His pale blue eyes flitted behind his glasses from table to table as if searching for old friends who might spirit him away from his predicament, from this odd small person, his daughter. He seemed perpetually restless, unable to settle at a single task, concentrate on another human for enough time to understand we walked and talked and felt emotions. I worried about Patrick, a physical clone of Mel. Would he lose his affable disposition, his social graces? By the time dessert arrived—a piece of strawberry rhubarb pie and ice cream topped with a gritty pink birthday candle he fished out of his pocket and lit with a paper match—I wanted to slink out the door. He did say "Happy Birthday" after I blew out the candle, but the sentiment ended with an upsurge in his voice like a question mark that left a whiff of smoky uncertainty in the air. I dawdled home along the beach and arrived a half hour after Mel. Grace met me at the door. "How'd it go, dear?" she asked. "Dad said you enjoyed yourselves."

"Sure," I answered, then headed out to the back yard and my refuge, the tree house my brothers had built me when I was seven and that I should have outgrown long ago. "He brought me a candle," I mumbled as I walked past my mother.

I looked at Rainbow. She couldn't put a name to her father, let alone a face or an accusation. "Yes, I have a dad."

"Where is he?"

"In Qualicum."

"I don't have a dad."

"Everyone has a dad."

"I know. About sperms and eggs. Mary says I'm like baby Jesus. He didn't have a dad." She took three hops ahead and whirled around. "Mary doesn't always tell the truth." She twirled in a circle on one foot. "Is he small too?"

"Baby Jesus?"

"Noooo." She raised both arms in irritation and let them flop to her sides. "Your dad."

"He's a bit taller than Paul."

"Is your mom small?"

"No."

"Do you have brothers and sisters?"

"Brothers and they're not little either. Keep walking."

"How did you get small?"

"An evil fairy godmother put a spell on me. I used to be taller than your mom."

She stopped and swung around to face me. "Truly?"

"No, not truly. I was born this way."

"You were a big baby," she exclaimed.

"I was a little baby. I grew and . . . I stopped."

"Will I stop too?'

"You ask too many questions."

She ran ahead, bent over to peer between her legs and waddled backward. "How much farther?"

"About five minutes."

Suddenly, she straightened, turned around, and wailed. Huge sobs wracked her slender body as she shuffled along, head down, shoulders slumped forward.

Bewildered, I trotted up beside her. "What's the matter with you?"

She continued to weep, face hidden in the folds of her sleeve.

I turned her toward me and cupped her chin. "Rainbow, what's wrong. Are you hurt?"

She peered out above her forearm, pupils clear and cheeks dry. "I'm practising for Mary."

I failed to hold back a smile. "Here. Give me your hand before you fall on your face."

For once she complied and we trudged hand in hand along the road, the dwarf and the wailing child, trees a living roof above our heads.

My station wagon appeared around a curve in the road ahead. Paul drove alongside and rolled down the window, knees up at shoulder level.

"You could have taken the extenders off," I scolded.

"I like the challenge," he answered with a grin. "I came to pick up Rainbow," he said. "What's wrong with her?"

I smoothed the hair plastered to Rainbow's forehead and patted her heaving back. "She's upset her mom left her behind."

"We didn't want to wake you up. Sorry. Hop in and I'll drive you the rest of the way."

Rainbow tugged on my hand and continued up the road.

"I think she prefers to walk." I fell into place beside her. "What's happening up there?"

"Not much," he answered. "A company pick-up pulled up an hour ago, turned around and left. I guess I'll see you back there." He did a U-turn, and glided past, waving like the Queen, his antics eliciting no response from Rainbow.

We arrived at the entrance to the upper valley road to find the protesters milling about, talking, in front of the locked gate—a single bar of red-painted steel. Rainbow received a great deal of mileage out of her theatrics, Mary beside herself with guilt at her daughter's distress. Protesters carried placards over their shoulders. Three men were chained to the gate. No sign of loggers, logging trucks, or machinery.

Paul drove me back to camp and we spent a strained afternoon checking traps, avoiding talk of the protest, the subject of Mary. At the end of the day, we walked the trail through the buffer zone and counted the timber marks. Five trees. I wanted to cry.

"Marbled murrelets are nesting in here," Paul announced as we stood at the base of a giant fir.

"What?" I asked, surprised he hadn't told me earlier. Nobody cared about arthropods, but marbled murrelets carried threatened status, their nests and eggs protected. An occupied nest could mean no road building, no cutting of trees. "Why didn't you tell me earlier?" I asked.

"I'm wasn't sure, but I've heard adults call and"—he dug in his pants pocket and pulled out a piece of tissue, unfolding it into his hand to reveal a delicate green-hued fragment of shell blotched with purple—"I spent an hour yesterday searching the base of these trees." He handed me the shell fragment.

I held the near weightless shell in the palm of my hand. "Any idea which tree?"

We peered again up into the canopy to study the green confusion above. Which tree, which ancient limb, which moss mat held the shallow depression where a murrelet would lay a single egg?

"I'll inform Roger in the morning," I said. "He can't ignore murrelets."

"This fir sure is a giant," Paul observed, head craned back. "Makes me feel like a dwarf."

"Me too," I said.

He nudged my boot affectionately with his toe. "Sorry, I forget."

I nudged him back. "Me too."

Late the next afternoon, I received an email reply from Roger. *Interesting about the murrelets. I'll send our ecologist in soon to check it out. Roger. P.S. It's a boy!*

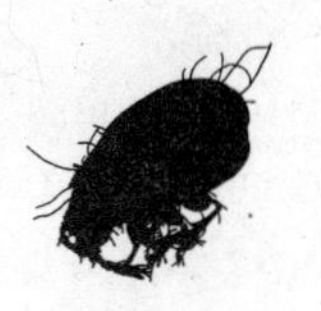

7

After the fifth day of occupying the road with no signs of loggers, the protesters—who referred to themselves as forest defenders—straggled back at dusk, dirty after days of camping and no showers and discouraged by the lack of progress. A meagre dinner of pasta and canned tomato sauce fuelled a growing frustration.

"This is crap." A middle-aged man overturned his bowl on the ground; the sauce splattered like blood across the stones and forest litter at his feet.

A woman burst into tears. "It's not our fault. All we had was pasta."

"I'm not talking about the food," the man growled. "I'm talking about this whole damn thing. It's a waste of time."

"I agree," a plump woman soaking her foot in a cooking pot full of warm water echoed. "Let's go home. I need a shower."

Marcel heaved himself off the ground and banged his bowl and cup together. "If we go, we will be playing into their hands," he argued. "The company, they are trying to outwait us, eh."

"Yah, aren't we in this for the long run?" an older man called out.

"The multinationals are the ones in it for the long run. Seventy-five per cent of the island's old-growth's gone," a young woman with a mass of wild black curls retorted. "If we don't stand up and say no, they'll keep cutting until it's all gone to toilet paper and tabloids. I'm staying."

"Twenty-five per cent left, Sue?" the man who dumped his dinner argued. "I can hear them. Still twenty-five per cent old-growth left? Plenty for all of us, toothpicks, you tree-huggers and the birds."

"Bull-shit. Their head office is in New York. They don't care about the animals," Cougar chided. "Or us."

"What do you think, Faye?" Terry turned to me. "You're the scientist. Is twenty-five per cent enough?"

I had avoided their political discussions, feigning disinterest to keep them at bay. Weren't the issues too complex to solve by civil disobedience? Processes existed to deal with the problem without breaking the law. But my research had uncovered more questions than it answered. "We don't know much about these old rainforests," I said. "We're finding new species of arthropods in the canopy all the time. I'm for keeping all the bits and pieces."

"Yeah, how many species have gone extinct before we know about them?" Sue said.

I squirmed at the comment the way I did when Mel observed I spent my time recording species before they disappeared. Underneath my well constructed and scientific counterarguments, I heard the cruel truth in his words. Protecting small tracts of land in parks wouldn't prevent a loss of biodiversity. How much intact wild land does a wolf, an elk, a goshawk, a canopy beetle need?

"My job will go extinct if I'm not back to work by next week," the plump woman argued.

"Mine too."

"Okay." Terry held up his hands. "We can't expect all of you to hang in here forever. Do we have a core group of people willing to stay as long as it takes? The rest of you can leave for home and work from there. If it gets hot on the road and they arrest people, we'll need supplies, new recruits, and support from outside."

A number of people bobbed their heads in agreement.

"Raise your hand if you can commit to stay."

A smattering of hands went up, among them Marcel, Mary, Rainbow, a white-haired Japanese man dressed all in black, Sue and two of her student friends from Vancouver, the dreadlocked man, Cougar, and his silent companion who went by the name of Squirrel.

"Excellent," Terry said. "We should manage to keep the road closed. I'll let the Victoria office know if we need backup. If you leave, keep in touch with them."

A black bear hung around the perimeter of the camp, attracted by the smells of cooking, curious about the increased activity in its territory. At night, his grunts and footfalls sounded through the thin walls of the tents, and as he grew braver, he ventured farther into the clearing, tongued huckleberries off bushes, raked open logs for ants, left claw marks in tree trunks, knocked over gear and brushed past tents. The campers took extra care to cache their food supplies up a tree or in a car, and I insisted they rinse all the dishes three times to remove temptation from our night visitor. One afternoon before dark he appeared at the edge of the clearing. His big shaggy head rocked back and forth, nostrils flaring.

"Git," I yelled, clanging together a pot and its lid as I stepped toward him; I prayed he wouldn't charge.

He swivelled his gaze in my direction, stood on his hind legs and sniffed the air, then dropped his front paws back to the ground and lumbered away into the forest without a backward glance, the fat and muscle on his haunches rolling as he walked.

The reduction in the number of people trampling the forest floor came none too soon, hiking boots and rain a destructive combination, the trail to the road and the latrine path rutted and muddy. I stopped my lectures on the danger of compaction at the base of trees and instead erected short fences of flagging tape and sticks around all the trees at the edge of the clearing. An unmistakable and effective message.

The remaining protestors spent their days on the road from pre-dawn until mid-afternoon when confident the logging crews had vacated the area in a crummy for home. Once back at camp, they pitched in with cooking and camp maintenance, took naps in their tents or the sun when possible, swam in the river, and sat around discussing strategy and the politics of cutting trees. Terry, who became more harried over time, spent endless hours on his radiophone, frequently dashing off in his car to find a clear-cut with better reception. He made pronouncements about the status of the court injunction, the political moves of the company who had hired a PR firm to greenwash their image and downplay the protest, and the progress of the letter-writing campaign to the premier and the forest minister. "Supporters are marching to the Legislature on Saturday," he declared one evening.

Mary spent most of her time nursing Cedar, rinsing diapers, and flirting with Paul. Marcel proved a willing cook. "I learned from ma mère, eh?" Sue, Chris, and Jen, the three biology students from Vancouver, played Hackey Sack between the tents or wandered around the forest identifying plants from natural history field guides during their spare time. Mr. Kimori, the Japanese gentleman, a handsome stocky man with salt-and-pepper hair, went about his day surrounded by an aura of calm, well dressed, always in black. He spent hours drawing and painting in a large sketchbook and in the evening after dinner he sat by the stream with a mirror and trimmed his moustache and narrow beard with a fine pair of scissors before his nightcap of green tea. When not on the blockade with her mother, Rainbow followed me around like a puppy. Cougar and Squirrel raised my hackles, their attitude militant and their social skills non-existent.

"Are you prejudiced against dreadlocks and eyebrow piercings?" Paul teased.

"I've never seen them offer to cook or do dishes, paint

signs or carry groceries." I suspected they were high on pot most of the time and was careful never to leave anything of value lying around.

After three days of clear weather, the camp awoke to a fresh deluge of rain. Leaky tents, damp matches, and wet clothing meant the protesters got off to a late departure. When they reached the road they found the gate unlocked and evidence of heavy equipment traffic. Terry and Cougar hiked up the road and returned an hour later, expressions grim, bearing bad news. The company had given them the slip and were cutting trees in the upper valley. The group huddled together to discuss the unexpected turn of events. A crew-cab truck with a company logo on the door roared past, spraying muddy water over the already dejected and sodden troop. The truck screeched to a halt thirty metres away and reversed, careening back and forth across the road, grinding to a stop mere steps from the protesters. The driver, a wiry dark-haired man dressed in jeans, a plaid shirt, and work-boots, leaped from the cab, brandishing a wrench.

"Can't take rain?" he leered.

Terry stepped forward. "Put the wrench away," he cautioned. "We have nothing against you."

"Hah." The man spat on the ground at Terry's feet. "I don't know whose welfare you're sucking off. I work for a living."

"You don't want to work yourself out of a living, do you?" Terry held his ground. "No trees, no loggers."

"You've already got your trees. Government don't allow logging in parks." The logger brushed water angrily from his forehead with his arm. "I got a wife, kids. Who do you think you are, you tree-huggers, coming here, interfering with things that ain't none of your business."

"The public owns these trees," Cougar yelled. "We have every right, you scab."

The logger's face twisted; he took three steps toward Cougar, wrench raised. Terry blocked his way and cautioned Cougar back.

"We don't want any violence. We're here to protest peacefully against the government and the company. We don't want anyone hurt."

"You better get the hell off this road then." He threw the wrench in the back of the pick-up, slammed the door shut behind him, and gunned the engine. A shower of gravel flew up from the back tires as he steered for the middle of the crowd. Everyone fled for the water-filled ditches. The truck veered off at the last moment and sped away.

Paul and I heard the whole story under the kitchen tarp when the protesters fled to camp, shaken, wet, and muddy.

"The guy's insane," Sue declared, wringing water from her socks. "He was this close"—she held up a finger and a thumb—"to cracking Cougar over the head."

"At least no one got hurt," Terry said. "It's no surprise the loggers aren't sympathetic. They take us as a threat to their jobs. But the whole upper valley's a tiny fraction of the company's tenure."

"More jobs are lost to mechanization and raw log exports than to the creation of parks," Chris added.

"But big trees," Marcel countered. "One tree is worth, what, fifty grand?"

"What about the trees?" Cougar stood and pointed out into the forest. "They're fucking out there cutting trees right now."

"We have to beat the workers to the road in the morning," Terry insisted.

"Not adequate. We failed once already. We need people in the trees," Cougar yelled. "We need a tree-sit. A round-the-clock tree-sit."

Silence fell at the new suggestion.

"Two lines of defence, the road and the trees," Terry said. "Brilliant."

A stir of excitement rippled through the group.

"Great plan. Who will go up?"

"Me," Cougar volunteered. "Me and Squirrel. We can do it." Squirrel raised his eyebrows but didn't object.

Jen stood. "I'll go too," she said. "We need a strategy. If we spread the tree-sit out they can't cut within a tree height radius of each tree without hurting us."

"We'll need equipment," Terry said. "And know-how."

All attention shifted to Paul and me.

"Will you help us?" Mary walked over and took Paul's hand. I nearly gagged, waiting for the woman to flutter her eyelids and pout.

He hesitated. "Faye?"

I forced my gaze from the saccharine scene between Paul and Mary to the ragtag gathering, the weight of their hope directed at me. They didn't know what they asked of me. To jeopardize my reputation, to step over the line of objectivity. I shook my head. "No, I can't."

Paul took my arm and steered me to the other side of the clearing. "They need us. It'll be safer if we help," he said, then added. "Do you want to see our trees coming down?"

"Of course not," I said, shaking his hand off, the rain pelting onto our heads. I pulled up my hood. "But I'm working through proper channels."

He gave a short laugh. "Your proper channels don't seem interested in talking."

"They have to," I argued. "We have the murrelets now."

He glanced back over at the shelter where the protesters had resumed talking among themselves. Mary watched us from the edge of the group. "A tree-sit might delay logging long enough for you to get answers."

I wavered, the suggestion compelling.

"Who will know?" he said. "They won't tell the company we helped."

Cougar? Mary? Could I trust any of them? I crossed my arms. "No, Paul, I can't."

"Well, I'll do it without you then," he said and stalked away.

I watched him return to the circle. The group cheered. Terry slapped him on the back. Mary threw her arms around him and kissed him on the mouth. My chest tightened. I was losing him. To Mary. To my principles. I checked my watch. Enough time for a call in to PCF's office. No signal and I'd drive to their yard, to Vancouver if I had to. I grabbed keys, wallet, and cell phone and headed up the soggy trail for the car.

I collided with two hikers around the first bend. They were shrouded in rain gear, appearing like bulging packs with legs. One of the hikers stepped back and called out a muffled greeting. Sodden wisps of white hair had escaped from the edge of her rain hat and were plastered on her cheek. She let her hood fall back from her face. Her glasses were fogged up.

"Hello, Faye," the woman said.

"Mother?" I gasped. "What on earth are you doing here?"

Terry and Paul left in Terry's four-by-four to drive to town to buy ropes, gear, tarps, and plywood. The rest of the group, buoyed by the new plan, maintained a presence on the rain-shrouded road. They dodged two loaded logging trucks hauling out of the upper valley and endured the posturing, taunts, and curses of homebound loggers at the end of the day. I spent the afternoon trying to convince Grace and her best friend Esther to go home.

I sat on a stump under the kitchen shelter and watched the two women set up their camp in the rain. In spite of the bulk of her bright yellow slicker and pants, Grace carried herself with an elegance I had always viewed with awe and envy, the fluidity of her movements suggesting her limbs were made of air or water instead of bone and tendon. She never dropped things, or stumbled, each step, each hand gesture a flawless choreography. I knew she'd danced with the Royal Winnipeg Ballet until she quit, at twenty-two, to marry Mel and have children. No regrets, she always said. I found the trade hard to believe. A life of dance, music, and fame for Mel, Qualicum, and three rowdy children? My birth a certain shock. Grace must have hoped for a girl. Ballet lessons and pink tutus, satin toe shoes. Instead, after two galumphing boys who preferred hockey and soccer, she got me. A tiny mutation on a single chromosome.

I was my mother's fall from grace. When I asked her about my birth, she merely described my emergence "more difficult than the boys"; that relatives and friends had exclaimed on sight of my week-old face, "but she's so pretty." My interpretation: the birth was hell, the relatives shocked. As a romantic teenager, I'd conjured the momentous occasion up with pen and paper. I remembered the embarrassing gist of it.

Unlike my elder brothers, who slid from Grace's womb with the ease of soft fruit dropping from a tree, I nearly killed my mother the night I was born. Twice.

In the hours between midnight and dawn, the time when all things mysterious and life-wrenching happen, after thirty-six hours of labour—and a crescendo of drug-induced contractions—I burst into the world with an audible pop that turned the heads of the nurses, Mel hovering in the hallway, the doctor waiting with gloved hands.

Pop. The sound of rectal muscle parting against the force of the baby's too-large head. The first sign of my lack of elegance.

I dropped, newborn, into startled silence.

Chaos erupted against the absence of a cry. While the room filled with monitors, machines, and an emergency medical team, Grace, confused, lifted her empty arms from the pillow. "Where's my baby?" The doctor, a kind woman with liberal leanings, focused like everyone else in the room on the scene in the corner—the oxygen tank, the wheeled incubator, the mutterings of the neonatal specialists—turned back to the bed, eyes tired above the white paper mask over her mouth.

"A girl . . ."

Of course I didn't know any of this. I didn't know if the doctor was kind, a woman or liberal. The precise instant of birth. Whether my father gaped at my stunted and bowed legs, willing me to die, or Grace's tears of regret mingled with the first watery stream of breast milk on my tongue. I had torn up the story into bite-sized pieces one day years later and fed them to my gerbil.

"I draw the line at sleeping on the ground." Grace manoeuvred a light folding camp cot through the door of their full-height tent. "We are over sixty." Grace appeared a decade younger, few wrinkles and slim, her hair—the white still streaked with coppery brown—swept up in a coil at the back of her elegant neck.

"Why don't you draw the line at camping altogether," I argued. "Go home and write letters, make phone calls. I can give you a list," I said. "I'm sure Terry would have lots of suggestions."

"After all the work it took to get here? Besides, didn't you get my email. I explained it all to you. Affirmative action. Peaceful resistance."

I mumbled about a lack of a connection. Rainbow, on sick leave from the blockade because of a runny nose, called out from Grace's tent where she was testing out Esther's cot, "Let them stay, Dr. Faye."

"You keep out of this," I shot back.

"I'm afraid you have no say in the matter, dear. Esther and I are here to do what we can to help." Grace shook her sleeping bag from its sack and tossed it through the door to Rainbow.

Esther, Grace's loyal friend for thirty-five years, looked her age and was quite capable of dropping things and stumbling. She hammered in a stake at the corner of the tent. "Your mother and I never back down from a fight for justice."

I knew Esther spoke the truth, she and Grace a formidable team at the endless marches I endured along with my brothers, Esther's four children, and a dog or two, the dogs tolerating banners with slogans like *Paws for Peace* or *I Bark for Human Rights. Save the Trees* was no different.

"What about Dad?" I whined, childishly.

"Your father can take care of himself for a few days. I told him he could bail us out if necessary."

"You're not going to get arrested, are you?"

"If need be," she repeated.

"It's not going to help," I insisted.

Grace fixed me with the gaze that never failed to stop me in my tracks, my mother's sharp opal eyes pinning me to the wall or in this case a tree. "'It is any day better to stand erect with a broken and bandaged head than to crawl on one's belly.'"

How could one argue with Mahatma Gandhi?

"Come on, Rainbow," I said. "Let's go make lunch."

As soon as the loggers abandoned the upper valley for the night, locking the gate behind them, the defenders packed the supplies needed to establish the tree-sit. Mary, Grace, and Esther remained at camp to watch the children and the belongings. I avoided the preparations, intending to hole up in my tent, get an early night, resume my aborted mission in the morning, find some answers. I made a quick visit to the latrine and was cinching up my belt, pondering the logistics of hauling half sheets of plywood up into a tree in the dark, when the sound of voices approached from the direction of camp. I peered around the crude privacy curtain erected by Esther an hour earlier and witnessed Mary, childfree and leading a feckless Cougar, run into view. The woman leaned back against a tree and pulled him to her, her hands tangled in his matted hair. He curved into her, grinding his pelvis against hers, and the two of them moaned and grunted like rutting bears, tongues flicking. Cougar lifted her skirt with one hand and tugged at his belt with the other. Horrified, I searched around for an avenue of escape.

"Maaaary." A voice called and Cedar's cry drifted from the camp.

The pair pulled apart, kissed again, and Mary ran off in one direction, adjusting her clothing, Cougar in another. My stomach turned as I thought of Paul and his tender heart, though I couldn't help but feel a sense of justice. Cougar and Mary. The two belonged together, joined forever by their nose rings.

When I crossed camp heading for my tent, I found Mary kissing Paul goodbye, jostling Cedar on her hip. Cougar watched from the trail, loaded down with a heavy backpack, his face twisted with contempt. "Let's go," he snarled.

While I read scientific journals in my tent, the group hiked along the haul road loaded with gear, hoping to find the new clear-cut, choose the trees, and set the ropes before dark, rigging them by headlamp to ensure the sitters climbed into the platforms before morning. Paul related the scene to me at breakfast the next morning. He described how the rain had abated, persisting in a fine mist that settled on clothing and hair in tiny glistening droplets. A rough track that ripped through the wall of trees along the road heralded the site of the afternoon's logging, a large opening full of equipment, logs, and stumps. They stopped at the edge of the clearing and surveyed the scene in silence. The view resembled a bomb blast: shattered trunks, broken branches, crushed shrubs and ferns, ravaged earth. Piles of delimbed trees rested by the yarder, waiting for the trucks.

Terry waded through the carnage to an enormous stump and climbed up between two jagged vertical slivers of wood that rose like daggers above his head. One by one they followed until all eight of them stood side by side across the span of fresh-cut wood. The sharp fragrance of cedar permeated the air.

"Jesus," Squirrel muttered, one of the few words he'd uttered out loud since he arrived.

"I feel ill," Sue said. "How can people do this?"

"Come on." Cougar stepped forward. "Dirt in their gas tanks'll put a stop to this."

"No." Terry grabbed him by the arm. "Vandalism works against us."

Cougar shook off Terry's hold. "Wimp," he growled and took another step toward the edge of the stump.

Terry moved in front of him. "Peaceful protest. No violence. Or you are out of here."

Cougar stiffened and clenched both hands into fists.

"Terry's right," Paul interrupted. "Your tree-sit's a great plan, Cougar. It's worked in California and Oregon. They can't cut with people in the trees and it doesn't hurt anyone."

Cougar turned to Paul, his face deformed by a malicious grimace. The rest of the group braced for an explosion and was surprised when he answered, "Sure. What are we waiting for?" He lifted his arm and pointed. "Hey, where's he going?"

Mr. Kimori had climbed off the slab and was picking his way through the slash to the yarder. He clambered up into the cab, his cap of silvery hair visible through the dusty window.

"What on earth is he doing?" Terry mumbled.

"The Buddhist has a mean streak," Cougar sneered.

"Shut up, Cougar," Jen snapped.

Mr. Kimori climbed from the cab and pushed the door closed. He brushed the dust from his black nylon pants, then made his way back to the stump, the expression on his face one of detached satisfaction. When he reached the group he said. "Shall we work?"

"Do you mind telling us what you did in the yarder, Mr. Kimori," Terry said. "We don't condone damage to equipment."

Mr. Kimori reached into the pocket of his vest and drew out his hand. He opened his fingers to reveal a cluster of tiny red and black ladybugs scattered across his palm.

"What the hell?" Cougar jumped from the stump onto the ground beside Mr. Kimori.

Mr. Kimori closed his fingers around the ladybugs, reached over and grasped the handle of the hunting knife that always hung in a sheath from Cougar's belt, pulling it free before Cougar could protest.

"Give me that back," Cougar growled, but Mr. Kimori held out his hand toward the man. He opened his fingers and inverted the knife point into the middle of his palm. The observers drew a collective breath. Mr. Kimori rotated the knife tip up; a single ladybug clung to the glinting metal.

"Fridge magnet," he said. "I left one on the dash. A peace offering."

Paul and Terry chose three trees, far enough apart to deter cutting in most of the area, but close enough so the tree-sitters could still communicate. Over the course of the night, the crew constructed rudimentary platforms high up in each of the trees, hauling plywood and tarps up with ropes and pulleys until they had three solid shelters. An hour before dawn, Paul talked Cougar, Squirrel, and Jen up to their makeshift nests. Squirrel balked halfway and Paul coaxed him the final distance. Sleeping gear and warm clothes were hauled to the platforms along with light backpacking stoves and fuel, a few days worth of food and water, and a bucket latrine each. One radiophone with spare battery was shared between the three of them. Supplies would be replenished nightly.

Cougar hauled his rope up for the final time. Paul called to him. "Would you keep track of any birds you see? Watch for marbled murrelets. Brown and white, big as a robin. Sounds like this . . ." He cupped his hand around his mouth. "Keer, keer."

Cougar grunted and withdrew to his sleeping bag. The team packed up and headed back to camp, the lights on their headlamps bobbing through the trees like fireflies.

8

Roger's truck was parked outside the trailer when I arrived. He opened the door at my knock, dark circles under his eyes. "Faye, come on in," he said, appearing unsurprised at my arrival. He returned to his desk, the surface a jumble of papers and empty coffee cups. "Sorry for the mess, I'm getting behind with the new baby."

"Of course," I said, embarrassed I'd forgotten. He was preoccupied, that's all the problem was. "Well, congratulations," I said lamely.

"Thanks," he answered. "Mixed blessing," he added quickly, nodding. "I know why you're here"—he shuffled through his papers—"I've asked the ecologist to check in with you, but he's busy for another week. I promise, he'll come out." He held up a scrap of paper. "Here's our correspondence."

His conciliatory manner disarmed me. "That's . . . great," I said. "Did you find out about the timber markings?"

"Haven't had time," he said, shaking his head. "Cal can do that when he comes out." He tapped his pen on the desk.

"Well"—I slid off the chair, relieved—"I guess that's all I need to know. I better let you get back to work."

He stood. "You've got quite a crew out there at the campsite."

I stopped, startled by the unexpected comment. “We do, yes.”

“What are they up to?”

“Protesting,” I replied warily. Wasn’t it obvious?

“These guys can damage equipment, blow things up. Anyone we should watch out for?”

“I wouldn’t know,” I said, heading for the door. “I do my thing, they do theirs.”

On the way back to camp I stopped at a rise in the road and walked a short distance to an outcropping where I could see over the valley. A family of sooty grouse, startled from the underbrush by my footsteps, scattered ahead of me. The mother zigzagged frantically back and forth to draw my attention while her babies scurried to safety. I sat on a large rock and thought about my conversation with Roger. I could wait a week. But not much longer. We needed to finish up our work and get back to town soon. Process the samples before they dried out. I was supposed to teach a summer course the beginning of July and was scheduled to speak at a conference in Lima in August. With all the distractions, I hadn’t worked on either. But I couldn’t leave until my trees were safe. A river of green flowed out before me across the landscape. No clear-cutting visible, easy to tell myself Roger was sincere. *A few trees. Keep the men working.* I didn’t need to worry. I bade farewell to the family of grouse hiding in the bushes and headed back to the car. I was glad I stuck to my guns over the tree-sit. Obviously, the company was watching.

Life in camp reached a state of strained equilibrium. The protesters manned the blockade during daylight hours. Terry checked in with the tree-sitters nightly, coordinating the delivery of food and water. Paul appeared to have forgiven me and we spent long days in the canopy. Grace and Esther turned out to be more than helpful, relieving the original members of the group of a number of tasks, performing most of the cooking and laundry, although I had to insist they stop ordering us all to wash up before dinner. The two women earned a place in Marcel's hall of fame by baking chocolate chip cookies in a tiny solar oven that materialized from Esther's pack. Esther carried a walking stick with a metal tip everywhere she went, which she used to pry PCF's survey stakes from the ground. "This messes them up," she'd say, tying the offending stake to her day pack for later disposal. They organized evening lectures on the history and techniques of non-violent civil disobedience, where they quoted Gandhi and Martin Luther King Jr. *ad nauseum*.

"How are things going with Bryan?" Grace asked one morning before breakfast, settling herself on a stump where I worked at my computer.

"Bryan?" I said absently, typing data into a spreadsheet.

"Your usual elusive self," she said. "You know who I mean."

"No one named Bryan here."

"Your internet pal."

"Oh . . . him." I hadn't read his last two emails.

"Do you like him?"

"We talk about his dog and rocks."

"Doesn't sound promising."

"It's not."

She took another sip of tea. "What about the other one."

"Other one?'

"On the list I gave you. What was his name? Jeffrey? John? The engineer."

"I hate engineers."

"Marcel likes you."

I snorted. "What a cute couple. He could carry me in his pocket when I got tired."

"Stubborn girl. There's a perfect man out there waiting for you."

I switched off the computer and jammed it into its case. "My size, right, Mom? Perfect." I stood and hoisted the bag onto my shoulder. "Lay off," I said, then went in search of Paul to plan our next day's work schedule.

I found him leaning against a large boulder, having breakfast with the forest defenders. Mary sat nearby eating a plateful of scrambled tofu and eggs, Cedar on her knee, the baby barefoot, wearing a folded handkerchief for a diaper, and a tie-dyed T-shirt. He pulled at her hair and she plunked him onto his bum beside the log. His fat fingers sorted through the pebbles between his chubby legs and he picked up a fist-sized rock, stuck it in his mouth, and sucked on it with great concentration. Mary replaced the rock with a rice cracker, which he promptly threw to the ground. He rolled onto his knees, pulled himself to standing on Mary's leg, and took four unsteady steps before falling backward onto his diapered bottom. We cheered and clapped, setting Cedar off into a startled bout of crying. The walking surprised us all, not least his mother. He had never ventured far from Mary's arms and always stayed wherever she put him, content to watch the world go by or explore within arm's reach, earning him the nickname Buddha Baby. Rainbow picked him up under his arms—his legs dangled below her knees—and cooed in his ear until he stopped crying.

"I worried I'd still be carrying him at twenty," Mary laughed. "Rainbow walked at nine months."

"You'll have no rest," Esther said. "I'll bet he's running in two days."

"Wait 'til the climbing starts." Grace raised an eyebrow and gestured with her chin toward me.

"Bon," Marcel said. "For a baby to learn to walk on this rough ground and in bare feet. He'll have a first-class balance."

Rainbow propped Cedar up beside the log again, backed up three steps, and held out her arms.

"Come on, Cedar bug," she crooned. "Walk to sister."

Cedar gurgled with pleasure. A smile lit up his fat cheeks and he took both hands away from the log and clapped his palms together. He lifted his dimpled knee and set his pink foot forward into the dirt, hands in the air. He wavered, caught himself, another step, another. Rainbow backed up and he took one more step toward her, then twirled around and tottered straight to Paul.

"Hey, wee man." He lifted the baby on to his lap and Cedar laughed and pulled at Paul's beard. "We'll climb trees together in no time."

"No!" Rainbow stood in the centre of the circle, fists clenched, eyes blazing. "No! No! No!" She stomped her boot in the dirt, turned on her heel, and marched off into the forest. Paul and Mary exchanged glances. Neither moved.

"Isn't anyone going after her?" I asked.

Mary moved over and sat beside Paul and Cedar. "She won't go far."

I recalled Rainbow setting off down the trail alone to find her mother at the protest site. This woman did not understand her daughter.

"There're cougars out here, non-human ones." I directed the comment at Mary, who stared back unabashed, the other Cougar out of trouble, twenty metres up a hemlock in the upper valley. "They like juicy children. Hell, I'll go."

I hunted the forest near the camp for over half an hour before I found Rainbow's hiding spot, a large western redcedar lightning struck decades ago, a cave worn smooth and deep into the trunk and big enough to fit a dozen people standing. The sound of crying led me to the base of the tree and I peered in through the dark opening to find her huddled at the back of the hollow, sobbing into her skirt. I crawled through the crude entrance, my knees scuffing through dirt and wood chips, and leaned back against the time-smoothed wall, breathing in the damp smell of decayed wood.

"Go away," Rainbow growled, her voice muffled in the folds of her dress.

"How do you know I'm not a bear and this is my den? Bears like cedar caves."

She lifted her head to reveal a red-rimmed eye. "You're not a bear. Bears are furry."

"You're smart."

"I'm not going back."

"Me neither. It's a lot quieter here."

Rainbow dropped her head back onto her knees and resumed crying, but her sobs soon became forced, then dwindled to half-hearted sniffles.

"Did you know this tree has a name?" I asked.

Her small head waggled back and forth on her knees.

"Do you want to know what it is?"

The top of her head bobbed slowly up and down.

"Rainbow's Hollow," I lied.

Rainbow's head shot up and she squinted from between narrowed eyelids. "Truly?"

"No, but would you like to name it Rainbow's Hollow?"

"Yes," she said suspiciously.

"Lots of the trees in this forest have names."

"Are trees people?"

"No, they're plants," I answered, glad to have her attention.

"But they're like people, aren't they?" Rainbow leaned her elbows on her knees and her chin in her hands.

"Well, they come from a sperm and an egg, like people,' I said. "Except for trees they're called pollen and seed. Trees aren't conscious like us, but they remember things. Their trunks record all that happens to them. Scientists can read what the climate was like from hundreds of years ago in the growth rings of trees."

"Trees grow and live and remember like people, but they're slower, right?" She jumped up, instantly bright with excitement. "Let's sleep here and make a kitchen." She stretched out her arms across the space. "It's big enough for both of us."

"Won't your mom miss you?"

The light in her face vanished and she hung her head. "She doesn't love me anymore."

"Of course she does," I said without conviction.

"She loves him."

"Who, Paul?"

Rainbow crossed her arms and turned away, chin thrust forward. "I don't want to talk about him."

"Okay, let's not. Let's talk about trees. When I was a kid and mad or sad or worried, I had a tree I shared my troubles with. This could be your tree."

"Could it?"

"Sure, if you promise to tell your mom when you come out here."

She hesitated. "Didn't your mom and dad love you?"

The question threw me off balance. *Trust a child.* "You ask too many questions," I answered. "How would you like to climb a tree?"

"Could I? Up a rope like you do?"

"Yup. But you have to ask your mom and we need Paul to help us."

She stuck out her bottom lip and scowled.

"He's our safety man," I coaxed.

"Okay, but I'm not talking to him."

Paul and I rigged one of the hemlocks at the edge of the clearing with two climbing ropes. Rainbow watched from her perch on an elbow of root and prattled away about whatever came into her head, leaping from her seat, then sitting again, unable to contain her excitement.

"Do mother trees care for their babies?" She batted at the soft floppy head of a seedling sprouting from a decomposed limb embedded in the forest floor beside her.

"In a way," I answered, adjusting the smallest harness to fit Rainbow's tiny hips, sobered by the realization that the length of webbing required for her arms and legs was not much shorter than my own. "Seedlings get nutrients from the roots of the adult tree. Try this."

After a practice session waist height off the ground, I followed Rainbow up; she scooted along like a monkey. Her pluck reminded me of myself as a child, always in a tree. Once adults, most of us lose our ease in trees, our feet less flexible, our bodies too tall and heavy. *Homo sapiens* are the only primates who don't live part of our lives in the canopy.

"Is this right, Dr. Faye? Is this right?"

"Yes. Push your feet straight down though, not out."

"I feel like a spider going up my web. Do you feel like a spider? Does the tree know we're climbing it? What's this tree's name? Can you feel the wind, Dr. Faye?"

Rainbow's enthusiasm reminded me of the first time I climbed a rope up a tree. My supervisor in grad school questioned my desire to study canopy bugs. "You're not serious," he said. "If you have to study canopy arthropods, hire a certified arborist to do your collections." I hired the arborist—an affable man named Al—took him out to the closest old-growth forest, and asked him to show me how to climb a rope into a tree.

"You?" he said.

"Yes, me," I answered. "I'm short, not disabled."

Al showed me how to rig the tree, how to shoot the lines, how to work them up higher and higher in stages, how to set the pulley. We hauled the climbing rope up and secured it.

"You're not so much climbing as walking up the rope." He demonstrated how to use the ascenders and the foot loops.

Easy, I thought, anxious to experience the rope. Ten minutes later I was dangling in mid-air, not three metres above the ground, clinging to the thumb-thick coil of polyester and nylon, terrified to let go, paralyzed in place.

"Put your faith in the rope," Al urged from below. "Let go and lie back."

I released one tentative hand, then the other.

"Breathe," he said.

I closed my eyes, listened to the air hiss in and out through my nostrils, and stretched my legs against the webbing. Tilting my head back I looked up. My body rotated around the rope; the canopy revolved above me; sunlight filtered through the ceiling of needles, the blue sky high above, flickering off and on.

"You okay?" Al called up.

I couldn't bring myself to look down.

"Try again."

I took another deep breath and started my jerky passage up the rope. As I climbed, the world of the forest canopy opened up in front of me like a hidden valley on the other side of a mountain and a feeling of elation slowly displaced my panic. I didn't make it to the top of the tree that day, but I was hooked.

"I've never balked at heights before," I had commented to Al at lunch beside a small stream.

"Don't worry," he answered, "my first time up a rope scared me too. It's the exposure, hanging in mid-air."

"It's all about trusting in the rope, I guess," I concluded.

"Yeah, but you know," Al replied, "if it breaks, the rope won't save you."

Rainbow and I climbed to where the trunk split into a broad crotch ample enough to accommodate us both. I showed Rainbow how to secure herself to the branch with a nylon lanyard and a carabiner.

"Wow," she crowed. "Paul, look at me." She waved at him.

"You weren't going to talk to him," I teased.

"Oh, I forgot," she said, then yelled down. "Don't look at me, Paul." Without a breath she babbled on. "This moss is as thick as a bed. Do you like being a tree doctor?"

"I like working as a forest ecologist. And that's not moss on the branch, it's tree-ruffle liverwort." The dark green shiny mat of flattened leaves hid the bark of the limb.

"Funny name. I have a wart on my knee. Can I be a forest cologist when I grow up?"

"Wort not wart and the term is e-cologist," I corrected. *The field of canopy research won't know what hit it.*

"Are there other little eeecologists?" She poked at the liverwort.

"I'm the only one I know."

"I hope I stay small like you."

I mussed her hair affectionately. "Here," I said and searched the lacy foliage along a branch above our heads. I plopped a hairless green-and-yellow-striped caterpillar, as long as Rainbow's baby finger, into her cupped hand. The caterpillar squirmed and she squealed.

"If you're going to study ecology you can't be squeamish," I cautioned.

"What is it?" Rainbow lifted her palm close to her face.

"A phantom hemlock looper larva."

"What does it do?" The looper inched its way across her palm.

"Chews on needles."

"Does it hurt the tree?"

"Only when there are lots of them." I plucked the larva from her hand and returned it to the branch. "It'll turn into a moth in the fall."

"How?"

"Do you know the word *metamorphosis*?" She shook her head. "It means a change of form. A crawling larva transforms into a winged flier."

"Like the Beast?"

"Beast?"

"Beauty and the Beast."

"You sure know your fairy tales," I said. "Let's see what else we can find. There." Amber-coloured sap oozed from a gash in the trunk. "We might find bark beetles."

"Ruff, ruff," Rainbow barked like a dog and giggled.

"Clown." I lifted the edge of a piece of bark and a flurry of tiny oval brown beetles scurried out.

"What's the sticky stuff?" Rainbow blocked the passage of the beetles with the edge of her hand and the shiny bugs scuttled up and into her palm.

"It's pitch, tree blood. When the beetle drills a hole to eat the wood, the tree fills the hole with pitch to chase the beetle out."

Rainbow watched the minute arthropods scuttle across her skin. "Could a beetle eat a whole big tree?"

"No. It would take hundreds. And they like old or dying trees and have lots of help from other creatures. And it takes a long time. Ready to go down?" I clipped in Rainbow's descender and unclipped the Jumars to ready her for the rappel.

"Ready spaghetti." She reached out, plucked a scrap of

fungus from my hair, her hand smeared with pitch, and giggled. "You're turning into a tree."

"You too." I tugged a twig full of lacy green needles off Rainbow's sweater, and mused how chlorophyll and human haemoglobin differed by only a single molecule.

"I'm a tree," Rainbow's high sweet voice rang out across the forest like birdsong.

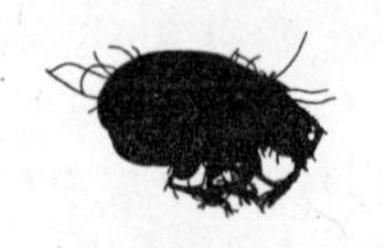

9

Paul and I drovc to Duncan for supplies. When word got out, a stream of people dropped by my tent with requests and I scrawled a list in a notebook. Mary sidled up, Cedar on her shoulders, bouncing his palms on the top of her head. I waited with irritation for the woman to speak, knowing she had no money. She lowered the baby to her hip and jostled him gently, although the baby appeared perfectly happy. I strained to hear her soft voice. "Sorry?"

She blushed. "Would you . . . talk to Rainbow?"

"About?"

Cedar squirmed and she set him onto the ground between her feet where he immediately stuffed a handful of moss into his mouth.

Spit it out, I wanted to yell to both of them.

"She won't eat. She says . . . she doesn't want to grow. She wants to stay small like you."

"Oh." I held back a smile. "What an imp."

"She thinks the world of you. I hope you don't mind her tagging along all the time."

"No bother," I answered. "Sure, I'll talk to her before we leave for town. She's got a mind of her own, though. Might not make any difference."

"I'd appreciate if you'd try." Mary paused. "I admire you too."

The statement took me aback.

"I watch you out here doing your work, climbing those skinny ropes into these huge trees. I'd die of fright before I left the ground." She picked at a strand of matted hair with her fingers. "You're a wonderful role model, a strong independent woman."

The sentiment, however banal, surprised me. "Don't." I held up my hand. "I'm no different than any other canopy scientist." I noticed Cedar, tottering on the top of a stump, hands sticky with pitch. "You might want to watch your kid."

"Oh, baby." Mary scooped him up into her arms. "He's been a terror since he started walking. I'd better get ready for the road," she said and took a few steps away, then pivoted on one foot, her skirt swirling around her legs, to face me again. "Don't worry about Paul."

"What do you mean?"

"There's nothing serious between us."

"Why would I care?"

"I've been honest," she said. "I don't do . . . domestic relationships." She rested her cheek on her child's head. "I didn't have much of a role model."

My heart softened. Grace always used to say one shouldn't underestimate the complexity of a human being. "Paul's a big boy," I said.

Mary ducked her head and lifted Cedar back onto her shoulders. "Thanks." Cedar waved his chubby fingers at me as they walked away, Mary's slender spine swaying like a sapling in a breeze.

I found Rainbow with Mr. Kimori. The two stood beside a young cedar, its branches curved gracefully downward close to the ground. Faces set in concentration, they dangled sheets of sketching paper in the air beside the tips of the branches.

"What are you two up to?" I said.

"Tree painting," Rainbow answered, tongue between her teeth, head bent, intent on her work.

"You're painting the tree?"

"Nope." Rainbow swung around and held out the sheet

of paper. "The tree's painting." Random swatches and spatters of blue and yellow like Japanese ink drawings decorated the page. "We put water colours on the needles and the wind blows them around and paints the paper." Rainbow shoved her picture toward me. "Here. It's for you."

Tenderness welled up in my chest at her gesture.

"Mr. Kimori showed me how." She smiled over at him. He smiled back and bowed. Rainbow chattered on. "Did you know a tree can move seven times around the world in a year?"

"Oh?" I accepted the gift. "Trees can paint and walk too?"

"No, silly." She giggled. "You add up how far all the branches swing in the wind," she explained. "Right, Mr. Kimori?"

"Right, Rainbow." Mr. Kimori held up his painting. Miniature black birds winging across a white sky.

I swallowed my breakfast speech. "Homemade granola?" I offered Rainbow a bowl. "I need a taster. It's got dried cranberries. Let's say it's a trade for the painting. Mr. Kimori?"

"Ah yes," he said. "A full stomach makes a happy painter. I'll get my dishes."

Rainbow scrutinized the gift with suspicion, but when Mr. Kimori returned and I divided the cereal three ways and added milk, she accepted. The three of us ate side by side on a log, the artwork spread to dry on a bed of moss at the base of the tree.

"What brought you here, Mr. Kimori?" I picked a cedar needle out of my cereal.

"I am a Buddhist," he answered. "We revere all life."

"That's it?"

"And, like you, I have a special affinity for trees," he said.

"What does your family think about you blockading a logging road and risking arrest?"

"I live alone." His placed his bowl and spoon on the log and folded his hands in his lap. "My wife died a decade ago and we had no children." He touched Rainbow's arm and his face brightened. "It is nice to spend time with children."

"Would your wife approve of what you are doing?"

"She would be right here beside me." He raised a finger up beside his ear. "Listen."

The song of a Swainson's thrush trilled like music from across the creek.

"Is it your wife, Mr. Kimori?" Rainbow asked excitedly. "Is she reincarl . . . re—"

"Reincarnated as a bird?" He tweaked her cheek affectionately. "She loved birds. It sings beautifully, doesn't it?"

The thrush sang three more times and was silent.

"What do you do when you're not blockading logging trucks or painting with trees?" I inverted my bowl to let the last of the milk drip into the duff at my feet, the white liquid seeping quickly into the spongy ground.

"I own a clothing store"—he patted his black fleece vest—"I cater to Asian men." His eyes glittered. "I call it Mr. Small and Short."

"You're teasing us," I said.

"Yes," he laughed. "I am."

Paul and I walked the aisles of the supermarket, cart loaded with bags of rice, instant oatmeal, dried juice packages, tinned food, and odds and ends requested by various people. I related to Paul the story of Rainbow's refusal to eat.

"She's spunky," he said. "It wouldn't surprise me if she willed herself to stop growing. I love those kids."

"Rainbow won't talk to you," I countered, peering ahead over the cart handle that came to the middle of my forehead.

"True." He frowned. "But she let me take her hunting for clouded salamanders in woody debris yesterday." He chuckled. "She used hand signals to ask questions."

"Don't get too attached," I cautioned.

"Why not?" he said. "They could use a bit of stability."

"Mary's not the one."

"What do you mean?"

"A hunch." I'd said too much. He could cry on my shoulder when he needed to. "Let's hope this is our last supply run." I checked toilet paper off the list. "My car is going to go on strike soon."

"We should finish in another five days if the weather holds," Paul said. "Where's that ecologist Roger promised?"

"I'll give him two more days," I said, climbing up on the bottom rack of the cart to reach higher on the shelf.

"I'll bet he never comes," he said. "What's with all the cookies?" Paul pointed at the boxes of chocolate chip cookies I was throwing one by one into the basket.

"The cookies are for Marcel," I said. "Give me a hand, will you?"

"How many? Three? Four?" he joked as he tossed four more boxes into thc cart. "I guess it's what keeps him svelte."

The drive back traversed a decades-old clear-cut environmentalists claimed was visible from space. A brown stain on a blue-green sphere. It reminded me of a battlefield: kilometres and kilometres of rotting stumps and slash, slumps of debris, colourless but for faint verdant brushstrokes where Douglas-fir seedlings replanted years ago struggled to survive.

"We'll have to give them proof," Paul said halfway through the desolation.

"I lost you. Proof of what?"

"The murrelets."

"We have the shell fragments."

"Not enough. I mean video footage of a murrelet in a nest," he said. "The tree-sit gave me an idea. I think I know which tree has a nest. One of the Doug-firs near where I found the shell. I'll spend a night in the hemlock next door. A few nights if necessary. If a bird comes into the nest in the morning, I'll film it or at least pinpoint the nest branch."

I considered the idea. "Murrelets are pretty skittish."

"Better skittish than no nest tree." He pulled the hood of his sweatshirt over his head and feigned slinking through tall grass. "I'll be stealthy as a ninja."

I ignored his shenanigans. The clear-cutting of critical

nesting habitat represented the murrelet's most formidable enemy, their numbers at sea plummeting over the past decades. "Okay. Let's do it. A nest should give ample evidence."

I swerved the car around a deep pot-hole at the top of a hill. Another expanse of clear-cut spread out before us. "We better do the filming soon."

"Tomorrow?"

"Tomorrow."

We stopped at the blockade and handed out chocolate bars and pop.

"Any action today?" Paul asked.

"One crazy logger drove by yelling insults this morning." Terry leaned in against the door, hands on the edge of the window. "Otherwise, it's dead around here."

"Those poor big men are frightened of a grandmother," Grace piped up. She wore a sandwich board that read, *Granny Against the Rape of Public Forests*.

"Do you think the company knows about the tree-sit yet?"

"I doubt it," Terry said.

"Any news about the injunction?" I asked.

"Our contact expects a decision soon."

Paul and I unloaded the groceries into backpacks in the empty parking area and lugged them down the trail. Halfway to camp, we found a jacket, ripped and muddy, in the middle of the path.

"I think it belongs to Chris," Paul said. "He must have dropped it on his way to the blockade." He picked it up and shook it out.

Around the next corner, we discovered a bag of oatmeal spilled across the ground, a few steps farther, a dirty sleeping bag and a headlamp with a smashed bulb. We ran the rest of the trail. Dropping the groceries on a stump, we stood, staggered by the state of the camp.

"Shit." Paul sucked in his breath.

Speechless, I took in the carnage. Slashed tents, food bins cut from ropes and upended, the kitchen tarp collapsed and torn to shreds, clothes ground into the dirt. Socks and underwear littered the rocks in the middle of the stream like strange displaced flower petals and the current swirled around a camp stove.

"The bear?" But I knew an animal could not accomplish this level of damage.

"Bears can't spell." Paul pointed to a placard painted over with the words: *Tree-Huggers Are Welfare Bums Crawl Your Butt Back to the City*.

"Our gear," I exclaimed. I carried my computer and cell phone at all times to protect our data, but we stowed the climbing equipment in packs under the tarp. We hauled aside the tangled strips of blue polyethylene and found the packs empty, ropes, lanyards, carabiners, strewn in the dirt, our best rope knifed in half.

I slumped onto a log while Paul continued to rummage through the mess. He strode around the clearing, muttering to himself, hunting under tarps, clothing, and sleeping bags. He lifted his head and faced me, a soggy pair of jeans in hand, cheeks drained of colour. "The crossbow's gone."

We drove to the blockade and gave Terry the news. He used his radiophone to call the RCMP.

The RCMP didn't show up until late the next afternoon, a single officer in uniform, his cap tucked into his belt, too late to witness the bulk of the damage, much of the mess already cleared away; a dozen digital photographs and a pile of equipment beyond repair the remaining evidence.

The officer introduced himself. "Sergeant Lange," he said. "You shouldn't have disturbed the scene." He lifted his hat and passed his hand over a balding pate fringed by grey.

"We had to eat and sleep," I pointed out. "We expected you sooner."

He shrugged with disinterest. "Anything missing?"

"One item of significance."

"Which is?"

"A high-powered crossbow."

The man raised an eyebrow. "A crossbow? What would a protest camp need with a crossbow?"

"It's mine," I said. "Paul and I aren't with the protesters. We're scientists. We just happen to be camped in the same place."

"Okay," he drawled. "I still don't see the connection. What do a couple of scientists need with a crossbow?"

I sighed. "We use it to set climbing ropes in trees."

"For?"

"Collecting samples from the canopy."

"Of?"

"Arthropods."

"Which are?"

"Bugs."

"I'll take your word for it. Anyone you know might have a vendetta against you?"

"Not us. You better talk to Terry Seybold. He's the guy over there with the phone glued to his ear."

Not an hour after Sergeant Lange left, Roger Payne walked into camp.

"We heard about your problems here," he said, scanning the clearing. "Is there anything I can do?"

"You heard where?" I asked.

"I golf with the police chief," he explained. "He called me this morning."

"For starters," Terry said. "You can tell us who did this."

"Hold on," Roger held up his hands in defence. "Our guys have strict orders not to interfere with your protest."

"Then who would?" Terry said.

"No idea. But your blockade has attracted a number of odd characters."

Terry scowled and stalked off, knocking the radiophone against his thigh as if to stun it into operation.

"Let's talk about those timber markings," Paul said.

"I thought it was only one," Roger answered. He picked a broken tent pole from off the pile and examined the scratch marks on it.

"Lots of timber markings," Paul corrected.

"I told you," I said. "In the park and the buffer."

"Definitely mistakes," he said. "I'll tell the fallers to stay out of there."

"That's welcome news—" I said, relieved, but Paul interrupted.

"Are you planning to log close to our site?"

Roger cleared his throat. "That's not what I meant," he said. "Everything's up in the air"—he gestured with one hand at the camp—"with this madness going on."

"Can we see your logging plans when they're ready?" Paul said.

Roger put his hands on his hips and scuffed the dirt with a boot.

"And what about the murrelets?" Paul pressed him. "I believe they nest all through there. Why don't you come with us now and take a look?"

"How long would that take?"

"An hour?"

He checked his watch. "I promised Pam I'd be home by five," he said, then flashed us a disarming smile. "But don't worry. Cal should be here tomorrow. Let me know how it goes."

He tossed the tent pole back on the pile and, with an apprehensive wave, strode back up the trail to the road.

"Why would he drive all the way out here for that?" I said. "To tell us not to worry?"

"Why indeed," Paul replied. "Why indeed."

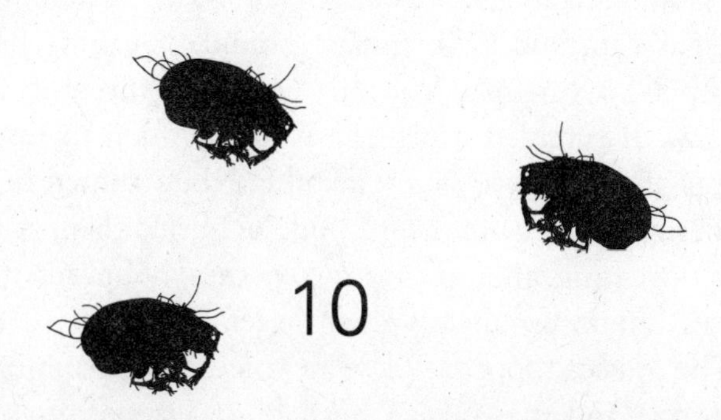

10

Three loggers carried chainsaws, jerry cans of gas, and packs with tools, food, and water into the new clear-cut, having bushwhacked for an hour cross-country from the north. The sound of music drifted through the trees, and they stopped and listened, scratching their heads in dismay.

"Weird bird?" the youngest of the three, a boy no older than nineteen, speculated.

"That's no bird, Billy," another answered, a wiry, bearded older man with a ponytail.

They resumed their strenuous journey through the underbrush, planning their strategy for the day, which trees, which direction of fall. The music grew louder and they could no longer deceive themselves about its origin.

"A damn recorder," the third man, heavy-set, in his thirties, and taller than the others, exclaimed.

They stood at the edge of the trees, tired and sweating, and surveyed the clearing. Other than the yarder, and the piles of logs and slash, the place appeared empty. They scrambled down the slope toward the yarder. The bearded faller tipped back his helmet and squinted up into the treetops at the bottom of the clearing. The muscles under the skin of his right cheek jumped.

"What the fuck." He stabbed his middle finger in the air. "Bastards," he screamed.

The other fallers stopped to locate the cause of their companion's outburst, following the direction of his angry gesture with their eyes. When they saw the three platforms high in the canopy, they dropped their gear and swore.

"Goddamn motherfuckers." The bearded man threw his saw, gas can, and pack to the ground. "Fucking bastards." He ripped his helmet from his head and threw it alongside the saw. It tumbled down the slope, coming to rest against a large stump where a tiny metal ladybug glinted in the sun. Gathering rocks from the ground, he hurled them at the three trees, swearing and spitting when they bounced off with a hollow klunk, well below their targets.

The music stopped. "Hey," a voice called from one of the platforms and the tousled head of Jen came into view, her short hair a cap of bronze in the morning sun. "Nice language to wake up to."

"You assholes turn around and hike right back out again," Cougar called, leaning against a branch in another platform, the recorder in his hand. "No cutting's gonna happen here today."

Squirrel sat cross-legged in a third tree, munching on an apple.

"What do you ejits think you're doing?" one of the loggers yelled up.

"Saving trees," Jen yelled back.

"How long you plan to stay up there?"

"Until this valley's a park," she answered.

The two younger fallers picked up their gear. "You might have a long time to wait." The tall one called to the bearded logger, who was on his knees gathering rocks. "Let's go, Donnie."

"No way, Chuck. No fucking way will I leave until I cut down a fucking tree," Donnie snarled. He lurched to his feet, grabbed his chainsaw, and scrambled over slash to the foot of Jen's cedar. He yanked furiously on the starter cord. The big machine roared to life and Donnie scored a deep slice into the base of the tree. The other fallers and the tree-sitters yelled.

Jen screamed. Donnie ignored them; sawdust spewed out from the saw in a continuous stream.

"Lunatic," Cougar yelled and chucked an orange at the faller, missing his head by inches. "You're crazy." Unfazed, the man continued with his murderous task.

Billy and Chuck dropped their gear and clambered over the piles of debris. The tree-sitters held their breath as the two men approached Donnie. The man continued to cut wildly at the trunk. Chuck put his hand on Donnie's back and Donnie pulled the saw free of the cut and swung around, the engine rattling in idle. Billy and Chuck stepped back. "Whoa, man," Billy said. He spread his arms and started talking quietly to Donnie, but the older man lunged forward, the deadly chain whining as he squeezed the throttle. "Get back," he snarled.

"Asshole," Cougar yelled and chucked another orange at Donnie, who turned and swore. Chuck leaped forward and grabbed Donnie's upper arms from the back, forcing him to his knees and the saw to the ground. Billy stepped in and hit the safety switch; the saw sputtered to a stop. The two pried Donnie's hands free, then wrestled him to the wood-chip-strewn ground at the base of the tree, pinning him face first in the slash. When he stopped struggling, they released him and the three stood, heaving and panting, brushing dirt from their clothes. Without warning, Donnie threw a punch into the side of Billy's head, picked his saw up from the ground, and stalked off into the forest in the direction they'd come. The others gathered their equipment and, without another word to the tree-sitters, followed.

Cougar radiophoned Terry, who relayed the story to the waiting group. Paul and I listened from the sidelines. "Hang in there," Terry yelled into the phone. "We'll come and get you."

"No way," Cougar insisted. "Things are getting hot."

"What about Jen?"

Another pause, then those gathered around heard the faint sound of Cougar shouting, "She says bring chocolate tomorrow."

Terry turned off the phone. "Whew." He sank onto one of Grace's camp chairs. "I guess the company knows about the tree-sit."

Grace and Esther arrived back late from the blockade for dinner with two strangers in tow whom they introduced as Billy Samson, a slight dark-haired youth with straight black hair and a wispy beard, and Chuck Ford, a stocky, older man. The men claimed to be fallers with PCF. They had walked up the road to the blockade, boots caked with mud, work clothes stained with sap and ground-in dirt, jeans soaked to the knees, and announced to the startled women they were changing sides.

Grace gathered us together. "Tell them all what you told me." Grace handed the two men each a cup of steaming tea.

They exchanged a glance. At a nod from his companion, Billy spoke up, "The company has their injunction. They're sending the police in tomorrow."

A ripple of excitement ran through the audience. I glanced around for Paul, but he and Mary were nowhere to be seen.

"Is this true?" Terry queried.

Steam swirled up from the cup in Billy's hands. "We got the word last night."

Terry clapped Billy on the shoulder. "Thank you."

"Tomorrow's our big day," Marcel declared.

Grace handed the fallers a plate of cookies. "Sit down and tell them the rest," she urged. "About why you're here."

"It wasn't our idea." Chuck stared at his feet. "Donnie talked us into walking in with him."

"I won't cut trees anymore," Billy said in a quiet voice. "Especially trees with people in them."

Sue jumped from her perch on the cook stump. "You're the jerks who walked into the clear-cut and tried to cut down the tree-sits?" She jabbed her finger at them. "You could have killed Jen."

Billy lowered his head and twisted his grease-stained fingers. "I'm sorry."

"Don't blame us," Chuck argued. "It was Ransom. We stopped him."

"Leave them be," Grace argued. "They're on our side now."

Terry stepped forward and put his hand on the boy's arm. "What else can you tell us?"

"We—they'll be at the gate at dawn tomorrow," Billy answered, then straightened. "I'll stand on the road with you," he announced. He glanced at his companion.

Chuck nodded slowly. "Cutting the big ones—" he confessed. "The sound when they hit the ground makes me sick." He put his mug on a stump. "Besides, once they're gone we'll all be out of a job."

Grace convinced Billy and Chuck to stay for dinner, Terry promising them a ride home before dark.

"We stay in town, but you can take us to my mother's house. She lives on the lake," Billy said.

"In the native village?" Terry asked, a note of surprise in his voice.

The boy dipped his head in acknowledgement.

Esther and Mary served bowls of pasta and bread fresh from Esther's oven. Chuck accepted the offer of a camp chair; Billy chose to sit on the ground against a log.

"Who's this Ransom guy who tried to fall Jen's tree?" Terry asked.

Billy opened his mouth, closed it, and then looked at Chuck as if seeking permission. Chuck studied his plate, then cleared his throat nervously. "He's our best faller."

"What's his problem?"

"His wife is sick."

"No excuse." Sue punctuated her words with her spoon. "He could have killed our friends."

"We can't speak for him." Chuck met her eyes. "But both of us kill trees every day."

"But trees are not people." Terry swivelled around to face Chuck. "There's a big difference."

Sue groaned.

"Is there?" Mr. Kimori said quietly from the back of the group where he leaned against the trunk of a tree.

"My grandfather taught me each tree has a song," Billy said quietly, digging the heel of his boot into the dirt.

"Leave the poor boys alone," Grace said,

Chuck set his bowl on the ground. "I do it for the money."

"The company says we're turning decadent forest into productive tree farms," Billy said, dark eyes focusing on a hole in the knee of his trousers.

"And you believe them?" Chris asked.

"No." Billy raised his head, expression defiant. "I do it for the money too."

Marcel leaned over and squeezed the boy's shoulder. "Hey, we all need to make a living. I helped fish the cod to extinction. What is important is that we are here."

Billy managed a thin smile.

"You know," Chuck said. "The older guys we work with, like Ransom, know more about trees than anyone."

"But they cut them down," Sue retorted.

"You use lumber, don't you?" Chuck threw back at her.

"There's a native group from the area talking to the province," Terry interrupted. "Our board's trying to connect with them."

"Why haven't we seen them here?" Chris asked.

"Lots of people from my village work in forestry like me," Billy said.

"Like you used to, you mean." Chuck nudged him with an elbow.

Sue whistled through her fingers.

"We should go." Billy handed Grace his plate. "Thank you for the food." Terry reached into his pocket for his keys. "But tomorrow morning," Billy added, "we will see you again . . . on the road."

I didn't know what to make of this turn of events. The police would be busy. I rinsed out my dishes. I planned on an early night; tomorrow was a big day for us too.

An impromptu party erupted. A substantial amount of liquor and pot materialized out of tents and backpacks.

Marcel pulled out a flute no one knew he possessed, Esther a harmonica. Chris and Sue lit a fire on the gravel bank. Mary leaped to her feet, twirling and gyrating to the music. Her long tangled hair, her skirt, swirled out away from her lithe body. She wore earrings and a necklace she and Rainbow had fashioned out of lichen, her feet bare. A fairy out of *A Midsummer Night's Dream*, dancing away the longest day of the year. A beauty. An irresistible siren to helpless men. She pulled Rainbow up with her, the girl laughing. The two grasped wrists and circled faster and faster until Rainbow's feet left the ground, airborne. An unexpected surge of affection for the child swept through me. *Heaven knows why she likes me.* I watched the pair, mother and daughter, the grip of Mary's hand on Rainbow's, the force of their revolutions pulling Rainbow outward, those tentative bonds, easily broken, the potential hurt. On the other side of the fire, Grace watched them too, clapping in time with the music, foot tapping, until Sue grabbed her hand and urged her to her feet. No ballerina in her fleece trousers and vest, knobby soled hiking boots, but her poise and style shone through, in the way she moved her arms, the tilt of her head. Marcel invited me to dance, but I declined. My repertoire of talents didn't include dancing, and never in the presence of Grace. Terry arrived back and before he could protest, Sue shoved a beer into his hand and slapped him on the back before dancing off. Before long he joined the frenzied mass in the firelight at the edge of the river. A full moon broke above the tops of the trees and shed an eerie glow over the scene of merry anarchy.

Rumour had it two buses of supporters would leave Victoria in the middle of the night and arrive on the road by dawn. Rumour also had it a group of loggers planned to blockade the buses on the way.

"Don't worry," Terry said. "The buses will have police protection."

"Until the cops, they arrest you," Marcel joked and nervous laughter ran through the group.

I kept to the edge of the party, sipping rum and orange juice made from crystals in a tin mug, uneasy, the mood tense, the laughter too loud, the dancing too furious. The trashing of the camp, the threat to the tree-sitters had unnerved the protesters; tomorrow they would lay their freedom on the road with their bodies. To what end? I watched Paul follow Marcel in a step dance, their heavy boots pounding down on the ground, Marcel in time to the music, Paul out of sync and elastic legged, their faces red with laughter. The sight of Paul made me want to weep. Tomorrow night he would go up the hemlock with the video camera. People in jail wouldn't stop the logging. But an elusive brown and white seabird just might.

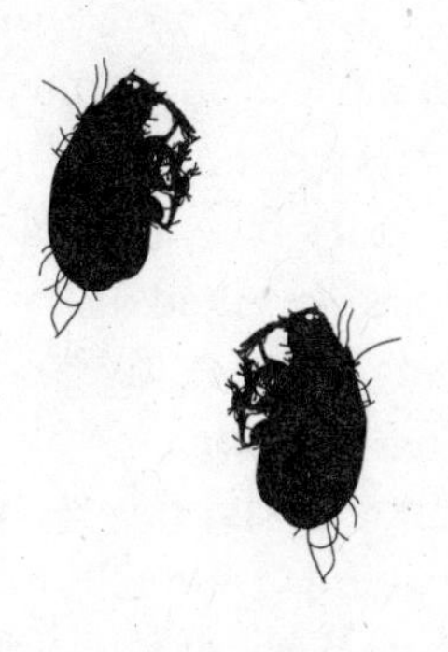

11

I made my way back to my tent to find Rainbow's sleeping bag missing; I recalled seeing it draped around her shoulders on the other side of the fire. Mary's kids didn't seem to have bedtimes. Flicking on my headlamp, I retrieved a journal article from a plastic folder and burrowed into my bag to read. The article described a new species of fly discovered in ancient temperate rainforests. *The male genitalia are distinctive, especially the broad posterior surstylus lobe with its scalelike bristles*. I yawned and read the line again. *The male genitalia are distinctive* . . . The words seemed to melt away before they reached my brain. I tried one more time. *The male genitalia* . . ."Oh, forget it." I snapped off the light and stuffed the paper and headlamp into a tent pocket. I zipped the sleeping bag up to my neck and listened for wild sounds in the dark, but other than the distant noise from the human revellers, the forest was quiet. All the animals had fled the party too.

I woke to the sound of unsteady footsteps shuffling through gravel followed by the whine of a zipper. A body fell through the doorway into the tent with a grunt. I jerked from a fitful dream where one step forward resulted in two steps back. Bear? I froze, heart racing. *Bears can't undo zippers*. "Rainbow?" I whispered and the mass at the foot of my bedroll whimpered in response. It was too large to be the little girl and it smelled of wood smoke, pot, beer, and sweat. I fumbled for my headlamp, a meagre weapon, and switched it on, ready to fight. Paul's face crumpled in a grimace at the sudden glare of light and he tilted away from me, his sleeping bag gripped in his arms like a teddy bear.

"Paul?" I jiggled his shoulder. "Wake up."

He half opened his eyelids, the blood-shot whites visible through the slit. Outside, I could still hear the distant sounds of partying, the raspy melody of a harmonica, laughter.

I shook him again. "Where's Rainbow?"

"Mary." He heaved his head and shoulders across my lap. "Mary doesn't want me anymore," he mumbled.

"She kicked you out, did she?"

His head rubbed against my legs in what I could only assume was a "yes."

I should tell him about Cougar. Cushion his heartbreak. He buried his face in my stomach. He was too out of it, the taletelling would have to wait until morning. I stroked his hair. He trembled, the heat from his body sifting into mine.

"You're my friend, Faye," he moaned moss-mouthed into my belly button. "I love you."

My fingers stopped their passage through his hair. His words conjured up a dust storm of emotion. *Give it up, Pearson*, I chastised myself. *The fool's drunk. He doesn't know what he's saying*. An addled declaration of affection the most I could hope for, this night a stolen gift, his head in my lap.

"I love you too, Paul," I whispered, his response a ragged snore. "Christ." I shoved him off my lap onto the bare floor and covered him with his sleeping bag. "Idiot," I said out loud into the dark night, not sure if my accusation was directed at him or at myself. I doused the light and burrowed deep into my bag. The music had stopped. Overhead the wind rushed through the tops of the trees. It would be a roller-coaster ride up in the canopy tonight.

I dreamed of falling. Drifting, weightless, a single needle from the top of a thousand-year-old redcedar, unheeded by the dark and silent world, spiralling through moss-laden branches like a lone snowflake before a storm. I accelerated, plunging headlong to earth through the canopy, whipped by limbs, breaking twigs, tearing sheets of ragbag lichen from the bark, the dusty white debris falling with me, a kaleidoscope of colours flashing by.

I didn't hit the ground. Instead I woke to find Paul's arm and a leg draped across mine, his body warm against my side, our sleeping bags in disarray.

Trapped under the weight of his limbs, chest hairs and the smell of him in my nose, I lay still, uncertain what to do. His ribcage rose and fell against me, and if I concentrated, I could hear his heartbeat; the rhythm burned into me, setting me afire. How long I had wanted this. *Flaming as I fall.*

I'm a fool.

"Paul," I whispered, then louder. "Paul." I pushed his arm away and he shifted, stirred, his lips in my hair. His hand slid across my abdomen. A wave of yearning swept over me. His fingers slipped under the bottom edge of my shirt, scrolling patterns on my skin. The night was black as coal.

"Sweetheart," he murmured against my cheek, his breath sour. His fingers inched under the waistband of my long johns and into the folds between my legs. I closed my eyes, the rising desire unbearable. He thrust the fabric below my knees in two clumsy movements.

He rolled on top of me and covered my mouth with his. His weight pinned me to the ground. Instead of pushing him away, I found myself kissing him back, his beard rough on my face. His musky scent overwhelmed me. I wrapped my arms around his shoulders, my reach inadequate. How many years had I wished to feel him like this? His amulet pressed into my skin. He rose up, the white glow of the tooth swaying in the air above my face as he entered me.

The briefest of moments. The first domino in a line of tumbling dominoes, stretching into the months and years to come. His body stiffened, he grunted and fell still, his weight pinning me beneath him. I suspected he'd fallen asleep, but then he slid off onto his side, stretched out beside me, and nuzzled my hair, breath hot in my ear. His fingers resumed their downward journey. His mouth formed words I will never forget. "Mary Mary, quite contrary."

A tsunami of anger crashed over me. I brought up my knees and grabbed his arm. "I'm not Mary." I forced his hand along my arm from shoulder to fingertip. "See, short arms, Paul." I sat up and wrenched the sleeping bag away. "Stunted legs. I'm Faye. Not Mary. Faye," I shouted.

Paul jumped away and onto his knees. "Faye?" he sputtered, head bent forward, hunched over, a spectral shadow against the blousy fabric of the ceiling. "I thought . . . aghh." His voice faded into the strangled sound of a snared animal. He fumbled for the flashlight and turned it on, the half-dome space illuminated by its indirect glow.

He stared into my face, eyes wild. He groaned, fumbled for the sleeping bag, and drew it around me. "I . . . are you all right?"

I dried tears from my face with the edge of the bag and pulled up my semen-soaked underwear, the air sharp with its musky odour. I wanted to gag. I wanted to suck the semen off my fingers. I wanted to push him to the ground and do it again. I wanted to hit him.

He raised his palms and gazed at them as if they were foreign. "I'm . . . I'm sorry."

What was I to do? Forgive him? Wind back time ten minutes? Forgive myself?

"I'm not," I answered.

Weariness overtook me. I huddled into my bag and turned my back on him. A few minutes later I heard him zip up his own sleeping bag. He clicked off the flashlight, plunging the small space into welcome darkness. I listened for the sound of his breath. After a long while, welcome sleep stole both of us away.

12

A pileated woodpecker drummed into the trunk of a nearby snag already riddled with insect galleries and beetle bores. Unable to sleep, I crawled from the tent at dawn, careful not to wake Paul, unwilling to meet his eyes, rehash the drama of the night without a chance to think. A ghostly figure in a white nightgown rattled a pot on a stove on the other side of the clearing. I was surprised to find any of the protesters up before dawn after the late-night festivities. But today was a big day. Their next night on a hard cot in a jail cell.

I grabbed an apple and walked the downstream trail west for an hour. The morning light expanded into the spaces between the trees. One day last year Paul and I had hiked the trail all the way to the ocean, a two-day trip there and back on a rough and muddy path. We'd camped in the open on a gravel beach above the high tide line and in behind a sheltering root wad at least the height of two men. Past midnight the scream of a cougar from the bush adjacent to the beach shocked us awake, the sound like the terrified cry of a woman. I shivered at the memory of the eerie call. Was it ten steps away? A thousand? We listened for the cat to scream again, the sky overhead crowded with stars and moonless, but heard only the grack of tree frogs in the grasses at the edge of the beach. We woke at morning light to find a grey whale feeding in the bottom mud near shore. Its calloused head broke the water's surface, the poof of its exhalation a quiet punctuation on the day's evolution.

I perched on a car-sized boulder above the creek and watched a stick twirl in an eddy. The current caught and swept it away. In the fall, returning salmon would batter their way up from the ocean to spawn in the gravel beds and die. The ultimate symbol of the cycle of life. Unlike the salmon, I knew I'd never travel that cycle. Sure, I'd been born, would live, and will die and rot like everyone else. But the rest wasn't in the cards. A mate. Reproduction. Not because I couldn't, I possessed all the right parts, a normal-sized torso, a vagina, a womb, the requisite needs and emotions. But men went for the best specimens. The biological imperative. Tessa, Mary. I chucked another stick into the eddy, and thought about an incident in high school. I couldn't recall the boy's name, but I remembered he was tall, athletic, and on the honour roll, all the prime genetic traits. Grace, in her usual Samaritan zeal, urged me to swallow my suspicions and accept his unexpected invitation out. "Give him a chance to get to know you. How could he not like you?" He left a note on my locker the day after he failed to show up at the movie theatre, poignant with its stick people illustrations and the scrawled words, *You've got to be kidding!* "We had a nice time, Grace," I'd reported to my mother, "but he's not my type." I understood why he'd done it. I was different, strange. An oddity like the white bears on the central coast, the golden spruce in Haida Gwaii, the rare albino crows on the island.

I started back toward camp. After the spawn, bears would drag the rotting fish carcasses up the bank and into the forest, as far as the top of the ridge, to feast on the protein-rich stomach and brain, leaving the remains to the gulls, the eagles, the decomposing insects, the bones fertilizer for forest trees. Nitrogen from salmon laced the heartwood of these rainforest trees, the boundaries between plant and animal blurred. Trees dining on fish, served by black bear waiters. But the banquet had dwindled, streams decimated by logging no longer supporting large runs of salmon. A dipper landed on a rock upstream. It checked the pool for food with its slender bill, its small grey body bobbing up and down, dip, dip. No salmon eggs nestled in the sediments today, the surviving fry long hatched and gone to the sea.

Each year on the birthdays of her children, Grace had recorded our heights in pencil on the kitchen door frame. The day I turned six, I noticed the measurements marked *Faye* weren't getting higher, unlike those of my brothers. I scrutinized the white-painted board, the terse black lines, the progress of my annual growth rings. The awareness that I was halted in time inched higher like water rising in a storm. My mother found me hanging by my fingertips from the door frame, face tear-stained and determined. Grace gave me one of her talks about individuality and the irrelevance of human differences. I learned I wouldn't grow much more than a few inches taller. Grace used the word *dwarf*. And the phrase *Good things come in small packages*.

I understood too about Paul. His reaction sent the same message as my high school suitor. *You've got to be kidding*. I stopped and threw a rock into the pool, frightening a red-legged frog from a crevice. He darted, legs pumping, across the surface of the water and under a ledge. Guilt swirled around in the pool with the twigs and the frog. I could have stopped Paul . . . and I didn't.

He stumbled white-faced from the tent around nine, hair awry, shirtless, barefoot, and belt undone. He squinted, then scanned the clearing until he spotted me by the stove stirring oatmeal.

"Hangover?" I said.

He limped his way across the gravel, grimacing with each step.

I handed him a bowl and he set it onto a stump, grabbed my arm, and steered me to the outer edge of the camp near the river.

"We have to talk," he whispered.

"You don't have to whisper," I assured him. "They left hours ago."

"We have to talk," he repeated.

"About what?"

"Come on, Faye. You know about what."

"What's there to say?"

"Lots . . . there's lots." He ran his hand over his dishevelled hair. "We . . . you . . . I . . . we had sex."

"I said you don't have to whisper."

He made a fist and struck it against the centre of his forehead. It felt satisfying to torture him . . . a little.

"We did have sex. You were drunk, stoned. Or you had a waking erotic dream. Could make headlines, man fucks in sleep. I think there's a term for that . . . sexomnia? Drop it."

"We . . . I didn't use a condom."

"I guess we'll have to hope for the best. I assume Mary doesn't insist."

He walked a circle in the gravel, waving his arms in frustrated gyrations through the air. "I don't want to talk about Mary." He dropped to his knees on the ground in front of me. "I want to know about you."

"This is a bit melodramatic." I gestured for him to get up. "What? What do you want to know? How did it feel? Were you good?"

The skin around his eyes collapsed as if recoiling from a blow. "You said you weren't sorry." He paused. "I want to know why."

I gazed past him at the curling tip of a sword fern, the uniform rows of spores on the underside of the fronds.

"I want to know, Faye. Why aren't you sorry?"

If I'd answered him things might have turned out differently. We might have spent the day in the tent, making love, this time with a condom, or more likely, he would have bolted, left for town, quit the project. Instead we finished breakfast in silence, cleaned up, and spent the afternoon rigging the hemlock for his night in the tree. Paul begged me to talk, but I couldn't, wouldn't, feigning concentration on my work.

Rigging the tree took longer without the crossbow; we used weighted lead bean bags on parachute cord instead, tossing them over branches, missing often, the bags less accurate and underpowered by my inadequate muscles, Paul's hung-over ones. He drank bottle after bottle of water and ate nothing but a handful of nuts. Late in the afternoon he clipped his Jumars on the rope to ascend for the night.

"Please speak to me," he tried one last time.

"Let it go." I ran through the check of his climbing gear, avoiding his eyes. "I'll see you in the morning after sunrise."

"We'll talk then?"

I turned away. He sighed, reached out and squeezed my arm, then slid his left ascender up the rope and headed into the canopy. Once he secured himself in the crook of a thick branch where he could hang his hammock, I sent up his gear. He hauled in the climbing rope for the night. "All set," he called. I couldn't make out his next words and didn't bother to clarify. I took one last look up at his nest in the trees and headed back to camp.

I made my way through the buffer zone and into the park, the low afternoon light melting into dusk. I was acting like a scorned teenager, my thoughts too muddled for intelligent conversation. We'd behaved badly. Both of us. I passed a high buttressed hemlock, young, a few decades old, its exposed roots wrapped like human limbs around the crumbling snag that gave it life. Their repose reminded me of a pair of lovers entwined, and the sight of it made me stop. Two as one. The natural pull of life. To merge with another. I wiped a tear from my cheek and vowed never to allow regret to taint the memory of my imperfect body entwined with Paul's perfect one, his breath on my skin. I stepped around a bend in the path and glanced back the way I'd come. The angle had shifted, the two trees no longer lovers, but mother and child.

The camp was bustling with activity, the protesters full of the events of the day. Two buses of supporters had arrived at sunrise minutes before the police, who trailed an empty yellow school bus of their own and a handful of company reps, followed by a parade of pick-ups and logging trucks. Terry instructed the core group to observe from the side. "We're needed for coordination and insurance." "He was scared," Sue confided later to me. Billy and four members of his family had drummed as police led, carried, and dragged eighty-six protesters off the road and transported them to the detachment in Duncan. Over a hundred activists were camped in the clear-cut prepared for more of the same tomorrow. Excited talk, descriptions of the arrests, and speculation about the next few days brewed in the background, but my mind was fixed on Paul rocking in his hammock high up in the canopy.

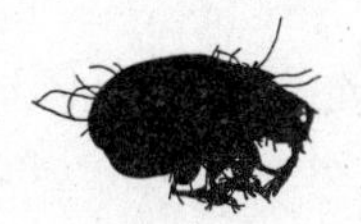

13

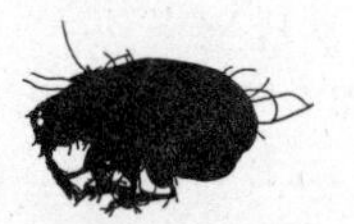

In the smoky light of the predawn hours of a June morning, a flock of brown and white mottled seabirds smaller than robins bobbed in the waves at the mouth of Otter Creek. The birds gathered at the edge of a raft of kelp. They faced the ancient rainforest and awaited the appearance of the sun above the trees. At their backs rolled thousands of miles of open water to Japan. The birds jockeyed, skittish in the open, watchful for falcons and owls. A bird on the outer fringe tilted its beak into the air, stretched its neck, and dove. An alcid, wing diver, it flew down through the green tinted water, webbed feet trailing, then circled up through a coil of Pacific sandlance. When it surfaced, a single silver fish glistened in its beak.

Sixteen kilometres inland, an archer stole through the thick underbrush of the forest floor. He travelled light, a crossbow slung over his shoulder, a handful of bolts stowed in a hip-pack. Alert, his ears picked out the slightest of sounds, feet and hands sensing direction under the faltering cover of night. The only sound, the shush of his pant legs past sword ferns, the rasp of boots on bark. He stepped into a small clearing. His nostrils twitched for scent. A barred owl swivelled its head and watched from its perch in a cedar. Patches of sky visible through the canopy above began their morning transformation from black to grey to pink to blue.

High up in a hemlock tree, Paul, cradled like a caterpillar in a nylon hammock suspended between two stout branches, retrieved a jacket from the bottom of his sleeping bag and slipped it over his head with care. He eased himself out of the sling and shifted his weight onto a branch, climbing rope trailing behind like a prehensile tail. He trained a pair of binoculars on the neighbouring Douglas-fir and scanned the largest branches in vain for signs of a tiny head, a fluffy ball of spotted feathers, a shallow depression of nest. A video camera dangled from his harness by a length of nylon webbing and he picked it up, flicked it on, and sited through the lens. A point of light on the housing flashed red. He covered it quickly with his hand, switched off the camera, and settled against the tree to wait.

The seabird lifted off the water, fish curved cross-wise in its bill, and flew east over land. The bird shot over the tree-tops at speeds up to a hundred and twenty kilometres an hour, covering the distance from sea to nest in a fraction of the time it would take a man to walk. It circled over clearings, calling out a high *keer keer keer*, the fish still clutched in its beak. Both archer and climber heard the call of the bird. *Keer keer*. The archer lifted his face to the sky at the sound of the call and the whirr of wings in time to witness the stunted silhouette hurtle like a bullet across the fragment of pale sky above him. As he scanned the canopy for another glimpse of the bird, he spied his prey. He slipped the bow from his shoulder and loaded a bolt.

Paul aimed the camera lens at the fir.

The bird dove through a narrow gap in the canopy and hurtled toward the ground, then curved up into a steep climb, the sound of air in its wings like the muffled roar of a jet plane. It stalled above a wide mossy limb and flopped onto the branch. A chick, half the size of the adult, stirred in a shallow depression in deep moss, called a quiet *psh, psh*, and rose to its feet, beak open, greedy for the fish.

Out of sight of the bird, Paul scaled the backside of the tree, moving with ease from branch to branch. When high enough to see into the nest, he inched his way around the trunk and wrapped his legs over a limb, raised the camera once more to his eye, and pressed a button. The red light flashed. The adult bird froze in place two steps from the chick.

Below, the archer focused through the cross-hairs of the bow, breath slow and measured, and followed the progress of his target up the ladder of branches. He steadied the bow against his shoulder and tightened his gloved finger on the trigger.

The trio waited in a silent triangle.

The bird broke the stalemate. It sidestepped the final distance to the chick, who snatched the sandlance from the mother's beak and swallowed it whole, tail last. Task accomplished, the adult bird waddled to the edge of the branch and dropped like a stone. It snapped open its wings in midair.

The bolt shot from the bow, whistling from understorey to canopy at a hundred metres per second.

Paul lifted his head at the odd sound. The bolt pierced his chest below the clavicle on his right side and with a grunt, he tumbled from the branch like a wounded waterfowl from the sky, the murrelet already high above the trees and heading for the sea.

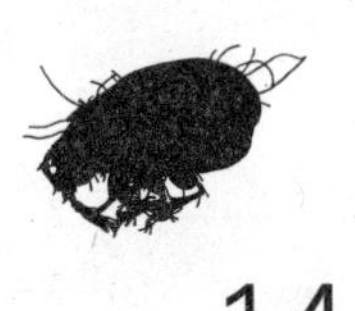
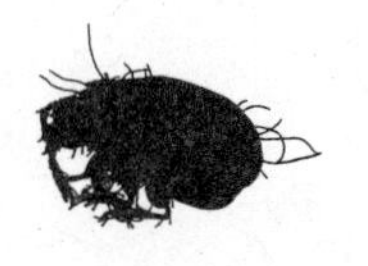

14

I slipped into a restless sleep, worn out from the previous night and the strains of the day, my dreams filled with wind, and the beat of bird wings, a vortex of restless sound; the suffocating tips of feathers swirled around my face. I would remember the dream for the rest of my life and imagine the drama unfolding in the woods while I slept. I woke gasping in the dark and lay staring at the curve of the tent above me thinking about Paul and what to tell him when he descended from the tree. I knew he wouldn't let the issue drop. The incident held the potential to forever alter our work, our friendship. I needed to lie. We would walk along the river after he showed me the murrelet footage. I'd ask him about his night in the tree. And explain what I had meant when I said, "I'm not sorry." I meant . . . What? *I haven't slept with anyone for years.* A half-lie. It might ring true to him. He knew all about my pathetic and absent love life. I could expect benevolence, but would he believe me? After my tears, my admonitions. *You thought I was Mary? Couldn't you tell the difference?* No expectations. *We're friends right? The work's too important.* End of discussion. We'd submit the video, our study area would be secured, and we could get back to work.

I dressed and crawled from the tent at first light, the sky

through the canopy a thin charcoal grey. By the time I washed my face and brushed my teeth I was anxious to find Paul, sort things out. I fixed sandwiches and a Thermos of tea by headlamp, packed a small rucksack, and headed up the trail to the study site. By my calculation, I should arrive well after the murrelet's dawn feeding, the departure of the adults. I'd not gone far when footsteps pattered behind me and Rainbow appeared, pyjamas under her Cowichan sweater, hair uncombed, her boot laces loose and trailing behind in the dirt. "Can I come?" she panted, out of breath.

"You're not dressed."

"Please."

"Aren't you going to the blockade with Mary?"

"Cedar threw up. She says we'll go later. They went back to sleep."

She appeared more relieved at missing a day at the blockade than disappointed. Was Rainbow's big adventure wearing thin? The arrests more than she could take? People dragged across the ground by police officers, her friends hauled off in handcuffs.

"Okay," I said, taking pity on her; she was just a child. "I'm going to meet Paul." Our talk could wait an hour or two. I dug in my pack and handed her an orange. "Hungry?"

She bit into the peel, wincing at a spray of juice up her nose. "Where is he?"

"Sleeping in a tree." I explained our plan as we walked, suddenly happy for her company, her curiosity a welcome distraction.

"Can I sleep in a tree one day?" she asked. "How do the murrelet babies get down?"

By the time we reached the study site, shafts of light from the rising sun angled in through the trees, illuminating tiny airborne insects and dust motes in the air.

"Shhh," I cautioned Rainbow, "we don't want to scare any murrelets away."

But we neither saw nor heard a single bird of any species, the forest eerily quiet.

"Paul?" We called from the base of the tree, expecting the end of the rope to come tumbling from above like Rapunzel's hair. When he didn't answer we tilted back our heads and searched for his hammock in the foliage.

"There." Rainbow pointed, finger quivering. "There."

I saw him then. He swayed in midair at the end of the rope, facing skyward, back arched. His arms dangled from his shoulders, legs twisted below, head flopped back. The video camera swung at the end of a length of webbing attached to his right wrist.

Rainbow whimpered and clutched the sleeve of my jacket.

"Paul," I called up crossly. "What are you playing at?"

Moisture from the tree dripped onto my forehead and I brushed it away impatiently with the back of my hand. Rainbow whined like a desperate puppy and tugged at my sleeve. She pointed to a pattern of red-brown raindrops splattered on the flared tree roots that tangled like long giant toes across the ground at our feet.

I cupped my hands around my mouth to call again to Paul; the words caught in my throat at the sight of blood on my knuckles.

I started at a run down the trail to get help, then remembered Rainbow. She stood immobilized, eyes wide and frightened, cheeks tear-stained. But I couldn't wait. Paul's life depended on me. "Stay here," I called out. "Talk to him. I'll find help." Rainbow stepped back against the trunk of the tree and slumped to the ground, her attention fixed on Paul's body swinging overhead.

I jogged the trail back to camp to gather help and equipment, my lungs burning, muscles aching. In less than an hour, I returned with Mary, Marcel, Grace, and a handful of others. Rainbow was still huddled at the base of the tree, hugging her knees. At the sight of her mother she scrambled, sobbing, to her feet and into Mary's arms. I geared up for the climb, my hands fumbling with the buckles in my haste: a rope clipped to my harness, a flip line wrapped once around the trunk, an end secured at each hip, and a bight of rope wound tight around each hand. On my feet a pair of climbing spurs. I'd practised the technique once under the guidance of an expert arborist, Paul. To walk straight up a tree trunk with spurs, a section of rope and brute strength to defy the force of gravity the way a lineman climbs an electrical pole. A dangerous proposition. Suicide for the inexperienced. I had no choice. Paul's rope hung coiled in the canopy. I had no time to rig the tree.

Paul's instructions played through my mind, as clear in my memory as if he were standing next to me. *Stamp the spurs into the bark, in one motion lunge toward the trunk and flip the line up, lean back into its support, step up, one spur in, the other, flip the line up.* I kicked the spur at the arch of my foot into the bark, the sound like a hatchet biting the flesh of a log. "Stamp the spurs in, lunge forward . . ." I concentrated on the tree, trying not to think about Paul, about my own precarious position. One slip, one wrong move, and I would fall. My body burned like fire—knees, biceps, wrists, elbows. The skin of my hands screamed with pain from the friction of the flip line. I struggled to move the rope ever upward. It caught on the bumps and nubs of old branches on the far side of the tree, the ridges in the trunk. My right foot slipped and bark rained from the sole of my boot. I cried out and jerked the rope tight, pulled my body flat against the tree. I stabbed the spur again and again into the bark, heart in my throat, but still I slipped. Through the knot of fear that gripped me, I heard Paul's voice again in my head, loud and insistent. *Lean back, always lean back on the line.* I pushed away from the trunk, opening the angle of my body with the tree and my spurs set firmly into the bark. Instantly stable. I fought tears of relief.

"Faye . . ." The sound of my name floated up from below, my mother's voice like an anchor. "You can do it."

I took another step. Another. I focused on the passage of the trunk, the ridges and dips, the variation in colour, the shape of each lichen, the feathery texture of moss. I imagined myself a mite on an epic journey up an old-growth tree. I recalled Billy's words. *Each tree has a song.* I closed my eyes and listened. Slowly I felt the vibration creep into my body, filling my bones, my muscles, urging me on. I continued up; the melody of the tree revealed itself in the rusty red lobes of the scissor-leaf liverwort, the moist edge of an olive-green mat of Menzies' neckera moss, the frills at the margins of a lettuce lung lichen. The rasp of the rope across bark on the other side of the tree, the bite of my spurs into wood. The sigh of the wind in the boughs above. The song of the tree moved through me, moved me upward.

The flip line resisted. A spray of needles scraped across my helmet and I knew I'd reached branches. The manoeuvre from trunk to the limb above my head sapped my remaining strength. I straddled the branch, lungs heaving, and anchored the climbing rope with a length of webbing, then collapsed back against the trunk, panting, clothes drenched in sweat. Below a dozen faces tilted heavenward, watching.

I could see Paul's body, hanging in mid-air, two body lengths above me, a body length out, his face the colour of ash, shirt soaked crimson with blood. The shaft of the bolt pointed skyward from the centre of a glistening red stain. *A wounded swan.* I couldn't rest. From here on up, the lineman's technique would no longer work, the branches too numerous. I had to free climb through the thick canopy, without a rope, setting anchors with webbing and carabiners for safety as I went.

"Paul," I shouted.

No response. No movement, no flicker of life, nothing to tell me he could hear. If only I could fly. Bile rose from my stomach into my throat. I spat, then swallowed the foulness. My goal: his hammock; my purpose: to find his rope and belay him down. Paul had fallen more than ten metres before his tangled line arrested his descent. His second mistake in two days. He had failed to use a safety lanyard to tie himself in. His third mistake—and a shock for me: Paul, the most safety conscious climber I knew, wore no helmet. His head was bare.

Free climbing was easier, safer than spurs and a flip line, but my short arms and legs restricted my reach, my progress slow. As I crawled my way upward, I recalled a film Paul showed me of orangutans travelling through treetops, smooth as flowing water. "One limb at a time," he explained. "Like a mountain climber. Never less than three points of contact with the tree."

When I reached Paul's gear, I tied myself in, looped his rope through a carabiner with a figure-eight knot, and took his weight. I unclipped his rope at the anchor webbing and dropped the loose end to Marcel. Marcel belayed from below and together we lowered Paul to the ground. I prayed the rope would not snag, but it slipped smoothly through my gloves. His body descended like a lead weight on a string. A dozen arms cradled him to the earth and bore him away, a centipede gliding on a bevy of legs along the forest floor. I slumped back against the tree trunk. Grief burst from me in great heaving sobs.

"Faye?"

I gulped air, fighting for control, the safety rope gripped in my gloves.

"Faye, it's Grace. You need to come down." My mother peered up from the ground, too far away to see her face. "Stop crying and come down."

I wiped tears from my cheeks with my sleeve at my mother's order. I dismantled Paul's hammock, folded his gear into it, and lowered the bundle to the ground, then rappelled myself down. At the moment my feet hit the duff, Paul was on his way to the PCF yard in Terry's four-by-four. Grace waited for me at the base of the tree. She helped me out of my gear and together we ran the trail. By the time we reached camp, an emergency helicopter kilometres away was lifting off the tarmac next to Roger Payne's trailer in a whirlwind of dust and pebbles. Nobody at camp could tell us if Paul was alive.

I collapsed to the ground, a helpless sack of muscle and bone. Others sat in shocked silence around the clearing. Esther and Sue embraced, sobbing into each other's hair.

"We need to find out where they took him." Grace laid her hand on my arm. "Come."

I lifted my head and considered the dubious band of activists, young and old, male and female, liberal and traditionalist, in the valley for selfless reasons. Why? To save a few big trees from the chainsaws? To protect a future they valued for their grandchildren? Paul might never have grandchildren, let alone children. I dropped my head into my hands. All I saw was the image of the crossbow bolt, the blood, his swaying body.

A warm hand settled on my shoulder. "You are a brave and strong woman, Faye," came Mr. Kimori's serene voice. "But you are not Buddha. Come."

He cradled my elbow and urged me to my feet, then led me to a cedar at the edge of the camp and positioned me in the shade of the tree. He arranged my arms doll-like, out from my sides, palms rotated to face the sky. "Look up," he whispered as he stepped back, arms folded.

I did as he asked; the striations of stringy red bark drew my gaze up the ladder of droopy limbs and into the canopy where swags of green foliage blocked the sky. "What?" I asked, confused.

"*Shin rin yoku.*" He opened his arms, palms up. "Tree shower. Close your eyes. Listen to the breath. Let the tree rain peace and calm upon you."

I did as he asked. The sharp fragrance of the cedar mingled in my nose with the stink of my own sweat. What peace? Rage tore through me. My eyes flew open and I whirled to meet the kind-hearted gaze of Mr. Kimori. "I'm sorry," I said. "I can't."

I strode across the clearing to a stack of placards and grabbed one from the top of the pile, not bothering to read it. "Screw process." I spat the words out to no one in particular. "To hell with the law." Without a backward glance, I strode up the trail.

Rainbow caught up with me at the road, breathless and panting, and fell into step beside me. Halfway to the blockade, she grabbed my sleeve and pointed back. Mr. Kimori,

Grace, Esther, Mary with Cedar, and the others followed. Marcel towered over them all, waving a placard of his own.

Esther's voice rose in song, strong and fine, a refrain that I recognized from my childhood. "We are peaceful, angry people. We are walking . . . for the forest's life."

Marcel handed his placard to Grace and pulled out his flute. Grace's high soprano joined with Esther. I turned back up the road and marched on, feeling the anger but not the peace.

Rainbow tugged on my hand. "Let's sing too, Dr. Faye," she pleaded. "Please." The words wedged in my throat, but when Rainbow's sweet voice rang out, "we are singing for Paul's life," I took her hand in mine and stepped forward. I sang my heart out.

Our song and our collective resolve faded as we neared the blockade. The road seethed with people, police cruisers, buses, and logging equipment. A dozen or more armed officers in flak jackets dragged, carried, or led protesters from the road to waiting school buses. Two constables worked with bolt cutters and hacksaws to cut chains off protesters locked to the gate. A half-dozen reporters and photographers recorded the drama with cameras, microphones, and video equipment. Billy and his family, wrapped in button blankets and eagle feathers, drummed and chanted from the roadside while behind the cordon of police officers, a crowd of loggers screamed insults and jeered when a new line of activists stepped in to fill a gap in the human barrier. The drums grew louder, the heckling stronger as the officers cleared the road again and again.

A logger sprinted from behind the police line and attacked a protester. He jabbed at the man's shoulder with his fist. "Scum, fucking traitor." The victim was Chuck, face blanched with fear, his assailant a stranger to me, not easily seen in the disorder. The police shepherded the attacker back behind the line, but he turned and raised a finger. "You deserve what you get," he hissed, then elbowed his way through the crowd.

We followed Esther and Grace onto the road, linking arms to form a human chain. An officer stepped forward and faced us. "In case you didn't get the message"—he waved a sheaf of papers in the air like a fist—"this orders all persons having notice of this Court Order be restrained and enjoined . . . any person impeding logging operations in the watershed, blockading the road to the upper valley, or standing within a metre of the roadway, will be arrested and charged with contempt of court for defying an injunction." He rolled the papers into a tube and stuffed them in his back pocket. "Here's your chance to avoid incarceration," he yelled. "I'm going to count to ten and we'll arrest anyone left on the road. We've got buses enough for the lot of you. One . . . two . . ."

No one moved. I glanced left to see Grace, head held high, three over, Mary at her side with Cedar in a sling. To my right, Sue and Chris, Terry, Marcel, Mr. Kimori. Where was Rainbow? *Four, five, six.* She hadn't left my side the entire march from camp. I scanned the crowds, spotting her the same time I heard her. She screamed from the ditch where she struggled with a police officer, kicking her feet at his shins.

"Mary," I yelled. "Get Rainbow."

Eight. Mary tightened her grip, drawing her neighbours in closer.

Rainbow's voice shrieked over the beat of the drums, "Let me go, let me go." I released my arms, but before I could run for her, Grace stepped forward and left the road. She spoke with the officer, picked up the weeping child, and whisked her away. *Ten.*

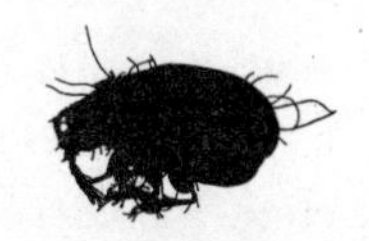

15

The main piece of evidence in my trial consisted of a segment of video. A cordon of uniformed officers advanced toward a blockade of protesters. The camera panned the line and zoomed in on the individual activists. It lingered on each one, my face, my profile unmistakable. My arrest a far cry from heroic. My recollection of the conversation with the officer went like this.

"What have we here? A tree-hugging dwarf? Where did they find you?"

When I didn't answer, he continued, "You are under arrest for criminal contempt of court. Are you going to walk, fly, or do we have to carry you?"

I slid to the ground. The next thing I knew I was hanging head down, pinned between the man's holster and elbow; the butt of his gun dug into my ribs.

I grunted in pain. "You can't do this."

"Our rules now, shorty," he replied.

"I object to the logging of this ancient rainforest," I yelled, "and the destruction of the habitat of all living creatures on this land."

"Tell that to the judge."

The officer carried me toward the buses. From my compromised position, I saw Roger Payne watching from a group of loggers and forest company officials at the side of the road. His eyes widened at the sight of me.

"Loser." A bearded man in a plaid shirt and dirty work khakis next to Roger yelled. "Freak, ever work a day in your life?" Roger elbowed the man in the chest and turned away.

The officer deposited me at the door of the bus. "Have a seat." I pulled my cell phone from my pocket, not sure who to call to find out about Paul or if there'd be a signal. "I'll take that." The officer leaned over and held out his hand.

"I'd rather not."

"You'd rather. Remember what I said, our rules."

The police arrested thirty-eight people on the road that day and transported us to the detachment in Duncan for processing. When I filed through the door with the others, I found Grace arguing with a uniformed clerk at the reception counter. Cedar, in diapers and a sweater, sat on the countertop in the crook of her arm, while Rainbow stood on a stool beside her, head resting on her forearms.

"Thank goodness." Grace hurried over. "I tried to explain about Paul. They won't listen." Rainbow jumped from her perch and wrapped her arms around my waist, face buried in my clothing.

At the mention of Paul, my knees buckled and I clung on to Rainbow, not sure if I could stand without her support. "Have you heard anything?"

"They've taken him to Victoria," Grace said. "I called the hospital. But they won't give any information."

The accompanying officer pressed his hand between my shoulder blades. "You need to move into the offices there."

I peeled Rainbow's arms free. "I'll see you later," I assured her and followed the man into the room.

"I've phoned your dad," Grace called after me. "He'll find you a lawyer."

One by one, the forest defenders were charged with criminal contempt of court, fingerprinted, photographed, and ushered into the segregated cells at the back of the detachment, bare barred rooms each with a single toilet, doors casually ajar.

Mary stood up from a bench in the corner and hurried over when she spotted me.

"Where are my kids?" she cried. "They ripped Cedar right out of my arms."

"Grace has them."

The woman's face relaxed, then clouded over again. "And Paul?"

"Don't know."

"I'm scared . . ."

"Faye Pearson?" A voice interrupted from the doorway. An officer beckoned. "You're wanted."

The officer escorted me to a small room at the back of the detachment where I found Sergeant Lange seated behind a wooden desk. He offered me a chair.

"I'll stand," I said, not wanting to suffer the difficult silence as I negotiated the climb into the chair.

"Suit yourself." He leaned forward, elbows on the desk-top. "You said you weren't mixed up in this protest."

"I wasn't." I paused. "Until this morning."

"You'll have to take the consequences, but I want to know about your partner, Paul Taylor."

"What do you know?" I gripped the edge of the desk. "Is he . . . ?"

The sergeant's face softened. "He's not dead."

I fought back tears. "Thank God," I blurted out. "How badly is he hurt?"

"Hard to tell. I talked to intensive care in Victoria. They've removed an arrow from his shoulder. They figured it was fired from a high-powered crossbow."

"Bolt."

"What?"

"An arrow for a crossbow is called a bolt."

"Whatever you say." He watched me curiously. "Your crossbow, I presume."

"The stolen crossbow," I corrected. "Was the bolt rubber-tipped? It shouldn't have penetrated. The bow might not be ours."

"Right. I'm sure there's an army of folks walking around in the forest carrying crossbows." He tapped his pen on the desk. "I don't know about the rubber tip. I'll check it out. You scientists work in a dangerous field. Weapons, shootings, vandalism. Why would anyone shoot your partner with a crossbow?"

"They mistook him for a tree-sitter?"

"Mistook? He wasn't a tree-sitter?"

"No. We were collecting data."

"On?"

"Marbled murrelets."

"Which are?"

"Seabirds that nest in old-growth trees."

"Don't you study insects?"

"I'd like legal advice."

He waved me out. "We'll need a statement."

After two hours in the cell, we were freed, without bail, on our own recognizance, instructed not to leave the province, and told to expect court notification of a trial date by mail in the next week. I didn't hesitate to sign the paper shoved in front of me at the front desk stating I agreed not to return to the protest, the alternative being automatic jail. Paul was my first priority.

I stepped into the crowded lobby of the police department where a second busload of protesters waited for processing. I spotted Grace across the parking lot through the window, her back turned; she was in conversation with a person I couldn't see. The officer behind the desk handed over my phone.

"Your husband's outside," he said.

"I don't have a husband," I answered.

"Boyfriend. Brother." The officer turned back to his work and mumbled. "Whoever he is, he's gotta be here to see you."

Confused, I stepped outside, the fresh air welcome after the claustrophobia of the lock-up and the reek of accumulated human drama. I picked out Grace again across the parking lot in the milling crowd. A man stood next to her; the scene before me difficult to digest. Grace turned and her face brightened when she saw me. My mother touched the man's shoulder; he swung around as Grace called out, "Look who's here."

From my vantage point on the station steps, I gazed at a person so like the image I saw in a mirror I felt lightheaded. A prominent forehead and square chin on a head and chest too large for the length of the forearms. Short bowed legs that stopped far too soon under a shelf of a bum. Stubby hands and fingers. Except my hair was straight, white-blonde, and fine as horsetail, his dark and cropped above the ears and wound into curls as taut as fiddleheads. I recognized the glasses balanced on a broad, flattened nose, and the neat half-beard familiar from his photos. His face lit up with anticipation as he walked toward me. I didn't know whether to turn back inside and lock myself in a cell or go to him and merge together like a scene in a crazy science fiction movie.

"Faye?" I heard Grace say. "It's Bryan. Don't stand there. Say hello."

Sap, dirt, and blood covered my clothes. I hadn't seen a mirror for days, my last shower a bucket of cold water over my head behind a clump of salal a discrete distance from the creek. I stepped forward, conscious of myself swaying in the same waddling gait as he, arms not swinging far enough, hips rocking from side to side. He moved easily, his body toned and athletic, stomach flat, face fine-featured, and when he drew closer, his grey eyes gave the impression of kindness and intelligence.

"What are you doing here?" I blurted out.

"Didn't you get my emails?" he said, smile fading from his face.

"The signal's been weak," I answered, my tongue uncooperative. How had I come to be standing on the steps of the Duncan RCMP detachment with another dwarf?

"I had a conference in Vancouver. I got directions from the university to your camp," he explained. "The people there told me where to find you." His face opened in a wry smile.

"The dangers of internet dating. They never tell you about their criminal record."

I grimaced. "I'm sorry, Bryan." I wiped my hand on the back of my pants and held it out. "You sure picked the worst time."

"It's all right," he answered and took my hand in his. "I'm happy to meet you, Faye Pearson."

"I have to get my samples, and then I have to drive to Victoria to find Paul." Grace listened patiently to my desperate appeal while Bryan waited in his rental car; Mary, the children, and Marcel in Grace's station wagon. Grace had offered them a bed for the night in Qualicum.

"What about Bryan?" Grace reasoned. "He's come all this way to see you."

I threw my hands in the air in frustration. Bryan's arrival had knocked me sideways. I had considered him a fictional character, existing in text on a computer screen, a one-dimensional image in a photo, a duty to satisfy Grace. But he'd walked into my life, warm and breathing.

"I have to see Paul," I insisted.

"Tomorrow, dear," Grace said. "It's late. Come home with me. You need sleep. Besides, I don't know if they'll let you see him."

Grace was right. When I dialled the hospital the receptionist asked, "Are you family?"

"His girlfriend," I lied. Grace let out an exasperated sigh.

"We give information to immediate family only," the woman said. "And never over the phone."

"But he has no one else."

"I'm sorry. You can try administration tomorrow."

I turned off my phone and shoved it into my pocket with a moan. My mother steered me toward the car. "Let's go get your samples."

Other than two RCMP cruisers parked off to the side and a scatter of protest signs in the ditch, the blockade site was empty when we drove past. A handful of arrestees lingered at camp, packing up gear, bidding tearful farewells to their friends. A few supporters from Victoria who had avoided arrest opted to stay in the valley to supply the tree-sitters and were setting up tents. "We're going to Vancouver to recruit friends to help Jen," Chris and Sue announced, shoving the last of their gear into a duffle bag.

Terry was on the radiophone. "Cougar," he announced when through talking. "The company has moved in and they're felling trees right around them. The police have read them the injunction and are telling them to come down. He knows if he does those trees are gone too."

"Tell them to stay put," Grace said. "The police won't allow them to hurt anyone."

I left Bryan with Grace, Mary, and Rainbow to pack up the tents and gear and hiked back to the scene of the morning's crime. My stomach churned with nausea at the sight of the spatters of blood on the shoulder of the tree. I looked up, half afraid to see Paul's body swinging above me in the canopy, the dark stain on his shirt. I hunted around in the undergrowth and found the video camera, still switched on but the battery dead, its contents to remain a mystery until back in civilization with an electrical outlet at hand. The crossbow was nowhere to be seen.

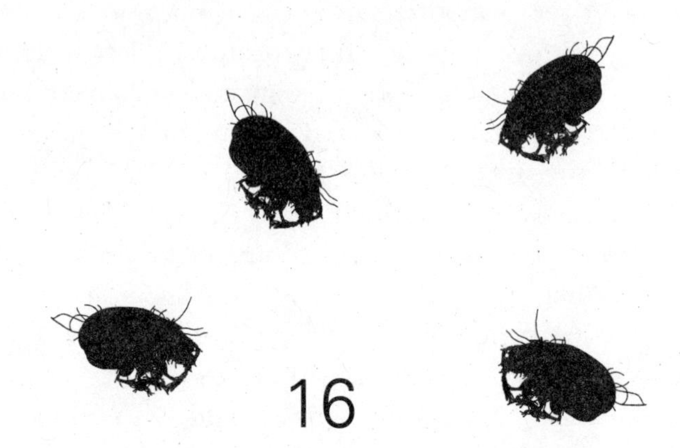

16

We reached the house well after dark. The headlights illuminated the steep, winding driveway through the trees to the house, which sat on a hill on the upland side of the east coast highway, the intermittent view of the Coast Mountains across the Strait of Georgia obscured by night. I helped Grace put out food and arrange towels and beds for the motley crew: Mary with a sleeping Cedar in her arms and a dirty-faced Rainbow in the guest room; Marcel on the couch in the family room. Mel, an early riser, was already in bed.

I showed Bryan to Steve's old room upstairs.

"I'm sorry about all this," I said. I handed him a folded towel and washcloth. "I can't spend any time with you. I need to leave for Victoria in the morning. My assistant's in the hospital."

"I understand," he said. "After all, you didn't know I was coming," but a flash of disappointment crossed his face and I felt a sting of remorse at the way I had used him. I couldn't deny a pull, a curiosity to know more than the name of his dog, his passion for rocks, his love affair with flat land.

"Well." He hesitated, and then turned away. "Good night." He reached up for the doorknob and the familiar gesture startled me. Up. Always up.

"How about a walk on the beach in the morning?" I said quickly.

"Love to," he answered. He gave a small wave and closed the door behind him. I lingered in the hallway, heart and mind a tangled web of confusion, and stared at the empty dwarf-shaped space he'd left behind.

My childhood room hadn't changed in the fourteen years since I'd moved out. Grace had hoarded all my childhood belongings: my wildlife posters, my fishing rod, the saxophone that I'd never mastered, and the rows of altered and hand-made clothes in the closet. I peered out the window and into the dark yard where I could make out the white bars of the rusted old swing set and the leaf-laden limbs of the apple tree. I wished Patrick and Steve were home, my stalwart knights, my guardian angels. The three of us had played for hours at a time in the yard, Patrick pushing me tirelessly on the swing, Steve coaching me in the fine art of monkey bar gymnastics. They taught me to catch a baseball, spit a metre, and whistle through my fingers. I cried the day they left, both the same fall, Patrick for university, Steve for a construction job near Port Hardy. I didn't see them much anymore. The occasional Christmas. Patrick taught college English in Manitoba, Steve was a building contractor in Powell River and the father of two boys.

The plywood and two-by-four platform they had built me in the apple tree appeared, in the dark, as a translucent skeleton in among the branches, my favourite retreat in my years alone with my parents. I wished I could hide out high in the branches now, avoid the inevitable persistent conversations with Grace, the uncomfortable silences from Mel, the complicated presence of Bryan. Where would the events of the past few crazy days take me? I climbed into the child's single bed I would never outgrow, followed the path of moonlight across the wall, and worried about Paul.

Bryan and I collided in the hallway outside the bathroom the next morning. "I'm ready for that walk," he said jovially.

My heart fell. I had forgotten, my thoughts on Paul and my departure for Victoria after breakfast.

"It will have to be quick." I cringed at the sharpness in my own voice. He'd come all this way. I could give him this one small thing. We found Mel hunched over the newspaper in the kitchen, cold coffee at his elbow, glasses on the table, scanning a column, nose inches from the type.

"Hi, Dad," I ventured, never certain of the reception I would get from him.

He squinted up at me, then slipped on his glasses. "Faye?" He gave me one of his inimitable smiles—a bit of a guessing game. "Can you explain what's going on? The house is full of sleeping strangers and she's gone out for groceries." The remaining colour in his already pallid cheeks drained away when he noticed Bryan.

"Dad, meet Bryan," I said. "Bryan, my dad, Mel Pearson."

"Nice . . . uh . . . to meet you," Mel managed. He folded and creased the paper down the middle, then addressed an apparition floating in the air above our heads. "I'm off to the office. Tell your mother I'll be late." He grabbed his briefcase from the counter by the door and left; the screen door banged in his wake.

Bryan watched the car turn the curve in the drive, headed for the college. "Is he always this . . . distant?"

"More." I pulled the paper toward me and read the date on the masthead. "Have I lost track of time. I can't believe it's Sunday," I said. "Mel likes to pretend I don't exist."

"No. He reacted to me, not you. He smiled at you."

"Well, yes. It's not me he likes to pretend doesn't exist, but my special attributes. You reminded him I'm a dwarf."

"Must be hard."

"I'm used to it."

"My parents treated me as special because I was a dwarf. My father's an LP too."

"LP?" I picked up the paper and stuck my face through a hole cut from the front page. "I wonder what *The Tribune* has done to offend Mel this time."

"Haven't you ever heard of the Little People organization?" he said with surprise. "What do you call yourself?"

I turned, still holding the holey paper in front of my face. "Faye . . . person. To tell the truth. You're the first dwarf . . . sorry, little person I have ever met."

"You're kidding." He gawked at me like I was from another planet.

"I grew up in small-town nowhere," I said in my own defence. "With a mother who acted like I was normal and a father who wished I'd disappear. After I left home, I was up a tree or lost in the library for ten years until I got my doctorate. Always the only dwarf on the block."

"Weren't you ever curious?"

"I contacted you, didn't I?" I didn't want to admit to him he was Grace's idea. I opened the cupboard door under the sink and plucked a ball of crumpled newsprint from the top of a handful of orange peels and egg shells in the garbage bin. I shook off the bits of trash, unfolded it, and smoothed it out on the table. Splashed across the wrinkled front page of the widely circulated daily was a photo of me, tucked like a sack of potatoes under the arm of a police officer who the paper identified as Constable Hanson. The head of the biology department at the university would later describe the photo as an act of humiliation worthy of a PHD. The headline read, *University Professor Arrested in Anti-logging Standoff.*

The events of the previous day crashed over me like a tidal wave. "I need that walk," I said and led Bryan out the door.

No wind on the bay and the sun beat warm enough to shed sweaters when we reached the beach. Seagulls reeled overhead and a seiner steamed out from the wharf in town, stabilizers up, engine at full throttle. The throb of the diesel engine thrummed across the water. We picked our way along a strip of pebble and shell beach, the extensive clam beds of the mud flat covered by high tide. Beach pea and grasses flowered on the foreshore. Other than a squawking pair of gulls and a young couple walking the tide line with their dog, the beach was deserted. The couple gawked at us when we passed, and when Bryan crouched to pat their dog, they whistled and the dog turned, tail wagging, and ran after them.

"I might bite," Bryan joked.

I forced myself to concentrate on the conversation, preoccupied by the irritation of the newspaper photo, my anxiety about Paul. "I came around a corner in downtown Victoria one day and the woman I ran into screamed."

"I don't blame them," Bryan said. "I'd scream if I met me in an alley too."

"Isn't it an issue of common manners?"

Bryan stooped to pick up a fragment of sandstone from a dry clump of sea lettuce. He turned it over in his hand, examining it closely. "Any fossils around here?"

"I know a place where you can pull them out of the cliff by the dozens."

"You'll have to show me next time." He tucked the rock into his pocket.

I struggled with the insinuation of *next time*. We reached the boulders at the end of the beach before I figured out why walking with Bryan felt odd. I didn't have to work to keep up.

"I've never seen this much water." Bryan gazed across at the mountains on the mainland. "Reminds me of the prairies. The long vista. I have to admit, the forest yesterday made me claustrophobic. All those trees and no view."

Forests claustrophobic? The views were merely closer, more intimate than the ocean. I grew up in the interface between forest and sea, comfortable in both. I tried to imagine living in a landscape with few trees. "Did you know the Inuit have twenty-six words for snow but only one to describe a tree. *Nabaaqtut.* The word means 'pole,'" I said. "Their term for forest, *Nabaaqutut juit*, 'many poles.'"

"Interesting," Bryan said. "The big trees are amazing though. I saw a picture in a book where eight couples waltzed on a stump. " He paused. "I could grow to like it?" The note of uncertainty in his voice drew my focus back to him. He wore jeans and a T-shirt with the slogan *I Have Rocks in My Head*, his sneakers wet on the toes. An educated, soft-spoken, easy-to-talk-to man.

"Why did you come here?" I asked.

"You know . . . the conference."

"No, why did you come *here*?"

"I wanted to meet you."

"Why?"

"I liked the photo you sent." The ocean and the clouds were reflected in the lenses of his glasses. "I think you're beautiful."

No one had ever called me beautiful. Not the few men I had dated. Not my brothers. Not Grace. Cute, strong, independent, smart. But not beautiful. I turned away, embarrassed by the tears suddenly streaming from my eyes, over my cheeks, and off my chin onto my shirt. Bryan stepped toward me. "Faye?" I held up my hand to stop him. I collapsed onto the sand and, amid the watery odour of seaweed, poured out to Bryan the events of the past weeks: the protest, my arrest, the timber markings, the marbled murrelets, the attack on Paul. My only omissions, my unrequited feelings for Paul and our night encounter in the tent.

Bryan listened, gazing out to sea. He offered me the edge of his sleeve. "May I hug you?"

I hesitated, overwhelmed by the sense of trust I felt toward him. He pulled me to my feet. The soles of our shoes crunched on a pile of dried kelp. Our bodies came together like two interlocking pieces of a puzzle, my cheek against his chin, my breasts against his chest, hips aligned, knees to knees, and his arms circled my shoulders. A perfect fit.

"Dr. Faye, Dr. Faye." We stepped apart. Rainbow sprinted along the beach toward us. Grace, Mary with Cedar, and Marcel were climbing down the bank beyond. Rainbow's hair flew behind her, her face flushed with exertion and she skidded to a stop in front of us. "Are you and Bryan going to get married?" she panted.

Bryan and I laughed awkwardly.

Rainbow danced in the sand, hips and arms undulating like a hula dancer. "Dr. Faye and Bryan sittin' in a tree, K-I-S-S-I-N-G. First comes love, then comes marriage, then comes Bryan with a baby carriage."

"You monkey." Bryan dove for her. "I bet you're ticklish." Rainbow screamed and ran laughing through the shallows, water splashing behind her with each step, Bryan after her, laughing too.

"I could get used to the coast," Bryan said later, after breakfast, while he packed his luggage in the trunk of his rental car. "Interesting rocks out here."

I rested my shoulder against the side door and slipped my hands into my back pockets.

"I'd need a view of the ocean, though," he went on. "You could teach me to appreciate trees."

You could teach me to appreciate you. But in a strange, twisted way I could admit only to myself, Bryan's disproportionate limbs, his dwarfish features, repelled me. *What's wrong with me*? I dug my toe into the grass beside the car. *I'm no different.* I longed to be back in the canopy with Paul.

"Can we keep writing?" Bryan leaned over and covered my hand with his. "I'd like to keep abreast of your criminal activity."

The warmth of his palm permeated mine. I liked his sense of humour. "Sure," I agreed with a cautious smile. "Why not?"

"Hey, there's an LPA conference in Seattle in September," he said. "Why don't you come?"

"Only dwarfs?"

"There's always family too. It's great," he said. "For three days you don't feel so different."

"I can't." I shook my head. One little person at a time was enough for me.

Bryan climbed into the driver's seat and turned the key. "Let me know if you change your mind."

As I leaned on the window frame, I noticed the extenders on the pedals. "Rental companies have extenders?"

"Are you kidding?" he said. "I carry them with me."

As I watched him drive away. I recalled a term he used in an email about the challenges of living in a big world. Environmental disability.

"There's no such thing as a disability," he explained. "Not when the environment is designed to accommodate everyone. Like extenders on a car. A blind man with a talking computer. Or a wheelchair ramp. Imagine an average-height person in a house designed for little people? Who's the disabled one then?"

Paul had fallen from old-growth rainforest straight into the ICU; his new environment was white, hard, and antiseptic. A high bed in a glass room behind locked glass doors. No twittering birds or wind through the branches, only the blink and bleep of monitors above the bed and the *hush-ha* of his breathing apparatus. The nurse checked his vital signs every ten minutes. His status, number 1 on the Glasgow coma scale—no response.

A visit to Paul meant a ride on an elevator—the buttons too high for me to reach without standing on my toes, arm stretched to maximum—followed by an endless walk along a quiet hallway to a boxy white waiting room. A buzzer on the wall for entry.

The two shift nurses assigned to Paul—Corrie, a sweet straightforward woman in her thirties, and Daniel, an older man whose solid presence reminded me of my brother Steve, advised me to assume Paul could hear. "He knows you're in the room," Daniel whispered. "I know he does. Talk to him."

I pushed a chair to the head of the bed and climbed up. He lay on his back, still as death, head shaved, burr hole drilled through his skull to relieve the pressure of fluid building up on his brain from the impact of the branch he must have hit during the fall. Head elevated to prevent the cerebral spinal fluid from leaking out of his body. His beard gone to accommodate the respirator. His naked face, ashen and smooth, appeared younger, more innocent, vulnerable as a newborn. I touched the dressing on his shoulder where the bolt had entered, his left femur—broken—a titanium rod pinned the ends of the bones together. The surgeon, whom I had convinced that Paul was my fiancé, had assured me the leg and shoulder injuries would heal with little if any residual effects. With physiotherapy and patience, he would climb again. But the head injury? No one could say. Until he awoke . . . if he awoke.

The mystery of the human brain.

"Did I ever tell you about my trip on Radeau de Cimes?" I watched his eyelids for an imperceptible tremor, his hand for the twitch of a finger. Nothing. *Paul, you in there*? "Did I tell you about the jungle from above?"

Radeau de Cimes. The raft on the rooftop of the world—a triangular web of inflated plastic tubing supported a mesh floor the size of a public swimming pool. Suspended by cables from the undercarriage of a multicoloured dirigible, it rose from the forest floor through the trees—a rainbow of colour illuminated by the ascending sun—and emerged above the Amazon rainforest canopy like an alien ship. The balloon cruised above the rumpled treetop where the tallest of emergent trees broke through the canopy like spires. The raft skimmed the brain of the world, the green cerebral cortex of living valleys, hills, and canyons. Gas hissed from the balloon on its descent and the raft settled onto the surface of the canopy. A flock of parrots exploded squawking out of the treetops. The arbornauts, roped to the raft with safety lines, scurried like spiders across the mesh floor. For an hour, we clipped branches, netted insects, read instruments, took notes and photographs. At a signal from the crew, we darted back to the balloon. With a roar, the canopy raft lifted from the trees and moved on to another patch of forest.

"We collected more data in one day, Paul," I said, "than we could collect in a lifetime with our climbing." I wished I could study Paul's brain the way the scientists studied the brain of the world in Brazil. Cruise his frontal lobes, his cerebral cortex in an airborne boat on a clear sea, hunt for damage, pinpoint the injury that held him captive, unconscious of the world, of me and my need for him to waken. I gathered up his hand from the blanket, struck by how it felt both heavy and weightless at the same time, as if he couldn't decide to which world he belonged. "Come back," I whispered.

I drew a bit of cedar bough from my pocket and crushed it between my fingers. The sharp scent displaced the cloying odour of antiseptic. I didn't know if Daniel, who sat outside at a desk where he could see Paul's monitors at a glance, would approve. I didn't care. "Do you smell the forest, Paul? Can you imagine yourself at the top of this cedar?"

Science had invented myriad ways to access the canopy. Ladders, walkways, towers, cherry pickers, cranes, and a metal-framed single cell designed to house a lone researcher in the treetops. Electronic probes to read the heartbeat of a tree, laser photographs, a conifer MRI, a botanical EKG. But what did science know about the human brain?

On the rooftop of the world, I had helped a female biochemist from Sweden collect plant material to study for potential medicinal properties. Had I cradled in my hands an emerald leaf, smooth and veined like a fan, a mistletoe or a crimson orchid, yet unnamed, that held the cure for Paul's wounded mind?

"Did you see the murrelet?" I longed for movement in his passive face, for the twitch of an eyebrow, a curl at the corner of his mouth, a sigh. "The murrelet," I repeated, seeing in my mind's eye the video camera buried in the climbing gear on my basement floor, its battery dead, the contents of the tape unknown.

17

A long row of white cloth extractors glowed like Japanese lanterns from the curtain rod in the lab. Inside each extractor, a core sample of ancient forest from one of my study trees lay scattered on a wire mesh platform—clumps of green moss and black soil, decomposed wood. Over the next two days, the heat from the forty-watt light bulb inside the extractor would force a migration of mites from the samples, the tiny arthropods crawling away from the light into a funnel where they would drop into a plastic vial half full of alcohol. Preserved and ready to identify.

I hung the last bag, secured the final vial, and turned on the light inside. It illuminated the translucent cloth like a weak sun on a cloudy day. I climbed from the counter and tidied up the lab, Paul, not mites, on my mind. But my field samples couldn't wait another day without drying out too much. The specimens might be dead, a field season down the drain. Paul would want me to carry on. I fingered my cell phone in the pocket of my lab coat for the hundredth time that morning. The nurse promised she'd call at any change in his condition.

I walked the row of glowing extractors and tightened the vials. I'd have to wait until the extraction was finished and the samples processed to know for sure if I'd caught them in time.

I switched on the lamp for the dissecting microscope and took a vial off the shelf. I spilled the contents into the sorting tray, dark flecks floating in a few spoonsful of alcohol. Last year's sample, unsorted and uncounted. I slid the dish onto the microscope stage and began the methodical counting and sorting of specimens. Normally I found the hunt thrilling—the discovery of an unusual specimen, a potential new species or an animal whose beauty took my breath away. Today I sought distraction.

A small black speck floated into the illuminated field of view, its tiny appendages visible. A mite. I plucked it from the sorting tray, and transferred it with a fine-tipped paint brush to a shallow depression full of alcohol on a ceramic well plate. I switched the sorting tray for the plate and adjusted the microscope focus, illuminating the body of the mite: medium brown, pear-shaped, it measured about a third of a millimetre in length. Too tiny to identify without slide mounting.

I can't say why I love mites. Any more than I could say why I loved Paul. Why do we love anything? Mites gave me no fame and fortune. No notoriety in science circles. No social standing. At parties, the conversation crashed when I mentioned mites, and people excused themselves to get another drink. Or asked if mites really lived on eyelids and cleaned crap from eyeballs. "Yes," I would explain, barely hiding my annoyance. "Mites do live on eyelids and in dust bunnies." I didn't go to many parties.

I scooped up the mite with a tool I'd fashioned myself, a tiny metal loop sticky with Hoyer's mounting medium inserted into the end of a moist balsam stick. I transferred the specimen into a drop of Hoyer's on a clean slide. Using the corner of a paper-thin glass slide cover, I carefully flipped the mite face down and floated it into position, then dropped the slide cover over it. A few seconds over the flame of a Bunsen burner to clear the soft tissues and the slide was ready to view.

I stood and stretched, my neck stiff from the intricate work. I glanced at the clock and was surprised to see that fifteen minutes had passed without a thought of Paul. I switched chairs and placed the slide on the viewing mount of a compound microscope, then flicked on the lamp, positioned the eyepieces, and adjusted the focus. The sample was perfectly mounted, all the internal organs and appendages visible and symmetrical. I recognized the specimen. *Cyrtozetes lindoae*, a fungus-eating oribatid mite. A new species identified from a sample I had collected six years ago from a section of stringy bark thirty metres up a six-hundred-year-old cedar and that took four years and several experts to name. I felt an odd affinity with this microscopic creature. It would be too easy to say it was because it was small like me. To a mite, I was giant. A square centimetre of fungus would appear to a mite like a mountain covered in trees or a vast plain. I adjusted my position on the stool, nowhere to rest my dangling feet. Unlike me, this mite was precisely adapted to her environment. I examined the large club-shaped antennae on the head used to sense wind currents and the long setae on the front pair of legs for smelling and tasting.

Maybe it was the mystery that attracted me to mites. My own sad life on display for all to see. Only twenty specimens of *C. lindoae* existed, all living on bark in old cedars, all in British Columbia. It didn't live with other mite species in the arm-deep suspended soils that formed in the crotches of trees, or with the wading mites that filtered nutrients from the sap oozing from a wound in the bark. It couldn't be found on the ferns and orchids that grow at the base of the tree on the forest floor, or on mushrooms and conks, on the epiphytic plants, between the hairs on leaves and stems, or in pools of water that collected in the cavities and depressions of the tree.

I labelled the slide with name and sample ID using a felt-tipped pen. "How did you get up there?" I asked out loud. "To the tops of those trees?" People likely wondered the same thing about me. Where did this odd specimen come from? Did I blow here like dust in the wind? A hitchhiker on a bird or a squirrel? In the nostril of a hummingbird? In the eye of a bat? Between the feather quills of an owl? I knew that mites were old souls, known to have lived with trees since trees appeared hundreds of millions of years ago, the association recorded in amber from the Cretaceous era. And the diversity of mites that had evolved over time was staggering, a dozen or more species on a single bee, forty thousand species of bees in the world. The math was simple. The implications to the forest ecosystem profound. What would decompose the mountains of organic matter, build soil, cycle nutrients? Under current careless logging practices, *C. lindoae* and others like her could soon go extinct.

My court date was scheduled for early August, along with two dozen other protesters including Marcel and Mr. Kimori. I had cancelled my summer course and sent a grad student to the conference in my place. *I'm tied up with personal issues*, I had explained in a brief phone call, suspecting the word of my arrest had spread like wildfire through the intimate canopy science community. The upcoming trials dominated the media. Mel refused phone calls from reporters to the Qualicum house and though I distrusted his motives, I was grateful to be spared the torment. At home I let the phone ring, left the communication with the world to Marcel, who had moved into my house to await trial.

I had taken the footage of the murrelets to one of the lawyers who had volunteered pro bono to coach protesters who, like me, declined legal representation for financial or personal reasons. The footage was perfect. I inhaled sharply when Paul's hushed voice dictated the date, time, location, and a description of the tree. A pan from ground to canopy, close-ups of the timber tag, the metal ID label. A murrelet keered, clear as a bell. The branch, its surface thick with moss, the murrelet, stubby wings open, landing on the broad limb. The bird frozen in place, the chick's fluffy head appearing from the shallow nest in the moss. The act of feeding, the adult bird stepping out into mid-air. Then a startled cry from Paul and the picture erupted into a dizzying confusion of colours and sounds: the crack of snapping branches, grunts, and bumps. The video ended with a shot of the ground far below, pitching violently back and forth, back and forth, the audio silent.

The lawyer talked throughout the viewing, making notes on a yellow legal pad.

"It's great evidence," he agreed. "The question remains how and when to use it?"

"What do you mean? Shouldn't it go straight to the government? Show the company's true colours. The sooner the better," I argued. "They could take out those trees any day if they haven't already."

"One option," he said. "Or you could use it to support your case in court." He rewound the tape and played the images again. Paul's hand swept across the field of view; I could see the life lines in his palm. I wanted to weep. "These kinds of mass trials are unpredictable. At Clayoquot, you blocked the road, you were guilty." He paused and leaned forward. "Listen, Faye, criminal contempt of court is a serious charge and an anomaly in our justice system. Sentencing is up to the presiding judge. There is no set schedule. Hell, a judge could impose a life sentence for this if he wanted to. In the past? A month of jail time at worst, fines and electronic monitoring at best. But you deserve the finest defence and this"—he pointed at the murrelet squatting on the mossy branch—"the proven destruction of threatened species habitat, could get you off and lots of publicity too."

"I don't know," I said. "It's still weeks to go. Can we risk the time? Can't we use it for both, the trial and a—"

"Possible," he interrupted, "but if the application is rejected out of hand, your video would lose its power as evidence. The trees are still standing. Think about this. You have a right to use the best evidence and to have your day in court."

I was drawn from my thoughts by the vibration of my phone in the pocket of my lab coat and I fumbled to retrieve it. "Yes?" My heart flapped in my chest like a trapped bird.

"It's Grace. Have you heard anything more?"

"No, nothing." I tried not to sound disappointed.

"Rainbow is asking about you." Grace had driven Mary, Cedar, and Rainbow from Qualicum to visit a few days before. They were refused entry into the ICU. Mary had cried in the waiting room, while Rainbow rang the bell for the nurse every five minutes.

"I have to tell Paul he's forgiven," Rainbow told the nurse who came to the door.

"No visitors except family."

"I am family. I'm his friend. I have to give him one of my dolls to sleep with."

The nurse held out her hand and smiled. "I'll give it to him if you like."

Rainbow frowned and snatched the doll back. "No. Not without me."

"Tell her I'll see her soon," I said to Grace and switched off the phone. I ticked a box on the data sheet labelled *C. lindoae*. Identification of specimens to species level was a precarious science. Taxonomists differentiated species by characteristics as simple as the curve of a hair beside another hair on the third section of a back leg. I tried to imagine an alien scientist from space attempting to categorize humans into species on the basis of our physical features: hair length, skin colour, the shape of the nose.

Height.

C. lindoae was one of three million specimens my colleagues and I had collected in ancient forests on Vancouver Island in the last ten years, most unnamed. The specimen might not be *Cyrtozetes lindoae* at all. An imposter. Mistaken identity.

I unclipped the slide and stacked it in a slide case, pondering the ability of female mites to reproduce without a mate. No suitable partner and *C. lindoae* might simply, like ten per cent of known mite species, forge ahead and make babies on her own.

18

Mary disappeared. She took Cedar and skipped town with Cougar. Grace called me to say that Mary hadn't returned from a planned meeting with Cougar to discuss their strategy for their upcoming trial.

"She left yesterday morning," Grace explained. "No phone call. No note."

"Where's Rainbow?" My stomach lurched at the idea of losing her.

"She's here," Grace assured me. "The poor thing's frantic."

"Damn woman," I cursed. "Have you told anyone yet?"

"No," Grace answered. "But she's asking for you."

I once found a newborn fawn in a patch of moss and twinflower while searching for big trees north of Port Renfrew. The hair was still matted from birth, the scatter of spots on the coat faint. Abandoned offspring in the wild most often starve to death or are killed by predators. If old enough to forage the young fawn might survive through its own ingenuity. In rare cases, I'd heard of does taking orphans into their care, nursing them along with their own. I left the fawn where I found it, hoping the mother would come back. When I returned to the spot the next day, the fawn was dead. I remembered the feel of Rainbow's warm body asleep beside me in the tent. Humans have the capacity to embrace another's young and care for them as if they are our own. Humans also have the capacity to abandon.

"Bring her here," I said.

Grace and Rainbow arrived at my door before dark. Rainbow threw her arms around my waist, her cheeks flushed and tear-stained. Marcel urged us all inside and made Rainbow a hot chocolate, the rest of us tea. I read her a story and put her to bed on the couch in my study, then waited until her breath slowed and deepened into sleep before I slipped out to the kitchen. Grace and Marcel sipped tea at the table, leaning in toward each other like a pair of old cronies.

"It's outrageous," Grace was saying.

I yanked out a chair and sat. "You're telling me, that woman is more than outrageous," I snapped.

"No, dear, I'm not talking about Mary," Grace explained. "I was telling Marcel about Esther's despicable treatment."

"What do you mean?"

"She refused to sign the form saying she wouldn't go back to the blockade and they put her in the drunk tank until her trial. I had to fight to get her permission to have even a pen and some paper. They give her no privacy."

"I'm sorry, Grace," I pleaded. "That's awful, but can we talk about Rainbow? What do we do?"

"For sure we don't tell the cops or social workers." Marcel set his mug of tea onto the table. "They will put her in foster care and we don't want that."

"Marcel's right," Grace agreed. "The child's had a hard enough time."

"You mean, let them think she's gone off with Mary?"

The two bobbed their heads in unison, as if they'd already discussed the possibility at length.

"Wouldn't the police need to know? Social services?"

"No, dear," Grace said. Marcel shook his head in agreement. They seemed to have it all worked out between them.

"But where will she live?"

Grace poured a third cup of tea. Marcel added milk and sugar and pushed it across the table. "Here, with you."

"Me?" My hand knocked against the cup and tea sloshed over the lip, forming a milky pool on the polished wood.

Grace went to the sink for a cloth.

"But I'm single, I work, I might go to jail soon, how can I babysit a child?"

Grace wiped up the spill and levelled her famous gaze at me. "Not babysit. Parent. You make it work, because you love them."

"But . . ." I didn't have any response to the statement. I had grown fond of Rainbow. But love?

"If you go to jail—a big if, you might get house arrest—I'll help." Grace tossed the cloth into the sink. "But she wants to live with you."

"Rainbow, she love you," Marcel said. "And I do what I can too."

I stared at the wet stain on the table. "She'll have to go to school."

Grace leaned on her elbows. "I'd love for her to go to school, but she can't. They'll want documentation, ask too many questions."

"You mean I'll have to home-school her too?" I stammered. "Don't home-schoolers have to register with a school?"

"If we tell them. We'll manage." Grace sat back and folded her arms. "You never know, Mary might come back soon." We all contemplated that possibility in silence.

Grace left the house and returned with Rainbow's belongings: a plastic bag containing a few pieces of ragged clothing, a toothbrush, and the two tiny dolls. "Not even a hairbrush," she muttered, handing me the bag. She hugged me and left for home.

Marcel washed up the dishes, stooping over the low sink I had installed when I bought the house. "You want to talk?" he asked.

"Tomorrow," I answered, my body drained of energy. "I need to sleep."

On my way to my bedroom I paused outside the study and pushed open the door a crack. The light from the hallway spilled across Rainbow's sleeping form. I tiptoed inside and sat on a chair, gathered her pathetic pile of clothes into my lap, and wondered how to explain abandonment to a six-year-old.

Discrete inquiries revealed Rainbow Cassidy did not exist; no certificate on record. The grandfather as tangible as Santa Claus. Grace bought her a wardrobe. "I never had new clothes before," Rainbow said, admiring a pair of brand new overalls in the mirror. We fixed up the study into a make-shift bedroom. Marcel, Rainbow, and I became an odd unit, drawing more stares than usual when we walked along the waterfront near my home. Rainbow delighted in my miniaturized kitchen and the preponderance of stools arranged about the rooms for reaching high shelves.

"It's like playing house." She giggled at Marcel, who was perched on a small chair at the kitchen table. "Marcel's like the giant with the little Putians." We went out the next day and bought him an extra-big chair at a thrift store.

On the third morning at breakfast she asked me point-blank, "Am I going to live with you until Mary comes back?"

I stopped spreading butter on my toast. "Yes," I answered cautiously.

"Is she going to come back?"

"Of course she is," I said, guilty for the lie, but unprepared for the conversation I had intended to broach at the opportune time.

Rainbow broached it for me. She swirled her spoon through her milky porridge. "What if she doesn't?" she said quietly.

I pulled Rainbow's chair toward me across the floor. *Precocious child.* I tipped her chin up with a finger. She deserved the truth. I breathed deeply. Could I keep the commitment I was about to make? "I don't know where your mother's gone. I don't know if she's coming back. But you can stay here as long as you want."

Rainbow slipped from her chair, threw her arms around my neck, and burst into tears. "Can I go to school?" she wailed.

"Yes, but—"

"With books and pencils and a lunch box?"

"Books and pencils and paints and a ruler too," I said, feeling Marcel's attention on me. "But no lunch box. You'll have to home-school, like you did with Mary."

Rainbow pushed away. "But why?" She rubbed her wet cheek on her shoulder. "Home-schooling was boring. Mary never taught me how to do anything."

"Marcel and Grace and I will try to do it better," I said. "You can learn whatever you like. But, honey, to stay with us, you have to home-school."

She scowled, but indicated her agreement with a dip of her head.

"And you must not tell anyone your mother has gone away."

Rainbow didn't ask why, didn't protest; she fixed her gaze on me and dipped her head once more. She didn't mention Mary again.

Marcel and I took Rainbow out and bought her a second-hand desk and two bags of school supplies. She spent the rest of the day organizing her school room, singing while she worked.

19

I listened to the doctor's blunt announcement with disbelief.

"No nasty viruses, no STDs"—she checked the clipboard in her hands—"but it appears you're pregnant."

"I'm what?" I managed to choke out the few words I could muster at the news. I gaped at the doctor, then at my abdomen, which was draped in a flowered print gown. What did I expect? A hand-shaped bulge, my belly inflating like a balloon as I watched. "How?"

"I expect the usual way," she said wryly. "Are you in a new relationship?"—she examined the chart in her hand—"Is that why you asked for these STD tests?"

I was unable to tear my attention away from my flatter-than-flat stomach. "Are you sure?"

"We found traces of hormone in your urine. If you want, you can confirm it with a home test. Come in next week and I'll do a prenatal physical. Any questions?"

Of course I knew how babies were made, for people, for trees, for mites. The union of a sperm and an egg; in plants: pollen and ovule. The process similar no matter how big or how small the species. The sperm of a blue whale and the sperm of a human were both invisible without the aid of a microscope. An African elephant started life the same way as a deer mouse. The largest species of trees on earth, the sequoia and the redwood, both developed from gametes that could sit undetected by the naked eye on the tip of a human finger. A male mite deposited a small packet of sperm, the spermatophore, which the female collected at her leisure. Fertilization in an old-growth conifer happened high up in the canopy. Windblown pollen from the male cone settled on the female seed cone, and over an entire year's span of time, the sperm moved in through the pollen tube to the ovule where it met with the egg. When released, the fertilized seed drifted to earth where it landed on a rock and dried up, or fell into a swamp to rot, or, if lucky, settled on a decomposing log, a patch of soil, or a gravel bank and when the time was right, the temperature warm enough, the humidity high enough, the ground fertile enough, the embryo opened and a seedling emerged.

The doctor rose and opened the door. "And once we're sure, let's set up an appointment to discuss your options."

My brain felt like mush.

"You might want to consider genetic testing."

"Testing?"

"You must know it's possible to test the fetus for achondroplasia. And"—she consulted the chart again—"if you are considering an abortion, you'll want to make a decision soon."

She left and I sat on the examining table, staring at the purple print flowers sprinkled across my lap. I hadn't needed a year for the microscopic sperm to wriggle its way to the microscopic egg but a few seconds of folly on a dark night in a rainforest. The fertilized egg didn't wait dormant until the substrate was wet enough, warm enough, or fertile enough. I was all of the above and the single egg divided once, twice, again and again to form an embryo, implanted in the wall of my uterus, growing and developing minute by minute. A silent secret mystery. I could imagine the miniature seedling of a spruce producing a fifty-tonne giant taller than a twenty-storey building, but couldn't bring myself to picture a fetus, another human growing inside my body. I counted back to the unmistakable moment of conception. Summer solstice. Four weeks and six days.

How could the beginning of life be a silent event? One would think this significant affair would at least send up a brief trumpet blast or a bar from Mozart. A girl in my high school gave birth at fourteen. Her family assumed she was gaining weight. How could they not know? Grace claimed she knew of her pregnancies within two days of conception with all three of her children.

How could I not know?

I sat with the thought until the nurse knocked on the door, needing the room for the next patient.

I waited outside the elevator on the main floor of the hospital. My stomach churned, my head ached with a thousand doubts and questions.

"Faye Pearson?"

"Yes?" I turned toward the voice, dazed, and tried to place the face of the man.

"Sergeant Lange from the Duncan RCMP." He held out his hand. "Remember?"

"Oh yes," I replied. "I didn't recognize you. You're not in your uniform." He seemed more like a grandfather in a casual golf shirt and tan cotton pants than an officer of the law.

"My mother had surgery on Monday," he said. "Listen, I'd like to talk to your partner, Mr. Taylor."

"He's in a coma." I punched the button again, reluctant to get into a conversation where I needed my wits.

The sergeant stepped back to allow an orderly to manoeuvre a wheelchair toward the next elevator. "Do you mind if I call you Faye?"

I shrugged.

"I have to apologize."

"About what?" I said, taken aback by the statement.

"I checked you out. Other than the blockade you're clean, more than clean. I'm afraid I didn't believe the story you told me. We examined the arrow that was used to shoot him. The bolt, I mean."

"And?"

"The rubber tip was sawed off and the end sharpened."

I steadied myself, horrified at the thought of Paul's assailant methodically whittling the tip away to a lethal point, the crime premeditated.

"Do you have any more information?"

I shook my head. I felt nauseous, wanting to escape, and was relieved when the bulb above the elevator lit up and the door opened with a ding. "I need to go," I said.

He fished a card out of his pocket. "Call me if anything new turns up." I stepped into the elevator. "One more thing"—he propped the door open with his foot—"about the picture in the newspaper. The constable's behaviour was out of line."

Heat crept up my neck and into my cheeks. "Thank you." I stood on my tiptoes and pressed the top button, feeling less than vindicated, my thoughts more focused on the future than the past.

"Nobody deserves treatment like that," he said as the elevator door rumbled closed between us.

I silently filled in the rest of his sentence. *Not even a dwarf.*

I sat in the corner of Paul's room and watched his chest rise and fall. I pressed the palm of my hand to my stomach. How big was a thirty-four-day embryo? Did it have fingers, a nose?

Corrie came in to check the monitors and change the IV bag. "Hi, Faye," she said. I wondered if a nurse could sense the momentous alteration in my body, but Corrie chatted about Paul's vital signs and the weather while she worked, then departed with a wave, leaving me alone again with Paul in the hiss and beep of the monitors and my own private ear-splitting shock.

I chewed on my bottom lip. "I'm pregnant," I said aloud to the silent room. His featureless face didn't flinch. "What do you think?"

Of course he'd be staggered by the news. Urging for an abortion. What man in his position wouldn't? He'd always talked about having children one day when he met the perfect woman. I moved to the end of the bed and peered over the edge of the crisp white sheets at the traction apparatus on his leg. I wasn't that woman. I had never anticipated having children, let alone a life partner, a husband. What if the baby was a dwarf? Destined to a life of being different. Of teasing and stares. Of not being able to reach the elevator buttons. Or sit on a chair without making a production of it. I'd marched through life acting like none of those things mattered. But could I put a child into the same position? I paced the room, then climbed on the stool and studied Paul's face. What if the baby was like its father? With a mother who couldn't lift and carry her own child past infancy? I tried to imagine parenting with Paul, our child toddling on unsteady legs back and forth between us, but the image evaporated before I could hold it steady in my mind.

On the way home, I bought a pregnancy test. The clerk lifted her eyebrows as she put the package in a bag, as if dubious about the implications of my purchase. After dinner, I locked myself in the bathroom. Rainbow haunted the hallway outside the door like a restless wolf, her radar uncanny. Without a doubt she would know the instant of conception of her own babies when the time came. I sat on the toilet lid and read the instructions on the box. Simple. One didn't need a doctorate in chemistry to pee on a stick. Arms longer than my own would help. I tried to ignore the intermittent tapping on the door.

"Dr. Faye?"

"I'm busy. Go find Marcel if you need help." Rainbow flopped onto the floor outside the bathroom with a thump and a sigh. The scoundrel. Did I want a child of my own? One I couldn't give back? I climbed half-naked into the bathtub, set the water glass in the bottom, hitched up my shirt, squatted and peed. Five minutes later my answer appeared, a faint flush on the end of the stick.

Pink . . . for pregos. Up the stump.

In trouble.

20

When I stepped through the door, the chatter and laughter in the classroom fell into silence. I heard the crinkle of newspaper being shoved into backpacks. My famous cover photo, no doubt. A blaze of scarlet filled the view outside the window, a Japanese maple in the university commons. Deciduous trees were rare in the rainforest. It was a splendid tree, but I missed the giants, missed my time in the field with Paul. I faced the group of summer seminar students from the biology department who had gathered to hear me speak about my research. The chair of the department had moved the date for my seminar up to allow me to squeeze it in before my trial, my fall courses cancelled. I hadn't been in front of a class in months.

All eyes were on me. No question they knew about my arrest. Many of the two dozen faces were familiar; a number had taken my undergraduate level entomology classes. I recognized Matt, a tall, thin, overly earnest boy I'd supervised for his master's thesis on ants, and Margie who worked on soil beetles up north. A few students were new to the department, doubly curious about their dwarf professor. At least I was certain they were in the dark about my pregnancy, a secret between my doctor and me. I intended to keep it that way.

I moved the podium aside, the stand far too tall. The room assigned to me was not the usual lecture theatre where the desks cascaded upward in a fan and all the students could see me with ease. This room was an older traditional classroom, small and square, the floor a single level. When I began teaching in classrooms like this, I had used a step stool, but it proved problematic, too limiting to my movement around the room, to the blackboard, the overhead projector, to engage with my students. Instead, I usually sat on my desk to lecture. But today I would stand, not caring if the students had to make an effort and peer around the bodies in front of them, crane their necks to see over the heads of their neighbours. I could imagine the gossip. *University Prof Arrested at Antilogging Standoff.*

My slides were already set up by the audio-visual technician. I collected the laser pointer from the desk and asked the student nearest the door to dim the lights, another to pull the blinds. I flashed a slide up on the screen. "My team and I have worked in Otter Valley for three . . ." I choked up at the photo of Paul in climbing gear ascending WR-3-3 on a rope. I paused to compose myself, to steer away from the onslaught of tears that seemed to be waiting in the wings ever since I'd left the doctor's office two days ago. An embarrassment I didn't need. "We've been in Otter Valley for three seasons," I repeated. "Our main focus of study is oribatid mites in the canopy of ancient rainforest western redcedar trees. Ancient, in the temperate west coast rainforest, is defined as two hundred and fifty years or older." I could hear a rustle of papers, the click of pens.

"No notes today. You're not going to be examined on this," I said testily, then regretted my tone. "Sit back and listen. I'll take questions later." I flipped to the next slide, a frontal view of a mite. "And for those of you who don't already know or who have forgotten what I taught you in your Bugs 340 class"—a smatter of laughter—"oribatid mites are a group of soil-dwelling mites in the order Arthropoda. Why are they important ecologically?"

Margie raised her hand; the girl was one of the brightest students I had encountered in my career. "Oribatid mites break down old plant material and recycle the nutrients back into the soil."

"Correct." I paced back and forth as I talked, not usual for me, but today I seemed unable to stand still. "Without oribatids and other mites, living plants would not have access to nutrients and could not survive, and we all know what that would mean. Plants as primary producers support all other life."

The next slide was one Paul had taken of me in the crotch of a cedar, my arm buried up to the shoulder in a deep pocket of suspended soil. "My primary study in Otter Valley," I explained, "focused on mites in suspended soils. Suspended soils are accumulations of decomposed plant debris over time in depressions and crotches in trees."

"How old is the suspended soil in the picture?" a student I didn't recognize asked from the back row.

"An accumulation of suspended soil like the one in this slide is deeper than my arm is long." I held out my arm to demonstrate, suddenly conscious of the attention on my shortened limb and the whispers from the back of the room. I raised my head and the whispering ceased. "This one's built up over a period of hundreds of years. In fact, we don't find appreciable accumulations of soils until the trees are well into the ancient category." I bent to fish a soil corer out of my briefcase and felt a sharp pain below my navel. I straightened slowly, my hand over the spot. *The baby?* I waited but nothing more. I pushed my concern aside. *It can't be bigger than an almond.*

I turned back to the class to find the students all gawking at me again. I cleared my throat and held up the corer. "This is a homemade soil corer, used to take samples from suspended soils in the canopy and from the ground. What did we find?" The next slide showed a series of charts and graphs. "One hundred and thirty-eight species of oribatid mites in ground and suspended soil samples. This bar on the graph"—I pointed at the chart with the laser—"are the ground mites and here the canopy mites. The top section of the bars show those exclusive to that particular habitat. Forty-two out of ninety-four canopy species were found only in the canopy. The remaining species found in both canopy and on the ground were collected from the lowest branches down. Not in the upper canopy. What does this tell us?"

"The soil conditions in the canopy are different than those on the ground?" a girl in the back called out.

"Yes. What else?"

No one answered.

"How did the canopy mites unique to the canopy get into the canopy?" I prompted.

After another brief silence, Margie ventured an answer. "Well, if the canopy mites aren't found on the ground, I guess they couldn't have crawled up? And they don't fly. Wind?"

"Wind is a possibility. Or hitchhiking on another animal," I said. "The important thing our study shows is that the oribatid mite community within suspended soils in the canopy are formed mainly by dispersal and colonization within the canopy system. In other words, canopy species originate within the canopy"—I waited for the revelation to sink in—"and"—I raised my finger to punctuate the point—"at least one-third of the canopy species we identified are undescribed or species new to science. Questions?"

Matt's hand shot into the air. "Dr. Pearson," he said. His beard, his optimistic energy reminded me of Paul and a wave of regret washed over me. "What are the implications of a Centinelan extinction when many canopy mites are new species."

I composed myself. The astute question had impressed me and I paused to consider my answer.

"What's a Centinelan extinction?" someone asked.

I leaned against the edge of the desk and crossed my arms, glad to distract myself with a story. "In 1978, two ecologists carried out the first-ever botanical survey of a cloud forest on a ridge in the western Andean foothills in Equador," I explained. "The ridge was called Centinela. The ecologists found ninety species previously unknown to science. These species lived nowhere else, a unique flora in an isolated ecosystem. Matt, tell us what happened when the ecologists returned to Centinela to continue their collections a few years later."

He seemed pleased at the question. "The forested ridge had been cleared for agriculture."

"And the implications?"

"The ninety new species had become extinct overnight."

"Yes." I took over again. "Many other isolated island ridges occurred in the area, which also must have developed species found nowhere else. These ridges were also cleared for farmland, but before anyone had a chance to carry out a botanical survey. A Centinelan extinction occurs when an ecological island, like the ridge in Equador, is cleared. Species go extinct in a virtual instant, including those unknown to science before they are gone."

"Could the rainforest canopy be like Centinela?" Matt asked, his voice rising with excitement. "Isolated and full of new undescribed species that provide ecological functions and services we don't know about yet?"

His question conjured up images of logging trucks loaded with old-growth cedar barrelling out of the upper Otter Valley. The image triggered a spike of anger that travelled up my spine and vibrated at the base of my skull. I struggled to push it away. "There's no doubt in my mind that the industrial clear-cut forestry allowed today results in Centinelan extinctions for canopy mites on a grand scale." I thought of the blue timber tags on my study trees and my voice rose. "How could it not? They are logging whole forest ecosystems before we can count and study the species we know about, let alone those we have yet to find. Not only that"—I went on, the floodgates swinging open—"they are doing it with impunity, breaking the law, breaking agreements," I shouted, "with no consideration for endangered species, for the benefits those forests provide. It's not science, it's greed, plain and simple greed." I paused to take a breath. Rows of stunned faces peered back at me. I caught myself. What was I doing? I fumbled around for a way to backtrack. I'd never before let my teaching cross the boundary into politics.

Matt's hand shot up again.

"Yes, Matt," I answered, hoping for a change of subject.

"That's why you got arrested?" he said.

I went still, the students fell silent. "I . . ." I groped for words. The image of Paul hanging in mid-air, blood dripping from his wound, appeared in my mind. How could I tell the students my arrest had nothing to do with greed, mites, or ecology? Nothing to do with conserving the forests. "I–"

Matt gave a single loud clap with his big weathered hands. The sound startled everyone in the room. He pushed his chair back, the legs scraping on the linoleum floor, and got to his feet. He raised his hands in front of him and clapped again, then again. One after another, the students in the room stood up and joined him until the room resounded with applause, like rain on a rooftop. I put up my hands to stop them. "No, please, don't," I pleaded. "You don't know." But they didn't hear me and they didn't stop. They kept on clapping until the students for the next class arrived at the door.

A handful of students waited for me outside the classroom. "Dr. Pearson," one of them asked. "Will you tell us about your arrest?"

"Sorry, I can't talk," I lied. "I have an appointment."

Margie held up the newspaper photo of me under the arm of the officer. "This was harsh. I'm going to write a letter to the editor and to the police."

Matt and the others agreed. "What else can we do to help?"

I carried on walking. I needed more than letters. I needed a miracle. I raised my hand awkwardly in a half-hearted acknowledgment. "Thanks for your support." I felt their eyes on me as I walked down the hallway and out the door.

I spent the next couple of hours in my office and lab organizing field samples and finishing up paperwork. I could be in jail the same time next week. The reaction of the students to my outburst had left me embarrassed, feeling a fraud. It was almost dark by the time I left for home. I fumbled with my car keys. The student's applause had thrown me off balance, their admiration undeserved. I'd stepped onto the logging road in a fit of rage, not virtue. A crossbow bolt flying through the air had carried me onto that road. I slid into the front seat and started the car. It was too late to go back to the hospital. Marcel would have dinner ready and Rainbow would be waiting. How had I accumulated all these responsibilities to other people? I drove out of the parking lot and headed for James Bay and home. I stopped at a light in the middle of downtown. I realized I was stroking my abdomen with my free hand. A baby grew inside me. Previously unknown to science. At least to this scientist. I stared through the windshield at the car ahead, at the red brake lights. The doctor had urged me to make a decision soon. I pulled my hand from my belly and planted it on the steering wheel. The light changed and I stepped on the gas. My chest filled with panic. What was I to do about this baby? Would it be extinct before I knew its name?

21

The first time I heard an old-growth tree fall in the forest was in the middle of the day in a windstorm during my graduate thesis project in the Carmanah Valley. The hurricane power of the storm couldn't mask the roar of the ancient hemlock a kilometre away as it toppled and settled to earth with an impact that left a crater as deep as I was tall. The second happened years later in the dead of a windless night when the rotted roots of a fifty-metre cedar tore from the ground and the mammoth whistled through the air like a dynamited building. I later walked the length of their fallen bodies in the aftermath of broken branches, young trees snapped off in the path of the descent, crushed ferns and shrubs. Around me, light streamed in through an opened patch of sky to touch forest floor that hadn't felt the sun in centuries.

The fall of SS-1-3, a.k.a. Bruce the Spruce, did not go unobserved. The scream of a forty-inch chainsaw blade serenaded the laying of the giant to earth. The saw whined while the faller worked at the massive trunk. He wore caulk boots, Kevlar pants held up with red suspenders, and a helmet with ear protection. He cut a V-shaped slice on the east side of the tree called a Humboldt undercut. He paused, removed a heavy plastic wedge from his leather belt, and hammered it into the cut with an axe, to ensure the direction of fall. He climbed around on the hummock to the west side of the tree and set to work. The saw-toothed chain carved small windows into the inner core of the trunk, then tunnelled through the damp layer of sapwood into the hard, dead rot–resistant heartwood that gave the tree support. The upper branches trembled. It was dangerous work. The threat of falling limbs—widow-makers—ever present. The sixty-tonne giant might shift without warning and trap the saw blade; the bottom of the trunk could kick out and knock the faller flat. He could lose a limb or his life. But the logger who felled SS-1-3 knew his job. The tree shivered and flexed with the final cut, and fell, as planned, away from the sea. Its top splintered on impact; the blast shot spears of fractured wood far into the forest.

As SS-1-3 fell, I was describing to Judge Marlene Robson the layout of my research site. Judge Robson, known during the past two weeks of trials as the hanging judge, had little sympathy. Her instructions to the crowded courtroom and the twenty defendants: "No more talk about trees. I'm tired of hearing about trees."

No one complied. Esther, ushered into the courtroom in handcuffs, sang about trees; Billy brought in his drum and played his version of a tree's song for thirty seconds before the judge silenced him; Mr. Kimori stood in *shin rin yoku.* Judge Robson issued an arrest warrant for Mary Cassidy and Tony Williams, alias Cougar, for failure to appear. Cougar was wanted in Oregon State on outstanding charges of wilful mischief and property damage in relation to anti-logging protests. He had blown up a skidder and a grapple yarder with dynamite. Throw in a few shoplifting and B&E charges and he had sufficient reason to avoid the contempt of court charges in Canada.

While I nervously waited my turn to address the judge who had dismissed the arguments of my friends one by one with a flick of her hand, the faller took a lunch break on the stump of SS-1-3: ham and cheese on brown and a Thermos of coffee.

"Faye Pearson," called the court clerk and I took my place in front of the judge's bench. The magistrate leaned over the front edge of the desktop to peer down at the infamous dwarf professor. The clerk read the charges. "How do you plead on the charge of criminal contempt of court?"

"Not guilty."

"Are you representing yourself?"

"Yes, your honour," I said and began my argument. I spouted science and its imperatives to society, the plight of a tiny seabird, and the significance of a blue paint mark on the trunk of a tree. Two more trees fell before I presented my evidence and while the video footage of the marbled murrelet played to the crowded courtroom, a faller cut into the cross point of the blue X at the base of the murrelet tree; the chainsaw blade sliced through centuries-old wood like butter. The ancient fir thundered to earth as the judge addressed me. "I don't know why you're showing me all this. Were you on the road?"

"Yes"

"Were you arrested for defying the injunction?"

"Yes."

"I find you guilty."

Judge Robson sentenced me to a fifteen-hundred-dollar fine and a month of house arrest on electronic monitoring beginning immediately.

Marcel was called next and when he rose from his seat in the back of the courtroom to come forward, the judge muttered "circus show" under her breath. In spite of his eloquent philosophical dissertation about cod, he was sentenced to sixty days, the lengthy jail time on account of his lack of residence.

I squeezed a clump of moss and green-tinged water dripped out into the Petri dish, the air in my makeshift basement lab fragrant with its earthy smell. I positioned the glass bowl under the dissecting microscope, flipped on the light, and adjusted the magnification to forty times. My back ached from four hours of cataloguing arthropods and I suffered a bout of nausea that hadn't eased for days.

A simmering fury smouldered under my skin and I struggled to keep it at bay. My trees were gone. With them years of research and untold species we might never find anywhere else. Lost along with the functions they performed that benefitted the forest, the world. The company had acted with impunity, the courts complicit. Marcel was still locked in jail, Paul unconscious in hospital. I wanted to gather them to me, rescue them, protect them from the pain of an uncertain future, but I couldn't, I didn't know how. My fledgling efforts at political activism had ended in disaster.

Swirling the dish in a slow circle, I concentrated on the tiny creatures that floated, twirled, and zigzagged through the field of view: rotifers, worms, protozoa, algae. About to discard the sample for another, I spotted a pear-shaped body a third of a millimetre in length lumber into view propelled by three pairs of legs. Instead of toes, the tips of its feet bore suction discs. Tardigrada. Water bear. The tiny aquatic animal resembled a caterpillar more than a bear. *Il Tardigrado*, slow-stepper. I checked my watch. Rainbow would be home soon from a craft class with a home-schooling group. Grace had discovered the loose association of families who got together for activities, people who didn't ask probing questions. Rainbow and I spent mornings doing "school." Three afternoons a week, a family from the group whisked her away for lessons. She never failed to return happy, dancing in the door full of enthusiasm. "I can float and paddle like a dog," she crowed one day after a swimming class. Rainbow would love the water bear.

I turned my attention back to the specimen. The discovery of water bears in forest canopies surprised scientists, the creature previously associated with ground soil, ponds, or the ocean: found between grains of beach sand, in leaf litter and algae, in sea-bed sediments. Now canopy researchers found them wherever they looked, at the top of old-growth trees, in water droplets trapped between the leaves of mosses and the thalli of lichen, in greater abundance and number of species the higher in the canopy they searched.

Rainbow rattled down the stairs, out of breath. She held a clump of blue dough in her hand. "We got to make play dough today." She spied the microscope. "Can I see? Can I?"

She pushed a stool over beside me and climbed up. Dropping the dough on the table, she peered through the paired lenses. "It's like a caterpillar," she said, her voice full of wonder. "What's its name?"

"Water bear. Its scientific name is tardigrade."

"Where did it come from?"

I showed her the moss. "I found it at the top of Bruce the Spruce last year."

Rainbow frowned. "But he's dead."

I smoothed the hair on the back of her head. "Yes, but isn't it nice to have one of his friends. The water bear dried up to a flake of dust in the sample bag with the moss. I added a drop of water and brought it to life again."

Rainbow lifted her head from the microscope, eyes wide. "You made it alive from dead?"

"It was dry, not dead," I explained. "Water bears can dry out for a hundred years and still come back to life in water."

"A hundred years?"

"It's called cryptobiosis," I said. "And that's not all. They can live in cold to absolute zero, temperatures up to one hundred and thirty degrees Celsius, six thousand atmospheres of pressure, X-ray radiation one hundred times the human lethal dose, and vacuum."

I had expected Rainbow to be impressed, or at least curious, but she turned back to the sample, hands gripped around the barrels of the eyepieces.

"They travel all around the world on the wind. Scientists call it *tardigrade rain*." I don't know why I continued on. She wasn't listening. In an odd way I felt like I owed it to the water bear to let Rainbow know how amazing it was. To impress on her that there were creatures in the world that could recover from almost anything. "We find them on mountaintops, in the deserts, and the tops of the tallest trees. They're the most resilient of species."

Rainbow slid from the stool and stood in front of me, her body vibrating, face bright with desire. "Could we?"

"Could we what?"

"Do the same to Paul? Bring him back to life?"

My throat tightened at the suggestion. "I wish we could, sweets."

"Let's try."

I pointed to my leg. Rainbow's shoulders sagged. I was trapped at home. I hadn't seen Paul since my trial, when a sheriff fitted my left ankle with a transmitter and my home phone with an electronic receiver that notified the corrections branch if I left the house without permission twenty-four hours a day, seven days a week. I had signed a form agreeing to keep the peace and be on upright behaviour. I wondered if ranting and kicking furniture fell into the category of upright. Grace drove from Qualicum once a week to bring groceries and take Rainbow on an outing. We missed our walks along the water and through the park. Two more weeks to go.

Rainbow turned and plodded to the bottom of the stairs, her feet scuffing across the unpainted concrete floor.

"Don't you want to find more water bears?" I swivelled around on the stool.

"No."

"Where're you going?"

"Homework." Rainbow spent hours writing up sheets of made-up math questions and answering them herself. Inventing stories about trees for Cedar. I worried at each ring of the phone, each knock on the door, in fear of a visit from social services, the return of Mary.

"Would you like to bake cookies?"

She whirled around. "Chocolate chip? For Marcel?"

"You and Grace can visit him on Saturday."

Rainbow ran back and hugged me with an energy that nearly unseated me. "I love you, Dr. Faye," she said. A warm beam of sunshine wrapped itself around my heart.

While we slept that night, the water bear dried out in the Petri dish and slipped back into cryptobiosis. Paul lay in a white-sheeted hospital bed on the other side of the city. The latest prognosis was discouraging. The longer the coma, the less chance of recovery. The doctors used terms like *persistent vegetative state*, *locked-in syndrome*, *brain death*. Talked of transferring him out of ICU and into the neuroward for *supportive care*. Daniel kept me informed by phone; his calm voice always ended with the same line, "Don't give up hope. Miracles happen in this place."

A few minutes after four AM, a miracle did happen. Daniel walked by Paul's bed and said to his patient, "Hey, buddy, want a brewski?" Expecting no answer, he carried on with his work, recording readings from the monitors. When he turned again to Paul's passive body, what he saw made his heart race. Paul didn't open his eyes, pupils working to focus on the machines, the lack of green, the weakness in his limbs. He didn't smile or whisper a name, Daniel's head dipping close to hear. Paul's resurrection from his personal cryptobiosis—initiated by beer, not water—was as subtle as the movement of tardigrade rain on atmospheric winds.

Paul moved his left forefinger.

22

Paul's hand moved, a toe, a flicker of an eye, like a restless seed in his body flowering into movement, into gradual awareness of his limited world, baby steps to recovery. When he could breathe on his own, the hospital staff moved him off the ICU and lifted the visiting restrictions. I had completed my sentence and visited daily, alone or with Rainbow, or Grace when she could make it. The doctors ordered low stimulation to allow the brain to heal. The nurses said, "Nonsense" and urged us all to talk. We played music and videos, read books out loud, something Rainbow, with her new-found skill, loved to do for him. She was reading the ending of *Where the Wild Things Are* about a little boy who runs away to a mysterious island only to realize he misses his mother when Paul opened his eyes and gazed around the room. Rainbow and I later argued about who he focused on first. "I think it was you," I said. "He noticed a new freckle on your nose." "No, Dr. Faye," Rainbow assured me. "I know it was you." We both insisted he had an upturned curl at the corners of his mouth. His first smile in three months.

The hospital piled on the resources. Speech therapy, occupational therapy, physiotherapy. Daniel warned us that Paul's personality might change, a common result of head injury. "I know one couple," he confided, "who separated three years after the husband's injury because she claimed he wasn't the man she married. She told me, 'his kiss wasn't his kiss anymore.'"

I stood on a kitchen chair and taped the end of a streamer to a curtain rod. Marcel, out of jail a few days, held the other end, his release ten days earlier than expected. "For my stellar behaviour," he insisted. Grace directed the placement of the decorations from the table where she sat blowing up balloons.

"Hurry up, you two." She tied a knot in the end of a large blue globe with a snap. "I need help. I'm too old for this. I haven't got the lungs. She'll be home soon."

We had guessed at the date of Rainbow's birthday based on her statement, "It's when the leaves fall." When asked to make a list of gifts she said, "Mary didn't believe in presents." I cursed the woman for the hundredth time.

"You're gaining weight," Grace commented, eyeing me as I balanced on the chair.

I gave no answer, afraid Grace would guess my secret hidden beneath the extra baggy sweatshirt I wore. I couldn't tell her, not before I had made a decision. For Grace, abortion was a choice for everyone but her own family. A few days before my trial, I had visited a genetic counsellor.

"There's a simple test for mutation in the FGFR3 gene, the gene responsible for achondroplasia. This gene makes a protein involved in the development and maintenance of bone and brain tissue," explained the clinician, a serious man in his fifties. "Is your partner a dwarf?"

"No."

He went on, "Your baby has a fifty per cent chance of having achondroplasia, a fifty per cent chance of normal stature. When both parents have achondroplasia, the chance of their offspring having normal stature is twenty-five per cent; having achondroplasia, also fifty per cent. There's a twenty-five per cent chance of occurrence of homozygous achondroplasia."

"What's that?

"Two copies of the mutated gene. It's most always fatal."

"You said the test is simple?"

"Yes, it's a blood test. It's best done in the first trimester. Routine periodic ultrasound can detect the bone abnormalities but not until the third trimester when it's too late."

"Too late?"

He paused. "For a termination."

The word settled on my shoulders like a shawl of nettles, a prickly comfort. It could be that easy. No one need know. Paul none the wiser. Life would go on. "How long do I have to decide?"

"The turnaround time for results is three to four weeks. If you choose to abort, it's best done by fourteen weeks, but we can push it later." He consulted my chart. "You're how many weeks?"

"Almost six."

"Decide soon."

I thanked the man. "I'll have to think about it."

"Don't think too long," he urged as I walked out the door.

I had cried all the way home.

I had the test a week later.

Now at eleven weeks, I had not yet heard the result. Time was getting short.

Grace continued talking. "And you're pale." She paused in the middle of ripping open a package of streamers. "Are you well?"

"I'm fine." I jumped to the floor with a thud to prove my robust health.

Marcel checked the cake in the oven for the tenth time. "Ma mére's recipe." Gobs of batter and a dusting of flour covered his paunch.

"The cake will fall if you open the oven one more time," Grace warned.

He eased the oven door closed. "I'll make the frosting."

Mel sat reading in the living room. I was surprised he had made the trip with Grace, his visits rare.

The phone rang. "Would you answer it, Grace?" I asked, my arms full of coloured napkins and paper plates decorated with comical bears in party hats.

Grace returned from the hallway. "It's the father who picked Rainbow up to go to the playground. She's been fighting." She collected her purse from the table. "I'll bring her home."

Rainbow traipsed red-eyed and solemn from the car to the house, a purple bruise rising on her right cheekbone.

"Grace told me not to fight," she declared, plopping onto a kitchen chair with a humph. "I wanted to punch those kids."

"Looks like they managed to punch you. Grace is right, no fighting," I said. "What happened?"

Rainbow pushed out her bottom lip and refused to speak.

"We can't have the party until you tell us what happen," Marcel wheedled. "My cake, he will get stale."

Rainbow lifted her head; her mouth dropped open at the sight of the decorations, the table set with colourful napkins and hats, the cake on the sideboard. "You made me a birthday?" she said. "With presents?"

"Yes, and we'll have it when you've explained about the fighting."

"I can't." She dropped back onto the chair and crossed her arms.

"Yes, you can," Grace insisted. "We're not going to spank you. We believe in peaceful resolution to problems. We're your friends. We want to know what's happened."

Mel appeared in the doorway and leaned against the frame, his hands in his pockets.

Rainbow swung her legs back and forth under the chair. "Freak," she whispered.

"What?" I said.

"They called me a freak."

"Why would they do that?"

"Your mother is a midget and your dad is a giant and you are a freak," she yelled, her face twisting with anguish before she burst into helpless sobs.

Anger rocketed through my body. *Midget*. The word transported me back decades. I was nine years old, alone and on my way home from school.

A red convertible cruised past. "Hey, midget," a voice drawled from the open window. My guardians, Patrick and Steve, were at baseball practice, nowhere in sight.

I walked on, feigning nonchalance, stomach churning like a wild, white river. The car did a U-turn and passed me again, then pulled into a driveway ahead, blocking the sidewalk. I stopped, heart thudding. Doors opened and four boys stepped out. I focused on the cracks in the sidewalk; I could see their legs as they walked toward me—black boots and jeans, a pair of sneakers, hairy legs with shorts. "Hey, freak. We wanna talk to you." I didn't wait. I turned and ran, painfully aware of each inadequate stride. I listened for footsteps, the roar of the car engine to overwhelm me, surround me like a net and lift me off the ground. The thud of my blood pulsing through my head drowned out all else. Warm pee trickled down the inside of my pants.

Patrick and Steve lied to Mel to borrow his car. "We're going for ice cream." We hunted town for the boys and their Mustang for an hour, driving every street, the back alleys. "Passing through, I guess," Steve speculated. "Bastards." "What's a midget?" I had asked. My brothers exchanged glances. "A mean word for a short person," Patrick said, staring straight ahead out the windshield.

Grace pulled Rainbow onto her lap and wiped the child's tears away with her apron. "They don't know any better, sweetie. We can educate them."

"Bullshit." I spat out. "They know exactly what they are doing."

The family looked at me in shock.

Mel walked over and placed his hand gently on the top of Rainbow's head. "You're a sweet girl."

The jolt of his gesture, the tenderness in his words, kept me rooted to the floor.

"Can I hit them tomorrow?" Rainbow sniffed.

Marcel opened his mouth. "Be my g—"

"Get the presents," Grace interrupted. "It's time for the party."

The damage was done. I kept a close eye on Rainbow during the festivities. She was a fine actress. She laughed at Marcel's trick candles that played Happy Birthday over and over when hot. When she squeezed her eyes tight for her wish, I wondered if she was asking for a boxing glove or a slingshot. She opened each gift with care: a red and blue store-bought sweater with pockets and a zipper from Grace, an insect collection kit from me, a recorder and a stuffed animal from Marcel, and a box of chocolates from Mel. She hugged each person in turn with a polite thank you. But I knew she was play-acting for the sake of her friends, and when all the presents were open in front of her, she lowered her head and said in a small voice, "Are there any more?" We all understood. *Is there anything from Mary?*

Nobody answered. I wanted to punch a wall but instead kissed Rainbow on her cheek and whispered in her ear, "You are a present for all of us." Sparklers materialized like magic from Marcel's coat pocket and we gathered outside where we wrote our names in fleeting script of light across the night sky. When Grace asked Rainbow what she would like to do next, she didn't hesitate. "Go and see Paul."

We trooped by the nurse's station laden with cake and ice cream, Rainbow trailing a bouquet of balloons. "What a loving family," one of the nurses commented.

"I got new felt pens and a hat and mitts Esther made me in jail"—Rainbow chattered on to Paul, not caring that he was unable to say more than a few words without great effort "and"—she held up a stuffed toy that filled her arms—"an old-growth bear."

Paul stroked the bear's head and managed a crooked smile.

"Marcel said he met the bear in jail," she said. "He's silly." She turned and beamed at Marcel, who leaned against the door frame.

Paul pointed at himself, his lips working to form words "No . . . present . . . from me."

She looped her arms around his neck and kissed his cheek, giggling at the half-day growth of beard. "Know what you can give me?"

He raised one eyebrow; his eyelid fluttered with the effort.

"Come home."

I wanted to kiss her.

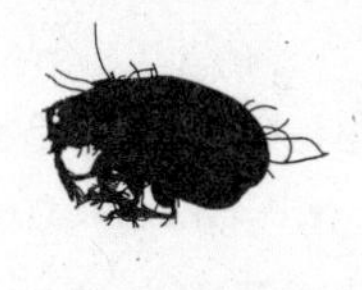

23

The baby was a dwarf, the test positive. I walked around in a stupor, unable to concentrate on anything else, the questions looming over me, time for decision short. I couldn't tell Grace, my fears about her reaction to the pregnancy palpable. Marcel? I didn't know him well enough. I had no close friends, except Paul. I'd done my best to alienate Bryan, the one person who might offer a unique perspective, his last few emails unanswered. I dialled his number late one night in desperation, hung up, then dialled again, hands shaking.

"I'm pregnant, it's a dwarf," I blurted out before he'd said more than hello.

He was silent for a moment, then asked cautiously, "What do you want from me?"

I burst into tears.

"Why don't you join me next weekend at the Little People's conference in Seattle," he suggested. "I'm sure I could get you in."

"How would that help?"

"There will be women you can talk to. Mothers. Doctors."

"I . . . I'm not sure," I stammered.

"Think about it,' he said. "What have you got to lose?"

The mid-September sun reflected across the tops of the waves as the high-speed ferry crossed the Strait of Juan de Fuca. The snow-topped Olympic Mountains rose blue and grand above the grey haze of coastline. I scanned the water with binoculars for rare seabirds or pods of killer whales, a distraction from my nerves. I wished the boat would slow down, take a detour through the islands to the west along an unnamed channel, and help me avoid my arrival in Seattle and the reunion with Bryan. In the past twenty-four hours I had almost backed out half-a-dozen times. One more dwarf in my life had been enough of a challenge. But hundreds? After another sleepless night I'd packed my bag, left Rainbow with Marcel, and caught the boat.

The customs officer glanced at my driver's licence and waved me through. No short jokes. No computer probe into my criminal record. Bryan waited outside the terminal, reading a paper in the sunshine. A huge smile lit up his face when he saw me. I hoped he hadn't misunderstood my precise words over the phone. "We're friends, right?"

He gave me a quick hug. "Glad you're here." He looked attractive, tanned, and fit, wearing a button-down shirt and dress pants, a sports jacket slung over his arm. We took a taxi to a conference centre out by the airport. "I've arranged for you to share a room with a friend," he said. "Her name's Leah."

I touched his sleeve in gratitude for the gesture. A true gentleman. I needn't have worried. The cab pulled up in front of the hotel entrance. I took a deep breath and got out, my attention on the grand entrance. Other than us, no little people in sight. Bryan paid the driver and took my bag. I stood at the curb as he moved toward the revolving door. When I didn't follow, he turned around and tilted his head quizzically. "You coming?" he said. When I didn't answer, he returned to my side, took my hand, and together we walked through the revolving doors.

The hotel lobby was a throng of little people milling about, chatting in circles, coffee cups and napkins of squares balanced in their hands. If Bryan hadn't held my hand in a firm grip, I might have turned and fled. What had I expected: instant rapture, a new clan, a rare weekend of anonymity? Everywhere I turned I saw myself, the template, the repeated pattern—stunted arms and legs, broad forehead, average-sized torso, flat face—not surprising, achondroplasia the most common form of dwarfism, a spontaneous mutation on a single chromosome. I felt like a paper doll cut-out in a room full of identical paper dolls. My chest tightened, my stomach rolled. I wasn't as unique as I'd always liked to think. Had Mel done the calculations? One in twenty thousand births. Three hundred thousand worldwide. I hurried behind Bryan, avoiding eye contact with the people we brushed past. I focused on the back of Bryan's head as we threaded our way through the crowd toward the front desk. He collected my key and dropped me off at the room, promising to meet me in the lobby in half an hour for lunch and a lecture by a physician who specialized in people of short stature.

Leah was not there. She'd claimed the bed by the window, her belongings neatly arranged on the dresser and side table. I slid my few items of clothing into a drawer. I hung up my coat in the closet beside a strapless evening gown. I cringed. "There's a banquet Saturday," Bryan had said over the phone, "Formal. Bring a dress." I didn't even own one. The dress was gorgeous, teal blue satin, low cut. A pair of midnight blue heels—shoes to kill, my brother Steve had always called them—on the floor below. A key turned in the door. The woman who walked in was as surprising as the dress, short-cropped red hair, green eyes that reminded me of the colour of spring buds, radiant face. She was smaller than me, legs badly twisted, her progress aided by forearm crutches. She lurched across the room, swivelling side to side; the tips of her crutches pressed small round dents into the carpet. "Hi, Faye, I'm Leah," she said and shook my hand, crutch hanging loose. "Welcome."

Leah sat on the bed and told me she taught elementary school, Kindergarten and Grade One. She lived in Colorado and skied in a disabled program in winter, canoed in summer. "I don't need legs for canoeing," she said without embarrassment. "I have clubfoot, hip dysplasia, scoliosis, and hitchhiker's thumb," she joked, wiggling her thumb in the air to demonstrate. She'd had twelve operations since childhood to straighten her legs. "My parent's idea"—she rolled her eyes—"I've had it with the surgery," she said. "The only thing they managed to fix was my cauliflower ear."

"You have lovely ears," I told her. When I described my work, she listened carefully, then asked, "Would you take me up a tree some time?"

"Bryan's a great guy," she said suddenly.

"I don't know him very well," I confessed.

She studied me. "I assumed you were an item."

"No, just friends."

She paused and fingered the crutch beside her on the bed. "Did he tell you we were engaged a couple years ago?"

"No," I said, surprised at the disclosure. "What happened?"

"He wanted kids, I didn't." She went on. "I'm with kids all day at work."

I turned away, aware I was blushing, aware of the elusive goldfish in my womb. Leah wasn't going to be any help. Could she even have children?

"I know what you're thinking?" she said. Was I that obvious? "Could a gimp like me give birth?"

I fumbled around for something to say.

"Don't worry," she said. "It's a logical question. Diastrophic women can have babies. Usually average height unless the father is also diastrophic. And by Caesarean section. But lots of us are mothers. I have chosen not to be."

I changed the subject. "Do you come to these conferences much?"

"I wouldn't miss one for the world," she said, then winked. "Great place to meet men."

The hotel restaurant was crowded and noisy with little people, many who called out greetings to Bryan as we made our way to a vacant window booth. I was aware of the eyes of several women following my every move. Did I have to stand on a table and make an announcement? Leah seemed like a talker. She'd set them straight.

"They all think we're a couple," I said irritably, sliding onto the padded bench.

"Who cares what they think?" he said. "Besides, it's great to be in the company of an accomplished and elevated intellect."

I grimaced. "Are size jokes popular at these things?"

He lifted his eyebrows and smiled. "Huge."

I groaned. "I wouldn't want to ruin your chances."

He handed me a menu and sought my eyes. "What are my chances?"

"You have to ask?"

He frowned, then spread his hands in contrition. "Can't fault me for being an optimist."

"You're a nice guy—"

He finished my sentence. "But you're not attracted to me."

"I didn't say that," I said, "but I am pregnant."

He dipped his head apologetically. "Point taken."

"Leah told me you wanted children." Did I detect a flash of regret across his face? "Under any circumstances?" I continued. "With the risk of the health problems associated with dwarfism?"

He sat back and pondered my question carefully before answering. "Any child can have health problems." He paused. "A dwarf baby would make me the happiest man in the world."

"A dwarf baby?"

"I would abort a normal-sized fetus."

"What do you mean?" I said, shocked. "Why?"

He paused again. "I couldn't handle having a child who's not like me."

"Let me understand this," I said. "If your partner got pregnant and the fetus tested to be average height, you would want to abort?"

"Yes."

The certainty in his voice infuriated me. "But there are lots of people here—little people—with average-height children."

"That's their option," he said. "Some dwarf couples terminate if the fetus is a dwarf. Genetic testing has given us choices."

"What about the mother? What about her choices?"

"We'd have discussed it before we ever got seriously involved," he said matter-of-factly.

Was that why Leah hadn't married him? I felt sick. The waiter was on his way over to take our order. Heat surged through my body. I leaned in toward Bryan. "What if she didn't realize how she'd feel? What if she changed her mind once she was pregnant?" I said sharply. "What if she discovered she didn't care one way or the other if her baby was a dwarf or a giant. That the fetus growing inside her was what she wanted after all." I must have been shouting. People had turned in their seats to stare. I lowered my voice. "Would you leave her?"

Bryan watched me carefully. He placed his hands on the table in front of him and focused on them for a long moment. When he met my eyes, his cheeks were moist with tears. "No"—his voice cracked—"no, I wouldn't."

The conference room was packed, wheelchairs lined up along the walls. Dr. Sanford, an orthopaedic surgeon from New York who worked exclusively with people of short stature, spoke from a podium at the front of the room, a PowerPoint presentation projected onto a screen behind him. Bryan and I stood at the back and listened to the doctor outline the pros and cons of limb lengthening, a painful, drawn-out procedure involving the breaking of bones, and a metal brace called a fixator that reminded me of a medieval torture device and involved the gradual turning of screws. Bryan shifted beside me. I was still shaken by our lunchtime conversation. I wasn't sure what had happened. After my outburst, we had ordered and eaten our lunch in silence. But I no longer felt angry, more of a confusion at my own words. *What the mother wanted.*

When he finished, Dr. Sanford announced he would hold office hours in an adjacent room. People rushed for the door. "Here's your chance," Bryan urged.

By the time I got there, people were lined up down the hall. I stood behind a young average-height couple with a baby.

"You fine here alone?" Bryan asked. "I've got a floor hockey game." We made plans to meet before the banquet and he hurried away from me toward the elevator. I leaned against the wall. What was I going to ask this doctor? He was a surgeon, not an obstetrician. The baby ahead peered at me over his mother's shoulder. Or a paediatrician. The child had sky blue eyes and blond curly hair that reminded me of Cedar. His flat face, high forehead, and large head tagged him as an achondroplastic dwarf. I waved at him and he chortled happily in response. His mother turned around. She couldn't have been more that twenty.

"Cute," I said.

"His name's Josiah," she answered swinging the baby around to her hip to talk. "I'm Carly." Carly and her husband, John, had joined Little People after they had Josiah. Josiah needed an operation to correct spinal stenosis, a spinal column too small to carry the spinal cord. She brushed her hand over his curls. "He's the best baby."

All around were wheelchairs and crutches, misshapen legs, hopeful faces. I brushed my abdomen with a finger. Would my baby have problems? I scanned the long line of people. I'd been wrong earlier in the lobby, these people weren't clones. Many had other forms of dwarfism. The woman behind me was as well proportioned as Paul, the height of Rainbow. She was talking to a man in a fancy electric wheelchair, his head the size of a baseball. Dwarfism occurred in more than two hundred forms, many of them here at the conference, in this hallway. The people around me were as different as creek gravel. Individuals with unique characteristics, personalities, quirks, passions, and values. Like any gathering of people.

Carly was sitting on the floor, nursing Josiah, love and dedication radiating from her like a sun. Genetic testing had the potential to decrease human diversity; how many of these people waiting here with me might not have been born if their parents had known what they were before they knew who they were. Would a world without little people be a better world? Without Josiah? Leah? Bryan? Without the baby I carried? I sucked in my breath. Without me?

I wished Carly and John the best of luck and left the hotel in search of trees. I found a neighbourhood park a few blocks away with a few squat ornamental spruce, a handful of birch, but trees nonetheless. I sat on a bench under their thin canopy. I thought about Paul, the damage he had endured, the long recovery ahead. I couldn't bring myself to add death to injury. I'd have to confess. To Grace. Paul. I couldn't imagine the implications for my work. But lots of women did it. And on their own. I placed both hands over my belly. Still too early to feel anything. "What do you think, baby?" I whispered. "Will I do for a mother?"

Dinner was a lavish affair, banquet seating, lots of wine flowing, everyone dressed to the nines. If Bryan cared about my fashion sense and lack of exposed skin, he didn't show it. He sat beside me through the meal, attentive, guiding the conversation with his friends at the table. Dan was black and a proportionate dwarf taller than I. "Call me what you want, but never call me midget," he said when introduced. Leah, his date for the night, poked at his leg with a crutch. "Dan's our resident comedian." Leah looked stunning, makeup, turquoise earrings, her dress showing her curves. "I can't believe you can walk in those shoes," I had teased earlier as we'd dressed for the evening. "I ski, don't I?" She had drawn a line of lipstick across her mouth, then looked askance at my conservative pant suit. "You didn't have anything else to bring?" "My high school prom dress?" I had laughed. She'd unbuttoned my jacket and draped a slinky red silk scarf around my neck.

Next to me sat Phyllis, an accountant originally from White Rock who was married to Mark, six feet tall and a nurse at a seniors home in Tacoma. They had five children, three average-sized, two dwarfs. Word must have spread about Bryan's availability; woman flocked to the table to claim dances, in dresses that made Leah's look like a nun's habit.

I couldn't concentrate on the conversation; the banal familiarity distracted me, the gathering no different from a group of my colleagues at a scientific conference, with their talk of personal issues, politics, sports, their last vacation. By the time the music started, I was wiped. I watched the parade pass by, the giggling girls in their backless dresses, all bums and boobs, the men in tailored tuxes.

Bryan leaned over. "Dance?"

I cradled my cheek on my palms. "Too tired."

He dropped his lower lip in a pout, but before he could say anything more, a hand reached in and grabbed his. He smiled apologetically. I dismissed him with a wave. "Go." The woman, a big-haired blonde in a mini-skirt that showed her bowed legs, towed him onto the dance floor. Gutsy. I hadn't shown my legs in decades. The lights dimmed, a disco ball lit up sending out undulating flashes of colour. Out on the dance floor couples gyrated and swayed, short couples, mixed-height couples, a woman the size of a doll sat in the lap of a man in a wheelchair, spinning around in circles. Leah shuffled side to side with her crutches, face aglow. A terrible beauty. The music slowed and the dancers moved together, arms not reaching, hips rocking. Phyllis leaned her cheek on Mark's stomach, his hands tenderly on her shoulders. Another man picked up his date and they swayed together in an intimate embrace, her feet dangling at his knees. I watched Bryan guide his partner in an elegant twirl. He was a good man. Easygoing, kind. He'd make someone a fine husband. But not me. I gathered my bag. The disco lights were giving me a headache. I missed Paul, Rainbow, even Marcel. I craved the smell of trees. I pushed through the pulsing crowd toward the door. As I waited for the elevator I watched a pair of short-stature teenagers necking in a doorway. Their sweet raw passion made me turn away. I knew I couldn't live in Bryan's little world.

I woke the next morning to find Leah's bed hadn't been slept in. I left her scarf and a note on the side table. *Best of luck with Dan.* Bryan was in the dining room eating French toast with the blonde woman who now wore jeans and a blouse, her hair pulled back in a ponytail. Bryan introduced her as Michelle. I pulled him aside. "I need to go home."

His eyes searched mine. He glanced over at Michelle, who watched us intently, then turned back to me. "Did you find what you came for?"

I kissed him on the cheek. "In more ways than one," I said. "Thank you."

On the ferry home, I took an aisle seat, oblivious to the passing islands. I neglected to scan for whales, watch for seabirds. *I'm going to be a mother.* A journey into the unknown. My head spun with a mixture of dismay and yearning. I'd once climbed in the California redwoods with a colleague from Humboldt County. Monty introduced me to secret trees known only to a select few researchers who feared a fascinated public and the recreational tree-climbing community would love the giants to death. They'd named the Titans after the Greek gods—Atlas, Pleiades, Kronos—redwoods more massive than any other living organism on earth, older than Christianity. Their canopy crowns supported complex ecosystems of interwoven limbs, where trees lived on trees, sprouting in the deep suspended soils high up in the crotches and crevices of the mammoths. I took a break at the hundred-metre marker on my way up Atlas and snacked on a handful of blueberries. A bumblebee buzzed past my head. Not far above, a Douglas-fir seedling taller than Paul grew from the redwood trunk, its roots drilled deep into the bark for nourishment. A pocket garden of moss and lichen the size of a birdbath hung beyond my reach. Above the fir, I unclipped from the main rope and entered the thick crown assemblage, swinging like a monkey from branch to branch, tree to tree on a length of rope and carabiners called a motion lanyard. I threaded my way through the dense tangle of wood and greenery that housed a whole community of species that never touched the ground: salamanders and squirrels, birds, epiphytic lichens and fungi. Millions of bugs. The redwood canopy overwhelmed me with excitement mixed with apprehension, the possibility for new discovery, fear of the unknown. A golden cache of biodiversity, an enchanted forest, a mysterious realm, a dangerous and wonderful place. After a time I stopped to get my bearings and realized I could no longer tell what direction I'd come from, my point of entry out of sight, and realized, in the tangle of life, I could easily become lost.

24

Paul came home. He moved into the guest bedroom, Marcel bunking with friends from jail. My focus shifted from hospital to home; my days spent observing Paul, his slow recovery like the opening of a bud.

We walked. Paul and I, sometimes Rainbow. Paul on crutches in a shaky, swinging gait from the guest bedroom to the bathroom and back to the bed. When able to make the circuit—living room, kitchen, dining room, hallway—without collapsing, forehead covered with sweat, he ventured out into the yard and sat for long hours on the garden bench watching the juncos and finches at the feeder. At times he retreated to the darkened bedroom complaining of headaches, but always game to try a few steps more the next day. I thanked the universe his spirit hadn't gone missing in the limbo-land of his coma. When tired, he garbled his speech, his thoughts confused, and it worried me. As he became more aware of the world, I told him stories about the forest activists and events at the university. I described the tardigrades, the water bears, and how Rainbow wanted to pour water on him to wake him up. His expression dazed, he smiled because I smiled and I stopped trying to make him happy. After a couple of weeks, he walked and talked with greater ease, and we left the yard to hobble back and forth along the street.

When he graduated to a cane, we went in search of trees. The bigger the better. Up the road to Beacon Hill Park, where garden specimens of redwoods towered in the middle of manicured lawns. Paul rested his cheek on the stringy rust-coloured bark; tears streamed down his cheeks and for the first time since his injury he said my name. "Faye."

I held on to the moment like treasure.

I waited until we walked in Mt. Douglas Park among the old second-growth cedar and fir to tell him about my arrest and sentencing, the loss of the research site, the buffer logged. He stretched out on his back in the middle of the trail and squinted up at the spreading branches of the canopy high above until the pain in his head subsided. He sat up and snapped a branch in two. "Bastards," he said, although the "ards" trailed off in a slur, which made him stab one of the sticks into the dirt.

Who shot Paul? The investigation had stagnated. "We're working on it" was the response I received from the police. I suspected the magnitude of the protest, the subsequent arrests, and the mass trials had overshadowed the shooting, another detail in a river of lawlessness teeming with chaos.

Sergeant Lange showed sympathy but little encouragement. "We haven't got much to go on," he explained. "No weapon other than a broken arrow, no fingerprints, no suspects. I'm sorry."

No sign of the crossbow. I had confirmed that the bolt belonged to me, its blunt rubber tip neatly sawn off and carved to a point with a knife. The few loggers questioned produced alibis. The majority of forest defenders suspected the crime was committed by Don Ransom, the disgruntled logger who threatened them with the wrench, the man who'd tried to fall Jen's tree. His wife suffered from an undisclosed illness—cancer, M.S., the doctors weren't sure—the fellow famous for his short fuse. He insisted he was home in bed at the time of the attack, the claim corroborated by his wife.

"He's lying. The guy's crazy," Jen insisted. "I saw his face when he attacked my tree with the saw. He didn't care if I died."

"It makes sense, he must have done it. Trashing the camp, stealing the crossbow, harassing the tree-sitters, shooting Paul, all of it," Chris added.

I doubted Ransom knew Paul's location, kilometres from the tree-sit. I hadn't told a soul about our plan to film the murrelets.

On Remembrance Day, Paul threw his cane in the trash and Rainbow and I took him in search of ancient rainforest. We packed a picnic and drove west through Sooke along the coast road to China Beach. The public trail led through old spruce and hemlock forest to the sea. The weak fall sun competed with the shifting cloud cover, the sea frosted with white caps. Paul limped along the trail, stopping frequently to rest. "I can't wait to get back up there." He pointed into the canopy high above his head. "Out of purgatory."

"Your leg might heal enough to climb by spring." I offered up the tidbit of hope.

"The doctor says it's doing well, but he thinks climbing will be too painful. I'll use the other leg." He worked his fingers into his shoulder. "This hurts like hell."

I had observed him in the basement working out: leg lifts, pull-ups, face streaming with sweat and contorted with pain. Difficult to watch but his determination was heartening. At Paul's last medical assessment, the doctor had expressed amazement at the speed of his recovery. "Head injuries often take two to three years before the patient regains fluent speech, the ability to think through issues," he'd explained. "Paul's already talking well."

We hunkered out of the wind in the shelter of a huge driftwood root wad high on the beach. Paul and I huddled under a blanket and ate sandwiches while Rainbow played barefoot along the edge of the surf, running onto the shimmering wet sand with each receding wave, scampering back toward land as the next wave crested and bubbled and boiled after her. Small polished stones clattered and tumbled in the surf. In spite of the cold, she stood in the retreating water, the sand sucking her feet down, body reflected in the shiny film of moisture remaining.

"No water above your ankles," I warned, although I had a pack of spare clothes in the back of the car.

"Nothing from Mary?" Paul asked.

I was unsure whether he wanted to know for Rainbow's sake or for himself. "Not a word."

"He kidnapped her."

"You believe that?"

"I don't want to think about it." He watched Rainbow drag a whip of bull kelp along the beach leaving a long, snaking track behind in the sand. "Poor kid." Rainbow cried herself to sleep most nights and spoke often of Cedar, but otherwise appeared content. "What's going to happen to her?"

"She wants to stay with me."

"Can you manage?"

"Grace helps," I said. My hand dropped to the bulge beneath the loose jacket I wore. I could wait no longer, my pregnancy nearing five months, my condition difficult to conceal. I had dressed in baggy sweaters and track pants for more than a month. Grace would figure it out soon. I needed Paul to know first. Two nights ago I felt the flitter of winged insects across my abdomen. I steadied myself. "I'll have to take a leave."

"For?"

"I'll have two kids to look after."

"Two? Did they find Cedar? Why didn't you tell me?"

"No, not Cedar."

"You're not making any sense." Paul pressed his fingers into his forehead.

I took a deep breath. "Paul"—I steeled myself for his reaction—"I'm pregnant."

Ridges of flesh appeared between his eyebrows. "What?" The light in his eyes receded like the outgoing waves, retreating from me.

Rainbow screamed and I turned. She was tumbling head over heels in the surf, bowled over by a cresting wave. I lurched to my feet and sprinted down the beach to fish the soggy, cold girl out of the swirling water. She spit sand from her mouth and swatted water from her face.

"That was fun." Water dripped from the hem of her sweatshirt, her bony shoulders quaked with the cold, her lips blue. "You're soaked too," she laughed, then wrinkled her forehead and pointed past my shoulder. "What's wrong with Paul?"

I turned around to witness Paul splayed out on the ground in the shadow of the root wad, torso jerking, limbs rigid, a strangled grunt issuing from his throat.

A number of activities are not recommended for people with uncontrolled seizures. Driving for one. Scuba diving. Piloting a plane. The operation of heavy equipment. Carrying an infant. Tree climbing. Paul retreated to his room, emerging only for silent meals and appointments with doctors. He lost weight, grew dark shadows below his eyes, developed new wrinkles and a scruffy growth of beard. I cringed at the strain in his face when the specialist talked about brain damage and the possibility of epilepsy, and prescribed anti-seizure medication. I tried to imagine how it must feel to watch your whole life breaking into shards of glass at your feet. Unsure of where to step. He didn't mention my confession at China Beach and I pushed away the nagging notion that my pronouncement had brought on his seizure. I assumed he didn't remember. He'd know soon enough.

Marcel came for dinner during a rare late-November snowfall and, we soon discovered, to say goodbye. We stood outside and watched Rainbow roll a snowman's head through the shallow white blanket, grass peeping through in the wake.

"I fly to Montreal tomorrow," he informed me. "I go to see ma mère until the New Year." His face lit up. "She does the best Christmas. Then I go north."

"Ice fishing?" Rainbow quipped, her arms full of snowman.

His raucous laugh made us all laugh too, except Paul, who sat on a bench in the corner of the yard watching rosy finches crack sunflower seeds at the feeder.

"No more fishing. One of my jail friends, he works for a conservation group who study polar bear around Hudson Bay," he explained.

"You're going to wrestle polar bears?" I joked.

"No, I will write brochures and grant proposals." He tapped his temple. "They want big Marcel for his brains, not his muscles."

After dinner Paul shook Marcel's hand and shuffled off to his room.

"Rainbow, time for bed," I said.

Rainbow skipped across the floor to Marcel and hugged him. He drew out a wrapped package from his pocket and handed it to her. "An early Christmas present," he said. She tore the wrapping free to reveal a copy of *The Little Prince*. "I make you into a philosopher yet."

She threw her arms around his neck, then jumped down and ran to the kitchen, returning with a handful of chocolate. "Here," she announced, pouring the candy into his hands. "You won't forget us?"

He blew his nose in a large white handkerchief and gathered her in his arms. "Mais non, I will never forget you, Rainbow. When I see one in the sky I think of you."

I tucked Rainbow into bed and poured Marcel a glass of wine, myself juice, then settled onto the couch.

"You've never told me about jail," I said.

"Not bad." He rubbed the evening stubble on his cheek. "Lots of time for reading. I thank you for all the cookies." He patted his ample stomach. "I need to smoke again."

"Bad idea," I said.

"And you?"

"What do you mean, and me?"

He stroked his belly again. "You think I wouldn't notice?"

"Notice?"

"Ma mère was pregnant most of the time. And who is the papa?"

I swirled the juice around in my glass. "Parthenogenic."

Marcel raised his eyebrows.

"My pregnancy. It's parthenogenic A scientific term," I said. "For asexual reproduction."

He swirled the wine around in his glass as he watched my face with skepticism.

"Some oribatid mites reproduce this way. In fact, the females ignore the males when they're around."

"They should write you up in the journals," Marcel teased. "I am happy for you." He lifted his glass in a toast and tilted his head to the side. "Okay, I ask no more questions. And Rainbow? She misses her brother. You let me know about the birth, eh?"

I changed the subject. "You know the court is going to expunge our sentences?"

"Oui. A hollow victory." Marcel tilted his head toward the hall. "Paul, he is not well."

"No."

"He'll be better soon. He's strong and he have you." Marcel leaned forward and lowered his voice. "They still have no suspects?"

"No."

"I spend time in jail together with Squirrel," he whispered. I had forgotten the silent, mousey companion of Cougar. "He tell me Cougar, he is elusive."

"We know. He's gone, isn't he?"

"Oui, but he disappears, without warning, without notice. In broad daylight, in the middle of the night. Like a wild cat."

"What are you getting at Marcel?"

"From the blockade in the middle of the day, from up in the tree after dark."

"What? Where?"

Marcel held the palms of his sausage hands up, the skin pink and criss-crossed with lines. "We can only guess. The cops, they might be interested."

The cops were not interested. Sergeant Lange considered my speculations dubious. "You think this Cougar guy climbed down a tree in the middle of the night, retrieved the stolen crossbow from a hiding place, stalked and found your partner, in the dark, in the top of another tree kilometres away and shot him?"

"Yes."

"Hard to imagine."

"It's a possibility."

"Why would he do that? Weren't you on the same side?"

"Jealousy. A woman."

"You?"

"No, not me. The one he's got with him."

"How did he know where to find your partner?"

"I don't know."

"I don't know either," he said. "We're doing the best we can with the flimsy evidence we have. If we ever find this Cougar guy, believe me, we'll have lots of questions to ask him."

"Sure," I said, "thanks," and hung up the phone.

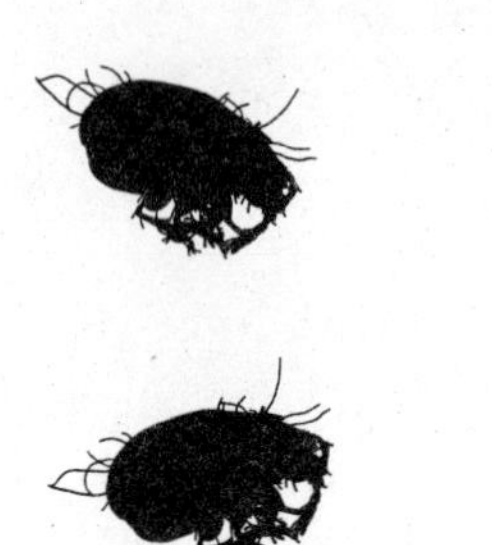

25

I declined Christmas in Qualicum. "Paul can't take the travelling," was my convenient excuse. Grace was undeterred. "We'll come to you. I'll bring the food. We haven't seen you since October." I hadn't yet managed to find the right time to tell my mother the happy news. "Don't you want to see your brothers?" she asked.

"Of course I do," I relented, resigning myself to the prospect of my entire family finding out about my pregnancy all at once. I couldn't avoid it forever, the way I'd avoided telling Paul again, walled up in his depression. It was a wonder, a testament to the extent of his isolation. My oversized clothes were becoming a farce.

Grace arrived Christmas Eve bearing a turkey and a tree, the others to follow with Mel the next morning. I was balanced on a chair in the kitchen pulling a stack of plates from the cupboard when she walked through the back door without knocking, arms full of packages. The house smelled of the shortbread and sugar cookies Rainbow and I had baked in preparation, the table covered with stars and moons dusted with red and green sprinkles.

"We might want to soak the turkey in brine overnight—" Grace stopped in mid-sentence at the sight of my bulging profile. I continued to transfer plates from the cupboard to the countertop, aware of my mother's intense scrutiny. Rainbow was reading Christmas stories to herself on the couch in the living room and Paul was resting in his bedroom. "Silent Night" wafted in from the stereo.

"Faye?" Grace set the turkey on the table. She wore her best coat open over a crisp white blouse and floral skirt, hair up. Each strand in place.

I opened the next cupboard door, looking for a salad bowl.

"Faye?" Grace grabbed my upper arms with both hands and forced me to face her. I gripped the edge of the bowl and resisted. Not until she cupped my chin in her hand did I meet her gaze. Grace's black pearl eyes with the perfect eyebrows misted over. Her lips quivered. Tears spilled over the lower edges of her eyes and streamed down her cheeks.

Grace never cried.

Panic rose in my chest. Grace never lost control. Grace the comforter, the purveyor of advice. She unravelled along with the bun in her hair, hairpins dropping like fir needles from a tree. She sobbed into her hands.

I couldn't get off the stool; Grace blocked my way. Fingers of anger displaced my panic, reached in and twisted like knives. What was terrible about the news that I . . . her daughter, would be a mother? A mushroom cloud of rage bloomed in me. I screamed, "Grace!"

She stopped crying and her hands fell to her sides.

"Damn you," I yelled. "What is so fucking bad about me having a baby?"

She raised her head, eyes red and confused. I half-expected her to scold me for swearing. Instead, Grace shook her head back and forth, a fresh cascade of pins and hair tumbling down around her. "Oh, sweetheart." She opened her arms.

I didn't move.

"Not bad. No. I—" Grace said through a fresh onslaught of weeping. "I never dared hope you would."

"Have you chosen a name?" Grace asked later as we shared a pot of tea at the kitchen table, her face washed, hair back in place.

"You're something else," I said.

"I suppose I am." She giggled like a schoolgirl. The sound caught in her throat, then exploded into hysterical laughter that sent her whole body into motion. I watched her, astonished, then found myself giggling along with her. Before long, we were both howling, red-faced and gasping for breath, cheeks shiny with tears.

Grace blew her nose in a tissue and reached over the table, between the tea cups and the honey and dirty spoons and grasped my hand. "I don't care what you name the baby if he's a boy. But if she's a girl . . ."

"What happened to your feminist principles of equality?" I teased through the last few spasms of laughter.

"Never mind." She dabbed at the corner of her eye with the tissue. "Your father picked out a name, but I had my heart set on Faye."

"Dad?" I stammered "Mel picked out a name for me?"

"We had a terrible argument," Grace admitted. "You're surprised?"

"I thought he would have preferred I died."

"What?" Grace sat back, stunned. "Why ever would you say that?"

"I . . . he . . . always acted sad or embarrassed or . . . Mel is ashamed of me."

Grace spoke with measured deliberation. "Your father loves you. Always has, always will."

"But he's never seen me, never looked right at me."

The skin around Grace's eyes softened. "Your father," she said. "Your father lives inside his own head. He rarely looks at *me*. He just never wanted you to get hurt."

"Funny way of showing it."

"After your birth he tried to fix you. He researched leg lengthening and gene therapy. When I objected, he gave up and let you be."

"Let me alone, you mean."

"Sweetheart, I know your father better than anyone. He's the most obtuse man alive. But he's proud of you, all you've accomplished. Your PHD, your work, your independent life. He loves you."

"The photo . . ."

"What photo?"

"In the newspaper, my arrest. He cut it out to save himself the embarrassment."

"No, he cut it out to save you the embarrassment. Enough about your father." She leaned in closer. "Do you know?"

"Know what?"

"If the baby's a dwarf?"

I scrutinized her face. "Yes."

She sat back and clapped her hands together. "Wonderful," she said.

"You're glad?"

"You sound surprised. Apart from your stubborn streak, raising you was a pleasure."

I pushed back tears. "Wasn't it difficult, though? You said my birth nearly killed you."

"Figuratively yes, I worked hard to push that large head of yours out. You popped my rectal muscle, which required five stitches and a couple of uncomfortable weeks. But I was afraid I might lose you. You had trouble breathing. Your air passages were too tiny. A minor virus could have been fatal. You were three before it got sorted out."

I was taken aback that the few details she shared mirrored my invented story from my youth. The large head. The stitches. Did Grace tell me more about my birth than I recalled? "You weren't sorry I was a dwarf?"

"Of course it took time to get used to, but we loved you from the second we saw you." She paused and caught the doubt in my expression. "Both of us. Mel *and* I."

"Mel attended my birth?"

"Yes, and not many fathers did in those days."

"How did he manage?"

"What do you mean?"

"His low pain threshold . . . ?"

"The poor man passed out." Grace chuckled. "He spent the rest of the labour in a chair." She handed me another cookie. "Eat. You have to keep your strength up." She brushed crumbs from the table and said, "There were no tests back then."

"Would you"—I needed to know—"would you have terminated the pregnancy?"

She shook her head emphatically. "Making that decision once was enough."

"What do you mean?"

She sighed. "I'd known your father for two weeks when I got pregnant with Patrick."

I was stunned by the confession, the puzzle pieces falling into place.

She reached over and touched my hand. "You haven't told Paul, have you?"

"You know about Paul?" I gasped, struggling to keep up with the revelations of the past minute.

"You've been so dedicated to him.

I twirled a spoon in a circle on the table, the metal scraping across the wood as it spun. "He's withdrawn. I tried . . . but . . ."

"Tell him, dear," she whispered. "He needs to know."

Rainbow stood in the doorway, hands in the pockets of her overalls. "Needs to know what?"

"Faye's having a baby," Grace announced.

Rainbow's face lit up. "I know," she said, then looked around. "When's dinner?" Grace and I glanced at one another and burst into fresh peals of laughter.

Paul stayed in his room Christmas Day, appearing only to greet my brothers, their families, and Mel upon their arrival. He missed dinner, the gift opening, the lighting of the tree. He missed the awkward moment when I announced my obvious pregnancy to the crowded table.

"Great news, Faye." Patrick broke the uncomfortable silence. "I thought you were getting chubby."

"Well, do we get to know the lucky man?" Steve quipped.

I smoothed my napkin, feeling Grace's gaze from the end of the table. "Not now," I said quietly.

"Pretty big secret," Steve's fifteen-year-old, Tim, whispered to his mother, Amanda.

"Never you mind." Steve swatted him affectionately. "I'm sure Aunt Faye has her reasons."

"Well, I propose a toast." Grace raised her glass. "To motherhood."

"Hear, hear," seconded Jean, a sociologist who'd been married to Patrick for two years. "Maybe we'll be next." She nudged her husband with her elbow and he blushed crimson.

"To motherhood."

Mel raised his glass with the others but didn't drink, watching me the whole time. He sat quietly through the questions about the due date, the speculation about sex and names. When Grace left with the children to fetch dessert he folded his napkin on his plate and cleared his throat. "Do you think this is the right decision, Faye?" he said. Everyone's heads turned at the unexpected sound of his voice.

I'm sure my face flushed the colour of the cranberry sauce on my plate. I opened my mouth but words failed me.

"What if the baby has problems?" he went on.

"All pregnancies have risks, Dad," Amanda said.

"But Faye—"

"Has a chance of making another dwarf?" I wanted to yell, to throw the turkey bone on my plate across the table at him. "Is that what you mean, Mel?" I wanted to ask him whether he knew achondroplasia could be inherited from one or both parents, most often the father. Had Mel carried the gene responsible for me? Did he ever try to find out? Not likely he'd have let the significant statistic go by unchecked.

"No—"

"Shut up, Mel," Steve ordered, cheek muscles twitching. "Fucking shut up."

Patrick pushed himself back from the table and stood. "Let's open gifts. It's Christmas."

"No," I stopped him. "Let him answer. What did you mean, Mel?"

Mel stared at his plate, at the brown scrape of gravy and mashed potatoes. "I meant . . . you'll be alone. Dealing with a baby all alone."

"That's right."

He lifted his head and met my eyes. "What will you do? There's no father. Your baby won't have a father."

The rest of the family stood, chairs legs sliding across the wood floor, and moved toward the living room. I stayed rooted to my chair; my chest ached. *No father.*

Mel excused himself, gathered his coat and hat from the closet, and left through the front door.

The family departed at nine for the drive back to Qualicum. I hugged Steve and Patrick at the door. "Call if you need anything," they said.

"I love you guys," I replied, my throat tight with emotion.

"And never mind Dad," Steve said. "He's . . . well, he's Mel."

"Your kid has two great uncles," Patrick added. "What more could it need?"

"Two great brothers." I waved them out the door, squeezing back tears.

I put Rainbow to bed and fixed Paul a tray of food. I tapped on his door. "Paul, you hungry?"

No answer. I eased the door open with my elbow. The room was dark; he didn't stir. He spent most of his time sleeping. I didn't blame him, sleep a state I wished I could retreat to most days. Block out the world. I left the tray on the desk and tiptoed out. I lay on the couch and surveyed the mess of wrappings under the tree; the few gifts left were Paul's. I should tie my confession up in a box with chocolates and a bow. Would he take the news any better than my father?

26

Rainbow brought Paul out of his depression. She made him snacks, crept into his darkened room, drew up the blinds, and camped on the carpet beside the bed to do her self-imposed homework.

"Paul, if you have five jelly bears and your mom gives you eight more, how many jelly bears do you have?"

"Paul, how do you spell *canopy*?"

"Paul, what colour should I use for this flower, a pink crayon or a purple one?"

When he didn't answer she would answer herself out loud, and then carry on with her task, humming while she worked. She knew to find me if he had a seizure. He responded slowly. Nothing, then muffled grunts from the depths of the pillow. Two-word answers. Rainbow emerged from his room one day and rummaged though the fridge. "Paul wants a carrot," she explained and returned to his room until dinner. A few days later I witnessed an exchange as I passed the open bedroom door on my way to the bathroom with a stack of towels.

"What do you want Santa to bring you?" Rainbow said to Paul. "I'm writing him a letter for next year."

"You don't believe in Santa."

"No," she paused. "But I don't know everything."

"You think it's possible he exists?"

"Could be?" She poised her pencil over the paper as if to say, *Do we want to take a chance?* "I'm going to ask for a wagon . . . for Cedar. How do you spell wagon?"

"W-A-G-O-N."

She formed the letters one by one, the pencil scratching across the paper, tongue between her lips. "Your turn. What do you want Santa to bring you?"

"A new brain," was his answer.

The day after New Year, Paul laughed at an inane joke I made at dinner. Later, Rainbow found me in the lab downstairs cataloguing specimens. "Paul needs to go for a drive."

"Paul's not supposed to drive, honey."

"No, you drive. He needs to go." She thrust a newspaper into my face. "Here." I studied the page, the tourism section of the local paper. A family posed in a stand of giant trees. The place, Cathedral Grove, a small park up-island protected for its old-growth, the giant trees bordering the highway and easily accessible. "He needs to go here."

Rainbow kept him in suspense through the drive. "It's a secret," she explained from the back seat, and when we reached Cameron Lake a kilometre before the park, she ordered him to "shut your eyes and don't peek."

We pulled into the empty parking lot, the day too blustery and grey for tourists. Rainbow hopped out, opened Paul's door, and guided him blind to an enormous weathered fir at the edge of the road, the trunk ridged with thick sheets of bark and clothed in green moss and lichen. "Tilt your head back . . . Okay. You can open them."

I hovered close by; his seizures often followed a shock or surprise. He stared up through the foliage and stroked the trunk, working his fingers between the ridges of bark as if trying to push through the thick skin of the tree into its living interior. "How did you know I missed this, you two?" he said softly.

"Surprise." Rainbow danced at the end of his arm, his fingers in hers. "Surprise, surprise." She pointed above Paul's head. "What's that?"

A black scar bruised the heavy bark of the fir. "A lightning strike," I explained. "Probably from hundreds of years ago."

"Was there a fire?"

"Without fire, these Douglas-firs can't reproduce," I said, imagining the scene. The lightning strike, the flame travelling along the ground like a lit fuse, devouring the dry underbrush, the years of accumulated branches igniting in its path. When the temperature of the fire reached flash point, flames exploded into the canopy like bombs. Whole trees splintering with the force of the created wind that flung entire trunks up and out of the fire and into the surrounding forest. Over days, the fire would have run its course, the ground sterilized by the intense heat. The only survivors a few thick-barked Doug-firs. The rodents would move in then from adjacent forest; deer mice and shrews would dig truffles from the ground and scatter the nitrogen-rich fungi across the forest floor, fertilizer for the sun-loving seedlings. Fire was a gift to this forest. A healing catastrophe.

We crammed together into a blackened hollow at the base of an ancient fir, my camera set on timer aimed from a stump on the opposite side of the trail. Rainbow and I stood upright, two forest elves, Paul jackknifed above us. "We're like a family," Rainbow said, linking her arms in ours. "A people sandwich." I stuck out my tongue, Rainbow stretched her lips sideways with her thumbs, and Paul crossed his eyes, two fingers wiggling behind Rainbow's head like antennae. The camera gave a click and a flash. Outside the hollow, a winter storm howled. We had ignored the sign at the entrance that informed visitors to vacate the grove in high winds. Windfall presented a constant threat to this vulnerable remnant of old-growth surrounded by clear-cut. Six years earlier forty-three trees had crashed to earth in a storm on a single night.

Paul came alive those few hours in Cathedral Grove. We wandered the trails, reading the interpretive signs out loud to one another along the way. *Wind and Fire: Natural Agents of Change. Nurse Logs: Nannies of the Forest.* I noticed Paul studying me throughout the day and found myself turning away from his gaze. We discovered a passageway cut through a recent windfallen tree, fresh sawdust in fragrant piles on the ground. Paul showed Rainbow how to count the concentric growth rings on the face of the cut. The task of calculating the age of the tree—one ring per year—took them half an hour. "Six hundred and thirty," Rainbow announced.

We walked to the far end of the park where a small group of protesters had held off the construction of a parking lot for more than two years before the parks department gave up. High in the canopy, the remnants of platforms remained, scraps of two-by-fours nailed to branches. A tattered blue tarp flapped in the wind. Ecojunk littered a small clearing full of logging slash: the shredded shell of a large canvas tent, a rusted metal chimney jutting out through the centre of the roof, a pile of empty tin cans and plastic bottles. To the north, clear-cut stretched from the road to the mountains.

"I guess civil disobedience can work." Paul kicked aside a broken lawn chair.

"A small victory," I countered. "I heard loggers burned one of the activist's cars."

We stopped at a coffee shop for a drink and a sandwich on the way home.

"Hot chocolate, please," Rainbow said in her politest voice.

"What size?"

"Small."

"Tall hot chocolate," the woman called out to her partner in the back.

"I wanted small," Rainbow protested.

"Yup, here small is tall," the clerk assured her.

Rainbow turned her questioning eyes on me. "Hey," she said. "Small is tall and tall is small." She slipped one hand in mine, the other in Paul's, and sighed with contentment.

Rainbow fell asleep in the back seat of the car halfway home, a chocolate moustache on her upper lip. Midwinter sun dipped behind the mountains and the light faded into dusk, into the dark possible only in winter. Rain speckled the windshield, the wipers sweeping the drops away with an intermittent swish. Paul turned the radio on low, leaned back against the seat, and closed his eyes. His face appeared strained. Had it been too much?

I drove along listening to a guitar solo. The news. An earthquake in Brazil. Fighting in Somalia. Grain prices dropping.

Paul switched off the radio. "Were you planning on telling me?" he said. "Or was I supposed to guess?"

I concentrated on the guiding lines of the road ahead, the reflectors at the edge of the shoulder.

"I know I've been self-absorbed, but I'm not blind."

"I tried," I managed. "I told you in hospital as soon as I knew."

"I was unconscious," he said. "Not fair."

"And I tried to tell you at China Beach."

"Your point?" he said. "It is mine, isn't it? Unless you met a guy while I was in a coma."

"I'm sorry. I didn't think you needed more stress."

We fell into a weighty silence, the headlights from oncoming cars illuminating our faces. My knuckles ached from gripping the steering wheel.

"I suppose you'll move back to your apartment soon," I said.

"You want me to leave?"

"No . . . no"—my heart pounded—"you can stay as long as you need to."

"What about—" He stopped in mid-sentence and switched the radio back on. "Never mind."

We drove the rest of the way home without a word between us. Paul carried a sleeping Rainbow in from the car to her room. I went to bed, my back sore after the long drive, and picked up a forest ecology paper I had neglected to work on for months, *Oribatid mites in temperate rainforest canopy*. I read through the abstract, crossing out words and sentences, scratching notes into the margin, a futile distraction from the playback of our clumsy conversation in the car that ran over and over through my head.

A tap came at the door. I put the paper onto the bedside table. Paul limped across the room, his expression unreadable, but his cheeks more full of colour than I'd seen since before his fall. Rainbow was right; he did need the big trees. I made space for him, plumping up a pillow against the headboard. In the early weeks after I brought him home from the hospital he had often visited me before bed like this to talk. "My shrink," he had dubbed me, but he hadn't visited since the onset of his seizures. I knew he wasn't in my room for idle conversation. I braced for his decision to leave.

"Time for the loony hour." He settled back against the pillow.

"Yes, the dwarf and the lunatic."

He propped himself onto his elbows and furrowed his brow at me. "Why do you make jokes about yourself?"

"If you can't beat them . . ." I avoided his accusing gaze.

"Hey, never mind," he said, his voice husky. "Thanks for today."

"Rainbow's idea."

"Do you think I can ever climb again?"

"Sure, a person can do anything they want to if they want it bad enough." I laughed. "I sound like Grace."

"Wisdom must be hereditary."

He slid his hand across the bedspread and onto my stomach; the heat from his fingers burned through the fabric of my pyjamas. "Do you know the sex?"

"It's likely a tumour."

He sighed. "No more jokes," he said. "I suppose everyone else knows."

"That I'm pregnant, yes. But only Grace knows about you," I confessed.

"What if I wanted to stay?" he said. "For good."

"You don't have to. I'll . . . we'll manage."

He reached over and put his hand again on my swollen

belly, tracing a circle around my navel. "No doubt you will. But I didn't say *have to*, I said *want to*."

I picked up his hand and returned it to his chest. "I don't want or need a reluctant partner."

"I don't see you twisting my arm." He trapped my hand in his.

I sighed. "The baby is a dwarf."

"Great," he said firmly.

"You don't mean it."

He cupped my cheek, his hand soft from a lack of physical work. "If this baby is anything like you, I'll be a happy man." I stared at him. "Besides," he went on. "I can't climb trees for a while and I expect you'll need a nanny."

"I don't want a nanny. Or an occasional father who comes by once in a while to babysit. Besides, you'll want to be free when your right woman—"

"Faye."

"—comes along. Remember Tessa. She's promising. Forget about Mary, though, if she ever comes back."

"Faye."

"She's abysmal, and you never know who's around the corn—"

He leaned forward and kissed me on the mouth. "When I said I wanted this, I meant the package deal."

He kissed me again, then slid down and rested his head on the package. "Two for one. What a deal."

A number of activities are not recommended for a man with uncontrolled seizures. Driving, flying, climbing trees. Apparently, making love is not on the list.

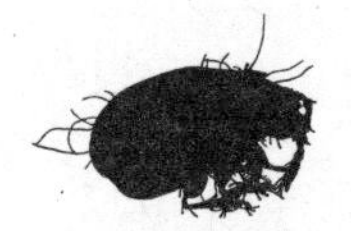

27

Mr. Kimori's house was sandwiched between two highrise apartment buildings downtown, the front garden of the brown stucco bungalow a tidy rectangle of grass, the brick walk swept clean of winter debris, a single ornamental plum tree in the middle of the lawn in early spring bloom. Rainbow swung the stone weight hanging from the bell chimes at the door, the metallic ringing of the clay circles mingling with the traffic noise from the street. Mr. Kimori opened the door dressed in a pullover the colour of moss and a pair of black sweatpants.

"Paul, Rainbow, Faye, Grace." He smiled broadly and beckoned us inside. "We're all here now," he said with satisfaction. "Happy Chinese New Year. *Gung Hay Fat Choy.* Welcome to my home."

"But you're not Chinese," Rainbow protested.

"I have many Chinese friends," he answered. "I embrace any excuse to celebrate. Come in, come in."

We stepped inside and he swung the door shut on the outside noise. Rainbow handed him our contribution of lilies, apple juice, and Grace's homebaked banana loaf.

"I thank you for this unnecessary gift." He patted her on the top of her head. "You're growing."

Rainbow beamed. "I'm in grade two," she said proudly and took his hand. He led us into the living room, where people filled the chairs, the couches, and the floor, or milled around a table in the corner.

"Hi." Terry walked over, a wineglass in his hand, and clapped Paul on the shoulder. Paul winced. "Oh, jeez, I'm sorry." Terry stepped back, wine splashing over the rim of his glass onto his corduroy shirt. "Great to see you, though." He pawed at the stain with a paper napkin. When he caught sight of my bulging belly, he exclaimed, "I heard you guys were preggo." A tense silence followed. "Faye," he said, unfazed. "I wanted to ask your opinion. I was watching this program the other day about dwarf tossing."

"Dwarf tossing?" I answered, bewildered.

"Guys in bars pay dwarfs to let them throw them as far as they can," he said. "On to mats, of course."

"Why are you telling me this?" I glared at him.

"I thought it was interesting that the dwarfs defended their right to be tossed. It surprised me—"

I was about to walk away when Esther interrupted. "Nice of Mr. Kimori to have a get-out-of-jail party. Here, Paul." She offered him her chair. "You need this more than I." He sat, face strained.

"It was a mistake to bring you," I whispered in his ear. "Let's go."

"I'm fine," he said. "Can you find me a beer?"

"No alcohol," I said.

He made a face. "Tea?"

I threaded my way through the crowd to the food table, aware of the furtive glances from people as I passed. Most of the original protestors were there: Chris, Jen, and Sue from Vancouver. Grace was talking to Billy and a small woman with dark permed hair. Squirrel sat alone by the door. We'd all done time, one way or another. There were three conspicuous absences. Marcel was still in northern Quebec; he sent frequent newsy letters and photos of snow and polar bears. No one had heard a word from Cougar and Mary since their disappearance.

The table was fixed with food and drink, including a variety of meats and a generous amount of beer and wine, noteworthy as Mr. Kimori was a strict vegetarian and tee-totaller. And a gracious host. I poured a cup of tea and loaded up a plate with sushi, a delicate ham sandwich with the crusts removed, and a handful of roasted soybeans. I returned to find Paul absorbed in conversation with Sue and Chris. "Stark naked," Sue was saying. She addressed me when I walked up. "Cougar stripped naked and smeared himself with shit, came down from the tree, and ran off through the forest with two officers after him."

"He's bad news." I handed Paul his teacup.

"Sue and Chris are getting hitched," Paul said and raised his cup in the air. "Cheers."

"Thanks," Sue said. "And congratulations to you too. Wow, a baby!" I sought out Paul's eyes and was relieved when he reached over and took my hand. Sue looped her arm through Chris's. "The protest was intense, especially when we smuggled supplies to the tree-sitters. No other partner could understand what we went through."

"My house arrest gave me a lot of time to think," Terry interjected. "I'm committed. The coalition is lobbying for a full moratorium on the logging of old-growth on the island."

"Won't help Otter Valley, though," Chris said. "I hear PCF finished the cut in there before it snowed. I guess your study's screwed, Faye."

"I'm not sure," I replied, wearying of the general conversation. "I haven't been out since the blockade." I retreated to an easy chair. My feet throbbed, my shoes too tight. I'd have to ask about the swelling. I rested my head on the seat back and listened to the conversation.

Esther, who had spent two months in the women's prison serving out her sentence, was unrepentant. "I'm going in there next spring. I won't give up until the last tree is gone. They can put me in jail a hundred times if they want to. Squirrel's coming with me, aren't you?"

Squirrel winced and upended his beer into his mouth.

"What was jail like for the rest of you?" Grace said.

"A lot of the inmates and the corrections officers resented

us," Jen said. "Damn greenies, they called us. We weren't serious-enough criminals. One of the corrections officers told me I wouldn't last long, but it got better. I worked in the kitchen." She giggled. "I was in a co-ed facility and a couple of the inmates sent me love-letters."

"Things weren't easy for me and Chuck," Billy's quiet voice came from the back of the room. "Too many angry men in jail. Marcel protected us."

"A lot of forestry workers are coming forward, Billy," Terry said. "We're talking with the unions. They see jobs disappearing to company downsizing, raw log exports. Things are going to change."

"I hope so." Billy smiled and turned to the woman at his elbow. "I'd like you all to meet my mother, MaryAnne."

The tiny woman, her friendly, round face softly wrinkled, circulated around the room and shook each hand. "You turned my boy into a tree-hugger," she said. "Thank you."

"What are you going to do, Billy?" Terry asked. "No logging operation will take you now."

Sue sighed, but Billy answered graciously. "I'm enrolled in a woodworking program for native youth."

His mother beamed. "The valley," she said, "was *eehmiis*, a precious place. The forest gives us gifts of bark and roots for baskets, woods for canoes and houses, food and medicines. Many of us have forgotten the importance of these places." She patted her son's arm. "Thank you for trying to save it. All of you. We need to work together."

Eehmiis. A perfect word to describe the forest, I thought. I'd better remember it. I was about to ask MaryAnne how the word was spelled when Terry broke the impromptu moment of silence for the loss of the upper valley. "I heard they kicked you out of school, Chris."

Sue pounded her forehead with her fist, turned and walked away, muttering to herself.

Chris laughed at her retreat. "I withdrew. I missed too much time. But I'm going back this term. I'm thinking of switching to environmental law."

"Fine choice," Mr. Kimori said from the couch where he was showing Rainbow how to make a paper boat.

"What about you, Mr. Kimori?" Jen asked. "What did you do for a whole month at home?"

"I tended my forest," he answered.

"Your forest?"

He stood up. "Come, all of you," he said. "I will show you." He led us through a tiny immaculate kitchen and slid open a door at the back of the house. I followed along, curious. We stepped across the threshold into the thick humidity of a greenhouse, the air heavy with the smells of fertilizer and flowers. Water trickled from a bamboo fountain in a clay basin in the corner. "My *tokonoma*," he said. A dozen or more miniature trees grew in pots around the glass room, their trunks and branches twisted and gnarled into a variety of shapes, upright and symmetrical or windswept and angled low to the ground.

"How lovely," Grace exclaimed. "A bonsai garden."

"They're dwarf trees, aren't they?" Terry said.

"A bonsai is not a genetic dwarf," Mr. Kimori explained. "If not contained and pruned, these would attain the height of a normal tree."

"Isn't it mean to the tree?" Rainbow eyed a spruce no more than thirty centimetres high.

"Ah, dear Rainbow, you are kind to other species." He placed his hand on her head. "But bonsai techniques are no more cruel than other horticultural practices. These trees will grow old and happy. We call them heaven and earth in one container. The centre of each pot is where heaven and earth meet and nothing must occupy this space. Notice"—he pointed one by one to three potted trees nearby—"the trunks are set off centre."

"Don't they grow up?" Rainbow asked.

"I teach them to stay small. But they grow old, old as Big Mama. This tree is one hundred and twelve years old." He gestured to a tree no taller than his knee. He picked up a pair of pruning shears from a tray and snipped off the tip of a branch. "*Shin-zen-bi*. The bonsai is a symbol of truth, goodness and beauty. Please, walk through and meet them. They are my children."

I wandered through the rows of stunted azaleas, a Japanese maple, pines, larches, junipers, and a crabapple with delicate pink flowers hanging from the sculpted branches. Each an exquisite work of art. Shaped and tended with love and care. Mr. Kimori's family.

Outside a window, a handful of bonsai conifers grew like a gathering of stunted old men around a neatly raked gravel rectangle. A single wooden bench sat against the wood and bamboo fence behind which the walls of the neighbouring apartment building soared upward. Peaceful but sad. I wondered how Mr. Kimori's trees got enough sun. I ran my finger along the trunk of an indoor cedar; the trunk tapered from crown to base.

"It is *bunjin* style. Comic." Mr. Kimori walked up behind me.

"It's exquisite."

"An old Japanese text says to appreciate and find pleasure in curiously curved and stunted trees is to love deformity."

I swung my head around and stared into his face, his pupils large and penetrating. My cheeks burned at his insinuation. I might have expected these words from Terry, who was unable to open his mouth without blurting out an insensitive comment, but Mr. Kimori? *Love deformity?*

"You . . . you think I'm deformed?" I stammered.

He placed his hand on my shoulder, the weight a warm ballast. "No, Faye, I speak of Paul." He handed me an ironed and folded handkerchief from his pocket. "Cry, it's about time. A tree loses a branch. It does not die or give up, but continues to grow and flourish, perhaps in another direction, but fully alive."

I brushed a sudden flood of tears from my cheeks. "He's a lot better."

"Yes, he is," Mr. Kimori agreed. "But he is not the only one who needs to heal. Buddha teaches us the individual is an illusion, a single conifer is a whole forest. Aren't the roots of one tree intertwined with all the others nearby and all fed by a net of underground fungi?"

I blew my nose. "Mycorrhizae."

"There, you see. Are we not all a single community?"

28

I paced the house, slept poorly, the time for the delivery growing nearer, a Caesarean section scheduled for the spring equinox, March 21, the baby's head too large for my narrow hips. Grace urged me to prepare the baby's room. "You need to nest."

"I'm not a bird," I argued and left the layette shopping to my mother and Rainbow, who talked incessantly about the upcoming event. I craved the outdoors and walked whenever I could. I missed my fieldwork, unsure when I'd be able to resume my research. At the beginning of March, after a sleepless night thinking about mites, I suggested an overnight trip to Otter Valley. Paul refused.

"You're too pregnant," he pleaded. "It's too early in the year."

"Pregnant but not sick." I yearned for big trees and the smell of moss, the rough texture of lichen on my fingers. "And when has a little weather stopped us?"

"We can do a day trip up to Cathedral Grove," Grace, who was visiting for the weekend, suggested.

"I was counting on Otter Creek," I said. "Who knows when we'll get out there again."

"Terry says the logging's pretty bad," Paul cautioned.

"I want to see for myself," I insisted. "Who can believe Terry? Besides, the park's still there."

"What if you go into labour?" Grace said.

"It's only an hour to the Duncan hospital," I argued. "Besides, the delivery isn't scheduled for three more weeks. The doctor told me to keep active."

"Can the baby be borned in Rainbow's Hollow?" Rainbow piped up from the table where she sewed baby clothes out of scraps with a darning needle, a preoccupation for the past weeks, along with lobbying to put the baby's bed in her room.

"Thanks, Rainbow," I said. "I needed an ally." I didn't mention I intended to search the area for clues about Paul's assailant. "Humour me, the rest of you. What better place for nesting?" When I declared I'd go alone if necessary, Paul relented. Grace threw up her hands. "Stubborn," she muttered, but set about packing enough food for a week.

Other than a faint trail to the latrine, the camp appeared washed clean by the winter rains, the events of the past summer a collective delusion. Patches of old snow scattered the sheltered hollows and new pools had formed where a freshly fallen hemlock spanned the creek. The drive in along the logging road had proven a nightmare. The last kilometres to the trailhead crossed clear-cut that ran from the upper valley to the road and as far as the river, a narrow riparian buffer the sole protection for the creekside soil. Winter had claimed many of the edge trees as windfall, the tributary streams clogged with debris, and in places the bank slumped into the channel. Root ends emerged from the ground like half-buried fingers. Kilometres of naked stumps and ravaged ground extended all the way from the intersection with the lake road to the park boundary. Clumps of scrubby trees had been left standing, a practice industry called variable retention logging, the survivors intended to act as a source of seed. But the rejects were never the best specimens, poor sources of quality genetic material, the exercise masking the high-grading of the best and the biggest. To the soaring hawk overhead, the park must have appeared an isolated island of green in the middle of a black churning sea.

Rainbow skipped ahead up the trail, flopped on her stomach on the natural bridge, and peered into the creek pools. Paul, Grace, and I rested on the former kitchen stumps and surveyed the remains of the camp: a plastic pole, bits of blue tarp, and a rusted pot, already silting over with needles and forest litter.

"Nature reclaims her own," Paul commented.

"Not the clear-cuts, though. They'll take generations," Grace added soberly.

"If they let them get that old," I concluded.

"I see frogs. And baby fishes," Rainbow called from the stream, a veil of hair fallen over her face.

"Should we set up camp?" Grace asked.

"I want to see the damage first," I said.

Remnants of yellow tape still flagged the trail in to the study site and we travelled it like a band of refugees. Paul favoured his bad leg on the rough ground, and I, the human beach ball, required help over all obstacles, big or small.

We passed the entwined lovers, the interior forest brighter than I recalled. Through the trees rose an abrupt wall of sunlight, the buffer zone gone, the rainforest severed at the park boundary. Hearts heavy, we made our way through our former old-growth study site. The loggers had punched across the park boundary to remove four of our biggest trees. SS-1-3 was a stump.

"How can they get away with this?" Grace fumed.

"They were charged with trespass and fined," I said. I'd read the news article to Paul over breakfast a few days ago. Roger Payne, the company forester, was quoted as saying the fallers had read their maps wrong. He offered an apology from the company for the loss of the park trees.

"A slap on the wrist. And they'll appeal," Paul said. "A fine will be a fraction of the value of a single tree."

I couldn't begin to place value on the loss of our long-term study site.

We stepped out of the trees into the buffer zone, reeling from the intensity of light and the carnage. I thought of the framed colour digital photo hanging on the wall in my office, a photo of space. Not outer space, but empty space. The forest space between branches, between needles, from the top of the tallest tree to the forest floor. The space where dragonflies hover, spiders build their webs, marbled murrelets race, seedlings sprout, pollen floats. Where rain falls, wind blows and sunlight creeps. Paul had constructed the photo a year ago while suspended between two hemlock trees on a traverse line, a series of horizontal ropes and pulleys rigged from tree to tree to allow climbers to move like sloths through the canopy without having to descend to the forest floor. Dangling in mid-air, he lowered a hand-held digital laser range finder from the upper canopy a metre at a time to the ground, recording measurements at each stop. When translated to a computer, the resulting electronic image of laser beams rebounding from matter resembled a Christmas tree ornament or a ship from another galaxy. What would a laser image of this place we called Otter Creek show today? A uniform bar of light? A flat line on a heart monitor? Not much left but space, the rest a memory.

We picked our way through the jumble of branches, splintered wood, and torn earth. I kept my head lowered, studying the ground, hunting for clues. Which stump marked the murrelet tree? Was the carcass of a chick trampled under the debris, or had it fledged before the cutting? Which piece of ripped and ravaged ground marked the patch of earth where Paul's hemlock had grown? Did his blood still stain the useless fingers of root? Impossible to tell in the chaos. My hopes fell. Would Paul's assailant remain a mystery forever? Not a single green plant grew in the injured land.

Paul and I collapsed onto the top of a stump, too depressed to move. Rainbow clambered over and under and around in the unstable landscape, trailed by a watchful Grace.

"Careful, child," she called.

"No point in carrying on," I lamented. "Let's go back into the park. This is too gloomy."

Paul massaged his thigh. "We could maintain an old-growth site in the park?"

"What's the point?" I countered. "We've lost half our study trees. Interior forest conditions are gone. New trees won't mature to old-growth for centuries. We'll be long dead."

Paul reached out and held his hand over the bulge that strained the buttons of my jacket. "Is she moving?"

"It's a girl, is it?" I teased. "He/she's a gymnast, I believe." I moved his hand over to the other side of my navel. "Here's the bum."

The fabric rippled beneath his fingers. "The swimmer swimmeth." He kissed my forehead. "We'll find a new site."

"Where? Only five intact watersheds left on all of Vancouver Island, all under threat of the axe."

"We'd better get busy."

"All right," I said. "Study site five hundred and sixty three a year from now." Could I handle an infant in a field camp? "I wonder if the university will fund a field nanny."

Paul laughed. "Why? You've got me." A light drizzle of rain in a darkening sky foreshadowed a downpour. "We should go," he said.

"Faye, Paul." Grace gestured from atop a pile of slash. She pointed to Rainbow, who knelt in the jumble, arms working between a pair of logs, tongue clenched between her teeth. Paul helped me up and supporting one another, we made our way through the slash.

"What is it?" I said. Rainbow grunted, wrestling an object from the hole. She gave one last tug, tumbling backward as her prize, mangled and caked in mud, came free. She held it up with a triumphant smile. The crossbow.

Paul and I lay in the tent after dark, our sleeping bags zipped together, his long body spooned warm against my back, a folded jacket between my legs to make space for the baby. We were like a seed within a seed, Paul the warm, protective pod enveloping us. We wore toques and socks and long underwear, the night near freezing. A steady rain drummed on the tent fly. "Who do you think did it?" I asked.

Paul remained silent, but I knew the discovery of the

crossbow, propped against his pack under a tarp outside the tent, must be on his mind.

"Someone tried to kill you."

"But they didn't." He paused. "I suppose it was a disgruntled logger."

"How did he find you?"

"He was hunting and stumbled upon me?"

"In the dark. With our crossbow."

"Can I go to sleep, Detective Sherlock?"

"I didn't tell anyone you went up the tree," I persisted. "The culprit must have known. You didn't say anything to anyone, did you?" His body tensed against me. "Paul, did you?"

His silence provided my answer. In my mind's eye I scanned the faces of the protest group, pictured Mary kissing Paul, Cougar watching from the trailhead, his eyes hot with jealousy. Mary. Paul would have shared our plan with Mary.

The rain stopped at dawn and the bleeding began. I discovered the spots of blood on my underwear when I crawled out of the tent to pee. I crouched on the wet ground and willed the stains to disappear, to evaporate, to reverse their journey. It wasn't fair. To end our time together in another bloody scar on the forest floor. The *rat-tat-tat* of a flicker hammered on a tree on the other side of the river and the sound pulled me to my senses. I woke Grace, who crawled from the tent to find me pacing between the trees.

"I'm bleeding."

"How much."

"Spots . . . a few."

"You need to rest." Grace dragged my sleeping bag and mat from the tent. Rainbow's sleepy voice called out from the second tent, "What are you doing, Nanna?" She'd christened Grace Nanna a month after Mary left.

By the time Paul emerged from the tent I was shivering inside the bag, propped against a log, trying to steady a cup of tea against my lips.

"We have to get her to a hospital." He slipped on a sweater and started yanking tent pegs from the ground. "Let's go."

"We can't risk driving. The road's too rough," Grace argued, her face creased with worry. "I tried the phone. There's no reception."

"What choice do we have," Paul said. "You hold her. I'll drive."

"You can't. I'll get the keys," Grace said. "I'll drive."

By the time the car was loaded and we were underway, the rain had resumed, steady and hard. It pounded on the roof, wipers thumping across the windshield, defroster on full in a vain attempt to keep the view ahead clear. Grace leaned forward and squinted into the downpour, driving at a snail's pace to minimize the vibration of the car on the rough gravel road. Paul supported me on his lap in the back seat as the car lurched through potholes and shuddered across washboard. Rainbow fell asleep, propped on a pillow beside Grace.

"Is it any worse?" Paul adjusted the sleeping bag and brushed my hair away from my forehead.

I couldn't tell, the space between my legs sticky but cold. No cramps or contractions. No flood of amniotic fluid. No river of blood flowing out behind with the rain. "I'm fine," I answered, reluctant to add to the level of stress in the car.

Paul's hand slipped under the blanket and stroked my heavy abdomen. "Hang in there baby," he whispered.

"Is she okay?" Grace asked, the strain in her face visible in the rear-view mirror.

"All under control back here," Paul answered. "You keep your attention on the road."

We drove in silence, the tension in the car palpable. Paul's thighs tight under my head, the muscles in his stomach taut.

Would he leave if I lost the baby? "Go ahead," I said. "Say it."

"Say what?" Paul asked.

"I told you so."

He waited a moment before answering. "No point in

that," he murmured. "Besides, I love you for your adventurous spirit."

Why else? I wanted to ask, but I couldn't muster the energy.

He massaged the back of my neck. "Why don't you try to sleep."

I drifted into a state of semi-consciousness, aware of the drumming on the roof, the swish of water on the undercarriage as Grace manoeuvred the car through deeper and deeper puddles. In the haze of my semi-dream state, marbled murrelets circled above a red canopy. The birds dropped purple eggs from the treetops to the forest floor, the eggs bursting open in yellow splatters across the ground.

I woke when the car came to a stop.

"Damn." Grace pounded her fists on the steering wheel. She swivelled around in her seat, face ashen.

"What is it?" Paul said.

"The road's flooded."

I struggled to sit up and leaned over the back seat to see the passage ahead a torrent of brown water and debris, the roadbed washed out for at least two car lengths. I wasn't surprised to see both sides of the road were clear-cut, no trees, no root system to modulate the flow of water across the land.

"Shit." Paul reached for his raincoat. "I hope it's not too deep." He glanced over at me. "You stay here."

"You can't go in there," I said, alarmed.

"Don't worry. I haven't had a seizure in weeks. Any better ideas?" He stepped from the car, turning at the last minute to say, "This time I won't do it in my underwear."

Rainbow sat up and rubbed sleep from her eyes. "What's happening?" she said, clambering onto her knees to peer out the window. "Where's Paul?"

Grace pulled her onto her lap and pointed.

Paul hunted around at the edge of the road until he found a solid length of branch. Standing beside the torrent, he thrust it out ahead of him and down into the swirling water. The current caught the tip of the branch and threatened to snatch it from Paul's grasp. He pulled it back and probed the bottom closer to shore. When he lifted his probe and measured it against his body, the watermark reached his kneecaps.

"He can't go in there," I said again.

Grace cranked the window open and called to him. He returned to the car, lifted the back hatch, and rummaged around in the jumble of gear. "I knew I brought this for a reason." He lifted a climbing rope from a pack. He tied one end to the front bumper of the car, looped the other around his waist, and, against our protests, waded into the flood waters.

By the time he was halfway across, the water had reached mid-thigh. He turned and raised a thumb. "He's going to make it," Rainbow yelled. Grace grabbed my hand. "Yes, yes," she whispered.

Suddenly, Paul's body stiffened. Rainbow screamed as he fell. We watched in horror as his head disappeared below the waves. His shoulders rolled to the surface and the current carried his body swiftly downstream.

"Paul." I heaved my bulk out into the driving rain, Grace close behind. We took up the rope and heaved, the loose untidy coils snaking in the mud at our feet. The line went taut. We followed it, hand over hand, until we found him, coat snagged on a half-sunk limb near shore, face submerged, body thrashing weakly. We stumbled down the embankment, turned him over, and hauled his torso onto solid land, legs floating. I knelt over him, my belly dragging in the muck and my ear to his mouth. "He's breathing." I burst into tears with a short-lived relief.

Keep him safe. I remembered the neurologist's instructions. *When he has a seizure your job is to keep him from hurting himself.* I removed my raincoat to shelter him. Rainbow appeared in her pyjamas and rubber boots, the tent flapping like a giant airborne bird around her. The three of us knelt under it in the muck and watched helplessly while the seizure took its course.

Somehow we managed to drag the weight of his unconscious body across the road and lift him into the car. Grace fetched dry clothes from the packs and we peeled his mud-soaked sweater and pants from his clammy body and wrapped him in sleeping bags. I struggled out of my wet things, my underwear spotted with fresh blood.

"What were you thinking?" Grace scolded. "What if—" She buried her face in her hands. Rainbow slipped her fingers into the crease in Grace's elbow. "Nanna?"

Grace pulled a tissue from her pocket and blew her nose. "What, dear?"

"I want to go home," she sniffed.

"I know." Grace drew her close. "Me too."

The rain continued, the floodwaters growing by the minute, and Grace backed the car away from the breach for fear the raging current would crumble the road bed further and take us with it. We huddled under sleeping bags and ate the dry remainders of our food. Grace boiled tea under the open back hatch for warmth, but we were reluctant to run the engine for fear of draining the gas tank. I checked Paul's condition every few minutes. He remained unconscious but breathing, skin pasty and cold.

"We should set up the tents," I ventured.

No one moved. The weight of our situation was suffocating. I reached again for my cell phone, praying for adequate reception. No signal.

Rainbow drew a picture with her finger in the thick grey film of moisture on the inside of the windshield. I punched numbers pointlessly into the dead phone. "Oh," Rainbow exclaimed. Her crooked house with a tree in the garden came alive with an eerie glow. "Lights," she cried out. A horn blared from across the washout. Rainbow wiped her landscape away with a single sweep of her sleeve and pointed through the glass. "A car."

Grace opened the window and peered out. "A crew cab." She bolted from the car and ran toward the torrent, arms waving. "Help us!"

Across the water, two people in heavy yellow slickers waved back. After a shouted exchange, Grace returned to the car. "I can't tell what they're saying." She slid in behind the wheel and started the car. "We can't wait. We have to try."

"It's too dangerous, Grace," I said, "We can't make it without a rope. Wait. Rainbow, crawl into the back and bring me Paul's gear bag, the one the rope was in." Within minutes she returned with the bag and I hunted around to find a length of parachute cord and a lead-filled pouch.

We climbed from the car and stood on the bank, loose gravel washing away below our feet with the current. I knotted one end of the line to the weighted bag, the other end to the rope that was still tied to the bumper. The two shrouded figures yelled encouragement across the water. I dragged the coiled rope to the edge of the torrent and threw the bag with all my strength, the cord looping behind. A cramp shot through my abdomen and I doubled over; the weight fell short in the middle of the stream.

Grace snatched the line from my fingers and reeled it back in. "I'll do it." She swung the bag in tight circles, then released it over the water. It too fell far from the opposite shore. On her third try, the weight cleared the water and landed on the crumbling roadbed at the margins of the flood. One of the men retrieved it and hauled in the line, followed by the climbing rope. They backed the truck to the water's edge and secured the rope to the rear bumper. The driver gestured out the window for us to proceed.

Grace and Rainbow and I piled back into the car.

"Open the windows," Grace ordered, starting the car. She paused, then added in a hushed tone that made my legs go weak, "in case we have to get out."

"Put the gear shift in neutral, Grace," I suggested with a tenderness for my mother I'd never felt before.

The rope stretched tight. The wheels turned. The car lurched forward in tot he rushing flood waters. "Mother of God," Grace whispered and then raised her voice. "Hang on."

"You can do it, Mom," I assured her. "All you have to do is steer."

The station wagon slipped into the current. I peered through the window and watched as water inched higher and higher on the hubcaps. At midstream, waves lapped at the bottom of the door. My heart banged in my chest and Rainbow's fingernails dug into my hand, her eyes clenched shut. None of us spoke.

A branch careened off the back passenger door with a thud. The rear end of the car jerked and pivoted. The back wheels floated free and the car listed downstream.

"Drive!" I yelled and Grace stepped on the gas. The engine roared and the back of the car slewed side to side while the crew cab churned up the hill, wheels spinning. Rainbow whimpered. The front wheels hit the far bank and the vehicle bounced and heaved from the water. The tires bit into rock and earth. The car came to a stop on solid ground. We sat in stunned silence, breathless.

A figure loomed outside Grace's door like an apparition and tapped on the glass. "You all okay?" The man stooped at the window and flipped back his hood. "Faye?" Roger Payne peered into the car. "What in God's name are you doing out here in this weather?" Behind him waited the second man, rain gear covering all but a soggy beard dripping with water.

"We need to get Faye and Paul to the hospital." Grace's voice quavered. "Paul's unconscious. Faye's bleeding. It's an emergency."

"They can come with me," he said. "The truck will be faster on these roads. I'll radio for an ambulance to meet us at Midnight Bay."

Roger turned and spoke to his companion.

"My partner here can drive the station wagon," Roger offered.

"No!" Grace shouted.

I stopped halfway out of the car and gaped at my mother. "It's a logical idea, Grace. It's pouring. You're beat. There's not enough room in the crew cab for all of us."

Grace rested her forehead on the steering wheel and mumbled something incomprehensible.

"Pardon?" Roger leaned forward.

"Take Rainbow," she repeated. "Go"—she flapped her hands with irritation—"go."

"I'll drive slow, ma'am," the man said. "Don't worry."

They transferred Paul with care to the back of the crew cab. "Careful." I hovered close by. "Don't hurt him." My whole body trembled. "Watch his head." They lifted me into the front seat, Rainbow following close behind. She curled up beside me. Roger honked the horn and we drove into the night.

I let my head flop back against the upholstery. "Thanks," I said, too fatigued to talk.

"No problem. We should reach the lake in a half-hour," Roger assured me. "You shouldn't be out here this time of year and in your—" He shook his head in disbelief. "It can snow through to the end of the month. You were lucky Donnie and I came out to see if it's clear enough to start timber cruising."

At his words, the losses of the past year poured down on me like the deluge outside, threatening to overwhelm me, drown me under their weight: the trees, our study, the nests, Paul's health, our baby. "Isn't it difficult to assess the value of standing timber in a clear-cut?" I snapped.

"Oh no," he said. "We don't cruise in cut—" He stopped talking without finishing his sentence and concentrated on the road ahead.

An uncomfortable stalemate followed. The big four-by-four sped along the road through the rain on its heavy suspension, absorbing the shock in a way my old station wagon couldn't. Rainbow slept curled up against my side. I wanted to yell at the man beside me, berate him for his lies, for aiding and abetting the demise of park trees and our study site, but I didn't have the energy. I focused on the baby inside, willing it to send us down another path from death and loss to life. My thoughts turned to Grace in the vehicle we'd left far behind. Had she ached for my life this way when I was a newborn? She wanted this baby as much as I. And I had forced her out here, put us all at risk. Guilt pricked at me as I recalled the fear on her face as we drove off. Her reaction to Roger's thoughtful offer was uncharacteristic.

My heart lurched with a sudden realization. "What was your partner's name back there?"

"Donnie?" Roger glanced in the rear-view mirror. "Donnie Ransom. He's a faller, and a wizard woodsman. He lost his wife last month. I hired him to cruise early this year as a distraction. Guy can track a deer through a snow storm and live for weeks with nothing but a knife."

Or a crossbow? The mangled bow was packed in the back of my car. The car that carried my mother . . . and Don Ransom.

"Stop." My yell startled Rainbow bolt upright. "Go back."

Roger looked over his shoulder at me. "What's got into you?" he said, then peered ahead through the windshield. "There's the ambulance." The truck slowed and bumped onto blacktop; the ambulance materialized out of the rain at the side of the road in front of an abandoned gas station.

"You need to go back," I repeated over and over as two paramedics hustled Paul, then me onto stretchers and wheeled us into the back of the ambulance, Rainbow in front with the driver. As the siren came on and the ambulance turned toward town, a bewildered Roger climbed into the cab of his truck, doing as I demanded, and headed back. I tried to sit up, to go to Paul, but the attendant, who was fitting an oxygen mask to his face, cautioned me back. "We'll get through this," I whispered. "You'll be all right." But I didn't believe my own words.

I awoke the next morning in the Duncan hospital to find my mother at my bedside, holding my hand. Grace appeared older, her hair loose and unbrushed, lips and cheeks without makeup.

"You're here," I mumbled.

"Where else?"

"Ransom," I said. "He didn't hurt you?"

"No. He was harmless. We talked about his kids." She handed me a plastic cup of juice with a straw. "Drink, you need fluids." Dark circles shadowed her eyes.

"You don't need to worry. The doctor said I can go home tomorrow, but lots of bed rest and no exercise until the baby comes." I drank gratefully, my body hungry for the cold, wet, sweet liquid. "You recognized him, didn't you?"

"He used to come by the blockade and swear at us."

"Do you think he's the one who hurt Paul?"

Grace paused. "Who knows? I didn't ask and I can't imagine he would have told me. If I'm not mistaken, the police don't consider him a suspect."

"He didn't mention the blockades?"

"Not a thing." Grace adjusted my blanket. "I doubt he remembered me." She paused. "The poor man's grief-stricken."

I sank back into the pillow and studied the pattern of lines in the tiled ceiling. An eye for an eye? I felt ashamed. The police knew nothing, the man likely guilty only of a nasty temper. "How are Paul and Rainbow?"

Grace fussed with my blanket. "Your father fetched Rainbow home about two hours ago." She gestured to a bag on the floor by the door. "He brought clean clothes."

"I had an ultrasound last night."

"Did they tell you the sex?"

The technician had shown me the monitor, the fetus curled like a fiddlehead inside my womb, the tiny disproportionate limbs apparent, the broad, flat nose. "Yes, Mother." I lifted Grace's long, elegant fingers and kissed each one. "She's a girl. But what about Paul?" I said. "You didn't tell me about Paul. Is he okay? Can I see him?"

Grace turned her face away.

"Grace." Alarm blossomed in the pit of my stomach. "Where is he? How is he?"

"He's gone, sweetheart." Grace gripped my hand. "He's gone."

29

Camille Grace Taylor Pearson was born on March 19, in an operating room at the Victoria Hospital, in the early morning hours most inconvenient for surgeons. She surprised us by arriving days earlier than planned and I experienced a few hours of escalating contractions at home and later at the hospital as the infant's too large head inched along the birth canal. The doctor—a kind woman with liberal leanings—checked the baby's heartbeat, then mine. "Everything's fine," she said. "The nurses will get you prepped for surgery." She ducked out the door to another birth.

Grace hovered close with offers of ice chips, massages, advice on breathing. Mel and Rainbow wandered in and out during the brief period of labour, Mel charged with keeping Rainbow—who had insisted on attending the birth—happy and occupied. In reality, Rainbow looked after Mel. Whenever he appeared unsteady, Rainbow hustled him into the corridor for a glass of water or another cup of coffee. She fell asleep on the couch in the hallway during the surgery, Mel with strict orders to "wake me up when my sister is coming."

I knew my daughter's precise instant of birth, 3:26 AM, the slippery body lifted from an incision in my pelvis by the confident hands of the paediatrician. I had opted for an epidural, awake when the doctor announced, "It's a girl," and handed her to Grace. The baby wailed and we laughed with relief at the lusty cry. In the recovery room after the stitches, Grace unwrapped her and eased her onto my chest. I felt my daughter's weight outside my body for the first time, her vernix-covered skin slick like butter beneath my fingers. We watched in awe as she crawled froglike toward the mound of breast, mouth rooting for milk. She latched on to the nipple, sucking hungrily. As the baby nursed, I inspected every square centimetre of her, her dark wet hair, her broad forehead and thick neck, her fat arms and legs.

"Her limbs don't appear abnormal," Mel commented.

"It's often hard to distinguish the bowing at birth," the doctor explained.

Grace stroked the baby's forehead, a tiny hand clutched around her free thumb. "Amazing."

I remembered every detail: the flavour of the frozen blueberries Grace fed me during labour, the cold, sweet juice in my mouth, the smell of antiseptic, the surprise of the curious nurses who dropped by to see the unusual infant and exclaimed, "But she's so pretty." The assurance in the doctor's expression as she announced the baby a healthy little girl. "We'll have to keep close tabs on her limb development and no question her air passages are small," she added, "but you've been fortunate."

"Excellent genes," Mel said from the chair in the corner.

Rainbow stood on a stool at my bedside. "I have a sister," she boasted. "I think she has Paul's forehead."

We had buried him in the city graveyard by the sea under an ancient Douglas-fir. The forest defenders were all present, including Marcel, who flew in from Hudson Bay. Paul's sister had sent a telegram, expressing her remorse at not being able to leave her own family to be present. It had taken Sue a solid week to track her down. The unexpected arrival of Roger Payne and Don Ransom caused a stir in the group, but the men only stayed for the short service, declining Mr. Kimori's invitation to his home for tea afterward.

Sergeant Lange had appeared as the pall bearers lowered

the coffin into the grave. He waited for me by the car and offered his condolences. "Anything new?" I said, not knowing what else to say. I had presented him with the crossbow a few days after Paul died.

"Sorry, the winter rains washed away any fingerprints."

I had cornered Billy and Chuck at the reception. "Did you ever see Donnie Ransom with anything suspicious?"

"Like what?" Chuck fidgeted with his drink.

"A bow, rubber-tipped arrows."

"Nope," he said. "He talked a lot about hunting, but only with guns."

"The police asked us all these questions last year, Dr. Pearson," Billy had added. "I'm sorry. If I knew who hurt him, I'd tell you."

I fingered the soft flannel receiving blanket swaddled around my daughter. Poor fatherless thing. I stroked the downy swirl of hair at the crown of her head. Rainbow was right. The baby had Paul's high forehead. Her pupils, the opaque blue of infancy, might turn lichen-green over time. Would she share Paul's happy-go-lucky attitude to life? A sense of humour was an asset for a dwarf. The ability to shed teasing like water off her back. On the bedside table a vase of mums and roses overflowed with colour. A gift from Bryan.

Mel was last to hold the baby. "What if I drop her?" he said from the easy chair in the corner.

"You won't," Rainbow insisted. "You're a dad, aren't you?"

Grace lifted the baby from my arms and carried her over. "Take extra care with her head and neck," she instructed as she transferred the infant into his arms.

"Her brilliant brain must be larger than average," Mel said. He shifted in his chair and peered into his granddaughter's face, at the thick eyelashes that fanned across her cheeks, as if she were a difficult mathematical equation he couldn't quite grasp. He removed his glasses with his free hand and bent closer. "She has my grandmother's nose," he said. "I wonder if she'll excel at math?"

"I'll teach her." Rainbow balanced on her stomach over the arm of the chair as if she couldn't get close enough to both of them.

We all laughed.

"Do you have a name picked out yet?" Mel asked, attention focused on the baby.

I hesitated. "How about . . . Camille?"

"What?" His head jerked up and he blinked, then returned his glasses to the bridge of his nose. "Camille was my grandmother's name."

"What a coincidence," Grace quipped. "Don't be greedy. Hand her back over here."

But Mel ignored Grace; he was looking straight at me. "It's the name I wanted for you."

Tears welled up in my eyes.

Mel touched the curled fingers of his sleeping granddaughter. "A beautiful name for a beautiful girl," he said.

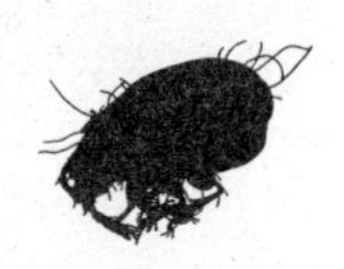

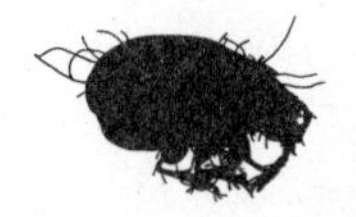

30

I stopped typing and leaned back in my chair. My home office had become a cross between a photography studio and nursery, pictures of Camille and Rainbow pinned to the wall, toys and stacks of laundry scattered over the floor and furniture. Camille lay asleep in her infant seat beside me, hand curled in a fist at her chin. She was growing well, but we had a bit of a scare a week earlier. She caught a cold and couldn't breathe. Middle of the night. Why do these things always happen in the middle of the night? I rushed her to hospital and they put her on a ventilator for two days.

I read over the last words I'd written. *An acre of old-growth stores as much carbon as a hundred cars emit in a year.* I'd laboured over the letter to the forests minister for a week, a summary of scientific evidence supporting a moratorium on the logging of old-growth forests on Vancouver Island. *There's no ecological justification for clear-cutting.* I wasn't hopeful, but I couldn't watch the old forests on the island disappear any more without speaking up. I stroked Camille's tiny foot. She needed big trees in her world.

I rubbed my eyes and yawned. The sleep deprivation was hard. I hoped to go back to work in the fall. Camille in day-care. Rainbow to school. Grace had asked Esther, a retired social worker, to make discrete inquiries about an application for custody. Still no word about Mary. Rainbow was practising ukulele in her room, the discordant chords and tentative strumming a tender reminder of her sweet and determined heart. A familiar pain flared in the vicinity of my own heart. Paul's assailant was still at large; no witnesses, no fingerprints. Not a half-believable motive. What did it matter who did it? Paul was gone. He'd been alive, well along on his way to healing, when I had forced him back to Otter Creek. If I had pushed him into the flood and held him under with my own hands I couldn't be more guilty of his death. Paul wasn't coming back. In the darkest hours of the night I convinced myself he would have left me in the end. The decision to stay out of a sense of duty, a fragile bond. Camille stirred; her tiny pink hand opened and closed like the wing of a butterfly against the curve of her chin. Camille was his perfect woman, not I.

Camille opened her eyes and yawned. I sat on the floor, my back against the couch, and gathered her in my arms to nurse. She suckled with an intense desperation that left me weak; fear and love shooting through me like arrows. What would the future bring? At six months Camille couldn't roll over. Would she walk? Would her legs develop problems? Would she need surgery? She relies on me for her every need, for life. On the darkest of days I would stand by the phone, receiver in hand, ready to call Bryan, but I never followed through. Sometimes I saw myself in Camille and imagined her a toddler, climbing spiderlike up the counter, the lattice, the drainpipe to the roof.

The doorbell rang. I threw a spit-up rag across my shoulder and carried Camille in my arms to the front room and opened the door. Sergeant Lange stood on the porch. Rainbow's ukulele sounded down the hall. I crossed my fingers she'd stay put.

"Faye," the sergeant said, official this time in his uniform. "Sorry to bother you, but could I come in for a moment?"

I stepped back to let him pass, cringing inside as the strains of "On Top of Old Smoky" floated from Rainbow's room.

He declined a cup of coffee, but accepted a seat in the living room.

"Cute baby," he said, taking the chair by the door.

"Thanks." I settled across from him onto the couch with Camille. "What can I do for you?"

"The Pemberton detachment contacted me a couple of weeks ago," he said. "Someone reported a young couple with a child squatting in a cabin up on the Duffy Lake Road. The neighbours suspected them of minor theft in the area."

"Mary and Cougar?" My heart skipped a beat and I couldn't help but glance toward the hallway and Rainbow's bedroom.

"We're pretty sure. The descriptions by the neighbours match the warrants. By the time officers got out to the cabin, they'd run. In a hurry. They left a few things behind."

"Oh?"

He glanced down the hallway to the bedrooms, where Rainbow had launched an all out assault on one of her favourite songs. "'B-I-N-G-O,'" she sang, her voice off-tune. "'And Bingo was his name, ho.'"

The sergeant smiled, then turned his attention back to me. "We found an envelope addressed to you," he said. "Our only real clue it was them."

I stroked Camille's back. "To me?"

He drew a package out of the leather folder. "I thought I'd drop it by."

I took the envelope from his hand and read my name scribed in clear, square letters, the address merely *Victoria*.

"Sorry, we opened it in case it contained evidence, but it's not of much use to us."

I draped Camille across my lap and opened the flap on the envelope. Rainbow thundered along the hallway and slid on stocking feet across the wood floor in front of us. Her smile revealed a gap in her mouth where she'd lost another tooth. "Can I have juice pl—" her voice petered out at the sight of Sergeant Lange.

"Honey"—I tried to suppress the fear in my own voice—"This is Sergeant Lange."

Rainbow's head swivelled back and forth between the officer and me.

"Your name's Rainbow, isn't it?" Sergeant Lange said, voice gentle.

She fidgeted with the buckle on her overalls.

This is it. He knows and we're going to lose her. I opened my arms. "Come here, sweetie." Rainbow slid onto the couch beside me.

"You're a great ukulele player," he said. "Well, I should go." He stood and replaced his hat. "I'll let you know if there's any more news about those two." He walked toward the door, paused, and turned back. "You know, Rainbow, your baby sister looks just like you."

Neither Rainbow nor I moved until the car pulled away from the front of the house.

"Is he going to take me away?"

I pulled her into the crook of my arm. "No," I answered, hopeful about the implications of Sergeant Lange's visit. *He knows and he isn't going to do anything about it.* I kissed the perpetual cowlick on the top of Rainbow's head. "Besides, I won't let him."

"What did he bring?"

I hesitated. In the end, the contents of the envelope might take Rainbow away from me anyway. "It's a letter from Mary."

Her face lit up. "For me?"

"It's addressed to me."

"Is she coming back?" she said.

"I haven't read it yet." I studied her, trying to read her thoughts. "What if she did? What would you want to do?"

Rainbow lowered her gaze.

"Don't worry about what anyone else wants," I said. "What do *you* want?"

She twisted her hands around in her lap. "I miss Cedar."

"I know you do." I caressed her cheek, touched by her honesty.

Camille stirred and grunted in her sleep. Rainbow patted her back. "Go to sleep," she crooned, her brow furrowed in a way a child's should never be. "Can we read it?"

I opened the envelope to find a folded sheet of paper with two swatches of hair taped inside. A soft white blond curl on the left, a poker-straight hank of brown to the right. Beside each swatch an infant handprint, the creases in the palm visible in the paint, and in careful script below, the names *Cedar* and *Rainbow.*

Rainbow stroked the blond hair with a fingertip. "I think these are for you," I said, offering her the sheet, holding my tears at bay.

Rainbow took the paper, slid off the couch, and disappeared to her room. I listened for the sound of crying, but all was quiet. "Poor sweet thing." I hugged Camille close. Rainbow's door opened and she stepped out, the paper in one hand, her watercolour set and a brush in the other.

"What's that for, honey?" I asked, surprised by the radiance in her face.

"Let's make a handprint for Camille too."

While Camille slept in my lap, we painted her chubby hand bright blue and made her mark on the paper beside Rainbow's, a wispy curl of infant hair taped below. Rainbow hung it in the kitchen on the refrigerator with two bird magnets from the junk drawer.

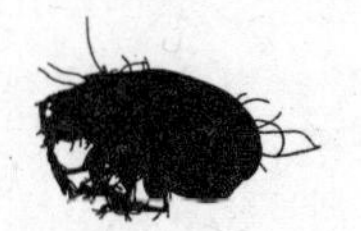

31

A temperate old-growth rainforest in spring is little different from a temperate old-growth rainforest in winter. No showy tropical orchids dripped from hanging gardens, no dramatic lanais, teeming with epiphytes, looping from the ground to the tree crowns and back again, no birds of paradise, no heady fragrance from gaudy blooms. Temperate rainforest flowers are shy and subtle—the solitary pink blossoms of salmonberry, a low carpet of white trillium at your feet, the tiny hidden bells of twisted stalk. Spring colour flits like ghosts through the green and browns of the forest understorey. Young fiddleheads unfurl beside last year's fronds, twinflowers inch along the ground, conifers add grass-green fingers to the tips of their branches. Migratory birds appear, mothers birth in hollows, under fallen logs, high up in trees on moss-laden branches.

Rainbow is pacing the perimeter of a tree. "One, two, three . . ." She places her feet heel to toe, one after the other, careful not to crush the forest plants beneath. "One hundred and twenty-one, one hundred and twenty-two, one hundred and twenty-three." She shouts out the last number and leaps into the air, arms raised. "One hundred and twenty-three." After two years of home-schooling, she can also add and subtract, and knows her times tables by heart to ten. At eight, she clears my height by her cowlick, and yesterday, she asked me eye to eye if she could live with me forever. When I said, "Yes," she hugged me with a force that left a bruise on my arm. We haven't heard from Mary since the handprint letter. I want to curse and bless the woman all at once. The temporary custody papers are due in a month.

The tree is one of the largest hemlocks I have ever seen. As far as I know it has no name. "Are we the only people in the whole wide world to see this tree?" Rainbow asks, reading my mind, this valley remote, with no established trails and difficult access. She's become adept at anticipating our thoughts, her abandonment making her sensitive to the moods and actions of those who care for her.

Jen measures the height of the tree with a clinometer. "It's over eighty metres." Twenty storeys high. I had hired her in the spring. The woman's tree-sitting experience during the protest had inspired her to become an accomplished and well-trained climber. Together we had discovered this remote rainforest. Dozens of ancient giants live here.

I scratch a number into the aluminum disk—WH-1-1—western hemlock site 1 tree 1, and below it in tiny letters and at Rainbow's insistence, Harry the Hemlock, and tack it onto the base of the tree. Nineteen more disks wait in a nylon bag for engraving and tacking on my way up. We set the rope in the tree with my new invention, a high-powered slingshot with a fishing reel mounted on the underside. As accurate as the crossbow, but lighter and easier to use.

"Yes!" The shot bag clears a high visible branch and I raise my arm in a victory salute while Rainbow leaps and cheers.

After the hemlock is rigged, I clip my ascenders to the rope and jug my way up. The long straight trunk rocks in the breeze. I bang the four-metre marker into the bark and signal to Jen, who waves, adjusts her helmet, and starts up an old crone of a cedar not far away. Grace supervises from a moss-covered nurse log, two-year-old Camille on her lap. The child spoke her first word this morning. *Dwee*. Her delay in verbal skills, according to Grace, has nothing to do with her dwarfism. "She never has to ask for a thing," she accuses.

The interpretation of Camille's debut into language inspired a contest over breakfast; Rainbow and I voting for tree, Grace for Nanna, Mel non-committal. Mel is off calculating diameter at breast height with a DBH tape for all the potential study trees and recording the measurements in a field book, happy I had invited him along. He can't get enough of Camille, a fact that both pleases and distresses me.

The ground below is hidden from view by a curtain of green. I lever myself to the other side of the tree with a convenient limb, retrieve my radio, and depress the transmission button. "Rainbow, can you see me?"

Her high voice crackles out of the speaker, "I can't, Dr. Faye."

"It's wonderful up here." *You're wonderful too,* I think to myself.

"It's nice down here too," she says. "I saw a wren."

"Lovely. Hey, I'm going to the top. I won't be down for a couple of hours."

"Okay. Camille wants to talk to you. Here, Cami, say hi to Mommy."

A gentle "dwee" floats out of the receiver.

"You've got it." I laugh. "Mommy's in the dwee. See you later."

When I reach the top, I tie myself in and wrap my legs around the branch for extra security. The crown rocks a metre to either side in the slight wind. Three trees over and halfway up I glimpse a flash of white where I know Jen is peeling sections of moss mats from a branch and rolling the samples like carpets into plastic sample bags. I will do the same at each marker on my way down. Moss mats full of mites. I retrieve a bag of orange sections from my pocket, pop one into my mouth, and admire the view. In the distance the ocean stretches west shining and blue to the horizon. All around me treetops sway in an undulating emerald carpet. Occasionally, an emergent crown spikes higher than the rest. The rooftop of the world. I suck on another section of orange and then tuck the bag back into the pocket of my vest. Juice drips from my chin. I can't see a single clear-cut. *Ancient forest forever.* A red-tailed hawk screes overhead and my mind expands at the sound; my body longs to soar above the canopy with the hawk. No, it wants to be the hawk, the sky. I am higher than any other earthbound species. I want to get higher.

I remove a small packet from another pocket and unfold the wrapping to reveal Paul's amulet. I lift it up. The yellowed orangutan tooth swings from the leather thong; a calm light emanates from the worn surface. People of the forest. I bring it to my lips, and then tie it to the drooping leader of the hemlock. *This is where you belong. Up in the canopy. Person of the trees.*

I raise my arms to the sky. Tears spill down my cheeks. "Wha-whoo!" I call out across the treetops.

An answering "Wha-whoo!" echoes from below and I can hear Jen laugh.

A barred owl hoots its drawn-out call, *who cooks for youuu.* I bundle a sleeping Camille into a fleece snowsuit and tuck her into the child carrier, which Mel swings onto his back. The baby's chubby legs dangle through the holes in the carrier and her head settles onto her grandfather's shoulders. Her eyes aren't green like Paul's but blue like her mother's, and hidden now behind closed lids. She'd spent another week in the hospital on oxygen at a year and a half, but has avoided other complications dwarfism can bring—compression of the brain stem, sleep apnea, leg complications requiring surgery. She hasn't walked yet, delayed mobility common with achondroplastic babies, but she pulls herself up on furniture and scoots along on her belly on the floor like a salamander. When Mel is around, he rarely puts her down. "It's different being a grandfather than a father," he said one day, patiently prying the arm of his glasses out of her hand. The expression on his face made my heart twist with regret at the rift between us, our conversations uncomfortable unless about Camille. A common ground of hope.

Grace, Rainbow, and Jen stumble from their tents, shivering

in the dark as they pull on sweaters and rain gear. It is four-thirty in the morning. Luckily, the sky is clear, the ground dry. I send up a silent thank you to the god of weather and hand each person a granola bar and a juice box.

"Ready?" They all nod and stash their provisions into a pocket.

I take the lead, Jen the rear, each of us with a flashlight, and the ragtag group heads off into the woods. Jen has already flagged the route and I pick out each loop of orange reflective tape circling a tree trunk there, a devil's club bush here. The going is not easy, the underbrush thick and, except for whispered conversation and the rasp of laboured breathing as we gain elevation up the valley or straddle a nurse log, progress in the deep duff of the mossy floor is slow and hushed.

We stop at a small clearing and disperse, each choosing a flat, moss-cushioned spot on the ground. Mel, two body lengths from me, removes the pack and zips Camille into his jacket, her back to his front. The baby's fat cheeks peek out of the opening at his collar. We lie on thermal sleeping mats and wait.

A finger of cool air brushes across my face, and moss at the edge of my matt tickles my scalp. The ground smells of rotting wood and humus. I roll my head toward Mel, Camille awake and wide-eyed. They both watch the sky; I can't see the expression in their eyes. Mel strokes the baby's forehead and tucks her hat over her ears. I try to imagine Paul in Mel's place, his daughter warm on his chest. Camille stirs and the image fades, leaving my body aching in its wake. My grief has diminished over the years since Paul's death, lost among the feeding, the toys, the endless laundry, the exhaustion that comes with parenting alone, but in places like this—silent and green—sorrow swoops in and pierces me like an arrow.

Sometimes, after a rare restful night, after a few hours in the lab, with a glass of wine in the kitchen, my thoughts turn to the future. Marcel wants us to visit him in Quebec. Bryan still writes. He has friends, he says, not all little. "I could introduce you." I assure him he has rocks in his head. He and

Michelle married last year. They're expecting a child. Perhaps when Camille is older, I'll take the children on a road trip. See the prairies. Introduce them to the endless wide-open skies and the land with no trees. Start a new story.

Above, stars twinkle through the opening in the canopy, bright pins of light on a black canvas. No clouds, no wind. A half-hour passes. 'I'm hungry," Rainbow whines. "Shh," Grace whispers and we hear the crinkle of paper as she opens Rainbow's granola bar. The sky lightens to purple, to blue; the stars fade and flicker out.

Whoosh. A murrelet hurtles overhead. *Whoosh whoosh*, two more.

"I see them," Rainbow cries out.

"Shhh," Grace croons. "Count to yourself."

Four, five birds circle and call above the canopy. *Keer, keer.*

Six, seven, eight. Another rockets through the trees, metres above our heads; the air sings through its wings. *Keer, keer.*

Camille scans the sky from the warmth of Mel's body, eyes wide and mysterious in the half-light. I imagine she must hear the beat of his heart beneath her. She turns her head as she tracks another murrelet across the heavens. Eleven, twelve, thirteen. "Dwee," my daughter gurgles. "Dwee, Dwee," and she laughs. The music of her laughter rises up, up, up, a feather on a breeze, up through the canopy, past the lichens that cling to the bark, the mites in their moss mats, past her father's amulet swinging from the top of the hemlock, and disappears into the sky after the murrelets, heading for the sea.

Keer, keer.

Acknowledgments

Faye is a creation of my imagination, unlike the hundreds of thousands of very real little people the world over who are parents, lovers, children, siblings, and friends, and who work in a wide range of fields: science, medicine, education, law, business, and agriculture, to name only a few. A number of books were of valuable assistance in helping me develop Faye as a character, in particular, *Little People: Learning to See the World Through My Daughter's Eyes* by Dan Kennedy, *Dwarfs Don't Live in Doll Houses* by Angela Muir Van Etten, and *Growing Up Small: A Handbook for Short People* by Kate Gilbert Phifer. I would also like to thank Little People of British Columbia (www.littlepeopleofbc.org) and Little People of America (www.lpaonline.org) for their fabulous websites full of excellent information.

While researching this novel, I literally went up into the trees, tagging along on five research trips into the old-growth forests of Washington State and Vancouver Island. I would like to give a huge thank you to my friends Nalini Nadkarni from Evergreen State College in Olympia, Washington, and author of *Between Earth and Sky: Our Intimate Connections to Trees* and Zoë Lindo from the University of Victoria for teaching me hands-on about canopy research. Nalini introduced me to tree showers, tree painting, and moss jewellery, was responsible for the quote "Unlike people, trees give back so much and require little in return," and took the time to count the number of references to trees in the bible. Zoë introduced me to the fascinating world of mites and spent an afternoon in the lab guiding me through the process of preparing a specimen slide. Appreciations also to Kevin Jordon of Arbonaut Access for double- and triple-checking the gear and for coaxing me forty metres up a veteran western redcedar in the Walbran Valley. The view was spectacular. A big thank you to Anne McIntosh from the International Canopy Network (www.evergreen.edu/ICAN/), who welcomed me along on her research, taught me how to rig a tree, and became a friend. I would also like to thank the following people for their assistance: Neville Winchester from the University of Victoria; climbers and canopy researchers from the International Canopy Network and other institutions including Bryan Torian, Hannah Anderson, Tara Chestnut (with Maggie and Molly), Traci Sanderson, Genevieve Becker, Janet Foley, Nate Nieto, DJ Cox, Matt Dunlap, Sage Dunn, Gabriel Horton, Judy Cushing, Lee Zeman, Aaron Crosland, and Katie Madsen; and colleagues I met at the Canopy Confluence who integrate canopy science with their creative expression including Jodi Lamask and Zack Bernstein (dancers), John Calderazzo (poet), Dana Lyons (songwriter), and Chuck Willyard (painter). The textbook *Forest Canopies* edited by Margaret D. Lowman and H. Bruce Rinker was an invaluable resource. I am grateful to Roman Dial, Nalini M. Nadkarni, and Judith Cushing for their chapter on empty space and the lovely line ". . . where rain falls, sunlight passes, winds blow . . ." that I shamelessly paraphrased. For details about marbled murrelets in old-growth forests I thank Dr. Alan Burger, Paul Harris-Jones for his book *The Marbled Murrelets of the Caren Range and Middlepoint Bight*, and Maria Mudd Ruth for her book *Rare Bird*.

While the Otter Creek protest is fictional, it is reminiscent of the long and ongoing tradition of forest activism in British Columbia. Examples of high profile conflicts include, among a host of others, the Walbran, the Carmanah, Cathedral Grove, and most significantly the Clayoquot—the largest protest in Canadian history—where more than ten thousand people from around the world participated in the protest and nine hundred and thirty-two individuals from children to grandparents, and from all walks of life, stood on a logging road on Vancouver Island in defence of old-growth and were arrested. The Clayoqout blockade resulted in the creation of the Clayoquot Sound Biosphere Reserve. I am indebted to Gary Moore, one of the arrestees, for lending me his folder of notes and legal papers and for telling me his story. *Clayoquot Mass Trials: Defending the Rainforest* edited by Ron MacIsaac and Ann Champagne, *Big Trees Not Big Stumps* by Paul George, *The Legacy of Luna: The Story of a Tree, A Woman, and the Struggle to Save the Redwoods* by Julia Butterfly Hill, and *Forest Giants* by Bob Van Pelt were invaluable references. I am grateful to John Vaillant, author of *The Golden Spruce: A True Story of Myth, Madness and Greed*, for his detailed description of the logging of an old-growth tree from which I borrowed heavily. I thank activists Nathan Clark and Tessa Helwegd, and filmmakers Richard Boyce and Rick Delgatty for sharing their stories. Thank you also to nurses Danielle Snowsell and Kory Boulton for teaching me about head injury, coma, and the ICU. Any errors are my own.

Gratitude and flowers to Ruth Linka, my publisher, for believing in my work. Admiration for Emily Shorthouse at Brindle & Glass for always answering my emails with patience and good humour and keeping the connections flowing, and to Kathy Page for her wonderful editorial skills and diplomacy. For critiquing the manuscript at various stages I am indebted to Nalini Nadkarni, Zoë Lindo, Kevin Jordan, Pearl Arden, Denise de Montreuil, Anne McIntosh, Lesley Pechter, Penny Joy, Leith Leslie, Peggy Frank, Tory Stevens, Barbara and Gary Moore, Elizabeth Blake, and Ken Wu. Thank you for your gift of time. If I have forgotten anyone, my apologies and appreciation.

As always, hugs to my children, Noah and Camas, for your unfailing support and for going up into the trees with me. I dedicate this book to my husband, Gary Geddes, who is firmly attached to the ground.

Novelist and biologist Ann Eriksson combines her background in ecology with her life experiences to create works of fiction populated with rich characters and grounded in nature. She is the author of novels *In the Hands of Anubis* (2009) and *Decomposing Maggie* (2003). Ann was born in Saskatchewan and grew up in the Canadian Prairie provinces, eventually migrating to the West Coast. Ann lives with her husband, poet Gary Geddes, on Thetis Island and in Victoria. Visit www.anneriksson.ca.